The Old English Peep Show

The Old English
Peep Show

Peter Dickinson

All the characters and events portrayed in this work are fictitious.

THE OLD ENGLISH PEEP SHOW

A Felony & Mayhem mystery

PRINTING HISTORY
First UK edition (as *A Pride of Heroes*) (Hodder & Stoughton): 1969
First U.S. edition (as *The Old English Peep Show*) (Harper & Row): 1969
Felony & Mayhem edition: 2007

Manufactured in the United States of America

The icon above says you're holding a copy of a book in the Felony & Mayhem "British" category. These books are set in or around the UK, and feature the highly literate, often witty prose that fans of British mystery demand. If you enjoy this book, you may well like other "British" titles from Felony & Mayhem Press, including:

The Killings at Badger's Drift, by Caroline Graham
Death of a Hollow Man, by Caroline Graham
Death on the High C's, by Robert Barnard
Death in the Garden, by Elizabeth Ironside
Dupe, by Liza Cody

For more about these books, and other Felony & Mayhem titles, or to place an order, please visit our website at:

www.FelonyAndMayhem.com

or contact us at:

Felony and Mayhem Press
156 Waverly Place
New York, NY 10014

The Old English Peep Show

PART I

OLD ENGLAND

Surely among a rich man's flowering lawns,
Amid the rustle of his planted hills,
Life overflows without ambitious pains;
And rains down life until the basin spills,
And mounts more dizzy high the more it rains
As though to choose whatever shape it wills
And never stoop to a mechanical
Or servile shape, at others' beck and call.

—W. B. Yeats, *"Ancestral Houses"*

10:45 A.M.

Pibble thought, I am the chosen vulture spiraling down onto a dying lion. A golf course rolled backward past the train windows, where three bright-anoraked couples marched in different directions across the dewy October turf, with the uninterpretable purposefulness of foraging ants. Then acres of birch and withering bracken, interrupted by ponds whose black-tinged water betrayed the sourness of the soil beneath—all so close to London, as though the Almighty had foreseen that His English would need expanses of agriculturally useless land within commuting distance of the money mart. And now, pat, terraces of tidy postwar development with long, thin gardens reaching down to the reedy canal.

In fact the canal—useless, beautiful, the romantic relic of obsolete needs, now stagnant and full of mosquito larvae—was a better image than the lion. Pibble turned a page in the folder of press cuttings on his knee but did not start to read; the greenhouse sensation of the mild sun beating through the carriage window made him mentally lazy, happy to wallow in the absurd melodrama of being the chosen vulture. He rejected the intrusive canal from his imagery, partly because he had recently been bullied by Mrs. Pibble into reading the Elsa books, partly because the stagnant waterway (though otherwise admirably suited to tone in with his own dim, suburban upbringing) provided no role for a visiting detective, but largely because of the comings and goings in Scotland Yard during the past twenty-four hours. That really had been like carrion birds squabbling over a carcass: Tom Scott-Ellis and Harry Brazzil had surprised even their enemies by their eagerness to go down to Herryngs and set Scotland Yard's seal of approval on the run-of-the-mill suicide of an old retainer, until the Ass. Com. had lost patience and sent old Pibble to spite them all. It showed you what a hold the idea and name of Clavering still had on the vulgar imagination.

And the not-so-vulgar, to be honest. Why, otherwise, go in for the melodrama, the picture of the princely quadruped expiring on the veldt while the broad wings loitered down toward it? Supposing Mrs. Pibble ever succeeded in her campaign to make him retire and write his memoirs, would he actually keep the Claverings out because the crime had been uninteresting? Scott-Ellis or Brazzil would milk a visit to Herryngs for a whole chapter, even if their task had been only to find a lost back stud. And *that* wasn't unlikely, either; witness Pibble's present mission. Sir Ralph seemed perfectly capable of sending for a busy crime-buster to come and grovel under his chest of drawers, and getting him, too.

So the lion wasn't quite dead, its limbs were not yet being reconnoitered by ants. But in any other sense the Claverings were finished, irrelevant, a figment of the corporate British Imagination (much like Beefeaters or Stratford-upon-Avon); they were heroes from the age of Sophocles who had survived with endearing absurdity into the age of Menander.

The absurdity was inescapable, seeming to permeate everything they had a hand in these days, witness the press cutting that now lay uppermost in the folder, dated 1958:

INCIDENT AT EPSTEIN UNVEILING
"Statue an Insult"—*Sir R. Clavering*

The unveiling of the memorial to Sir George
Murrow, R.A., at Framplingfield, Sussex, yesterday, did
not go off as smoothly as hoped. The soapstone statue
had been commissioned by Sir Cyril Blight, the Lord of
the Manor of Framplingfield (Sir Cyril is better known
for his extensive interests in property development), in
memory of Framplingfield's most aesthetically distin-
guished son. General Sir Ralph Clavering, hero of the
St. Quentin Raid, came out of retirement to perform
the unveiling ceremony. Murrow had been an official
War Artist attached to the Raid.

Opposite Trenches

In a brief speech Sir Ralph reminded his audience
of Murrow's achievements, and of his place in the affec-
tions of the British public as a painter of animal subjects. He spoke movingly of the fact that Sir Jacob
Epstein, who had spent most of his life in what Sir
Ralph referred to as the "opposite trenches of the art
world," had consented to bury the hatchet and produce
the monument which Sir Cyril Blight's generosity had
made possible.

Sir Ralph then unveiled the monument, and the
band of the 7th Marine Commandos struck up "Abide
with Me."

Photograph Confusion?

On seeing the statue, however (it is two-thirds
life-size and portrays the artist in striking pose with
brush and palette), Sir Ralph vaulted the rails of the
unveiling dais, seized the baton from the sergeant-con-
ductor, stopped the band, and ordered the Commandos
to reveil the monument. Sir Ralph is Colonel of the
Regiment.

While the reveiling was proceeding, Sir Ralph held an impromptu Press Conference and explained the reason for his action.

The statue, he alleged, was nothing like the late Sir George Murrow. It was an insult, no doubt unintentional, to a great artist and a great comrade-in-arms.

Sir Ralph suggested that perhaps Sir Jacob had confused the photographs from which he was working with those concerning some other commission. You could not expect artists to be as efficient as other folk. He knew of several stained-glass windows where a similar error had occurred.

Re-unveiling

Sir Ralph added as he left the Conference that he was most distressed that Sir Cyril Blight's attempt at generosity had miscarried in this way. One must, he suggested, learn to take the rough with the smooth.

As soon as Sir Ralph had departed for Herryngs, the statue was re-unveiled on Sir Cyril Blight's instructions. Neither Sir Cyril nor Sir Jacob Epstein was available to comment last night.

Our Art Correspondent Writes:

Sir Ralph Clavering's strictures on the Murrow memorial caused considerable surprise in aesthetic circles. The statue was shown last autumn as part of a one-man show at the Marlborough Galleries, and was thought by almost all Murrow's acquaintances to be an excellent likeness, carried off with verve and panache, the half-heroic stance made attractive by a strong satiric undertone such as one associates with a Sargent portrait. I do not know whether Sir Ralph Clavering visited the exhibition, but I certainly saw Sir Richard at the Private View.

Too many flaming knights, thought Pibble. No, Sir Ralph's a Bart. There was a photograph of Sir Ralph pulling the cord, and another of the disputed statue; Sir Ralph had chosen to sport tropical military uniform—whites—bedizened with every medal and decoration to which he was entitled, and had topped the confection off with a feathered cocked hat. The next cutting was from the following day's "Peterborough" column in the *Daily Telegraph,* a paragraph discussing whether Sir Ralph was allowed by military etiquette to dress like that in England, and whether it had ever been done before by a retired General. He was, the writer decided, and it hadn't.

Pibble leafed back through the folder for a photograph he remembered of Sir Richard in uniform, but when he found it it wasn't a fair comparison. The Admiral had been pictured in a very somber attire at his sister-in-law's funeral; the caption said he had flown in from his NATO command that morning. Sir Ralph was in the background of the same picture, just as soberly dressed; they were fairly alike, but not outstandingly so, compared with other twins. Of course Sir Ralph's mustache made a difference. You could see that Sir Richard was, in their nanny's famous phrase, "the quiet one." Pibble wondered whether there was a single retainer who had known the heroes of St. Quentin in childhood and whose reminiscences of them had not been taped and broadcast in the euphoria of that exhilarating defeat.

Most of the later cuttings were about Herryngs, and its recent blossoming into a Division One Stately Home. There was even an absurd correspondence from the *Times,* the Marquess of Bath and Sir Richard Clavering disputing about whose lions were wilder. There were gossip-column paragraphs about jousts and other tourist-attracting nonsense; the last cutting in the folder was a paragraph from "London Diary" in the *New Statesman,* in which Paul Johnson complained of the immorality of staging a mock hanging to earn a few dollars.

Pibble turned back to the yellow, fuzzy-pictured pages at the beginning of the folder, and was once again surprised at how Sir Richard had seemed the main hero at first. After all, Sir Ralph had undoubtedly been defeated, even if it was at a time when England was so starved of victories that a dashing defeat could set us dancing in the streets. We had made it Narvik and Dieppe and Dunkirk and Copenhagen and Quebec all rolled into one; and Sir Ralph, sent on an impossible enterprise which was shored by self-contradictory planning, had actually blocked two of the St. Quentin submarine pens and completely demolished the third; he'd lost 60 per cent of his force but had held out three days longer than anyone gave him a chance to; and then Richard, handling his miscellaneous flotilla with crazy precision among the puckered shoals, had disobeyed the express orders of a panicking Admiralty and brought the survivors off. Further on, the cuttings contained a reproduction of old Murrow's picture of that lump-in-the-throat moment when Sir Ralph had scrambled with his tiny rear guard into his brother's riddled boat, while a fantastic series of improvised demolitions and booby traps ("Ah, Master Ralph were always a one for practical joking!"—a pensioned undergardener) gave them a bare chance to escape. Murrow had made a mess of the episode, of course, except for a brilliantly sketched mule which he had managed (in defiance of history) to sneak into the scene, but Pibble found that the lump was in his throat all the same.

Then came the book reviews. At first they had been of I-was-there stories, but the myth was already powerful and the reviews were longer than is usually allowed for a drably written account of a senseless muddle. The competition from other war books stiffened, but St. Quentin seemed always to attract the worthwhile historians and the big-name critics. It had the distinction of being the first British exploit of the war to attract a full-scale debunking, but even the hardy young don who had flailed so vigorously into the myth, cataloguing order and counterorder, weighing the ineptitude of the War Office against the dilatoriness of the Admiralty in a prodigious libration of crassness, had excepted the Clavering brothers from his wrath. Pibble remembered reading the actual book, which had belied its notoriety by being a scholarly and well-managed account of the action; the reviewer quoted that phrase of Shaw's about the British soldier being able to stand up to anything except the British War Office.

Pibble picked about in the folder and found himself reading a cutting from *New Society* in which a well-known tellymath analyzed the position of the Claverings in the British social structure on the twenty-fifth anniversary of the Raid. It was an oddly mealymouthed bit of work from someone normally so glib with his condemnations, so ready to cast the first stone, so happy to pick the peeling whitewash off any sepulcher; evidently he did relish explaining why we all, even the unconnable writer, reverenced a pair of old war horses who had done nothing (unless you counted turning their ancestral home into a nine-month fairground) since that ambiguous adventure. He came to the conclusion that it was the nothing-doing which accounted for the nation's love; never had the Claverings attempted to turn their prestige back into action, to pronounce panaceas for the world's ills, to go globe-trotting and become pally with potentates, or even to make speeches demanding bigger and deadlier armies and navies. Occasionally they had written to the papers, as in the matter of the lions: there was another *Times* correspondence in which Sir Ralph defended his action of having a thousand cuckoos trapped in Africa, flying them into England in a friend's plane, and releasing them in Hampshire in the middle of February. He argued (as he had later in court) that a cuckoo brought here by airplane was unlikely to be more or less diseased than one which had migrated unaided.

But if Sir Ralph had done nothing except mar Sir Cyril

Blight's venture into generosity, Sir Richard had been even more quiescent. Apart from his sudden concern with the wildness of lions, his only interest during the whole generation since V-J Day seemed to have been, during the great debunking era, to write to the press to defend this or that scapegoat as a brilliant and courageous officer who had met with unforeseeable bad luck. Each letter was cast in almost the same terms as the last, except that he had reserved his most vehement praise for the most notorious buffoons. He had also steadfastly attended their funerals.

The train, after running through several miles of that southern parkland which suggests to the traveler that there are areas of England where Lady Catherine de Burgh still rules inviolate among her neighbors, ceased from its humming motion and began hawing. The brakes groaned as they took on the task of annihilating the momentum of four hundred tons of wood and metal and fellow travelers, in order that a measly Detective Superintendent should alight at Herryngs Halt. As Pibble slid the fat folder into his briefcase, he remembered the cutting in it which told how a Scottish Liberal had asked the Minister of Transport why trainloads of holidaymakers should be uneconomically stopped and started again at this tiny, nowhere-serving station. He had been booed from both sides of the House.

But when Pibble stepped down onto the sleeper-built platform he found that he was by no means the only one. Two reserved-carriage-loads of tourists were streaming out of doors farther up the train, some with cameras already clicking; the mere name of Herryngs in green-and-white B.R. lettering would make a grandly romantic introit to a half hour of film or a rackful of slides. Dragomans shouted and exhorted; a top-hatted station-master bowed and smiled, obsequious to the smell of dollars; two sleek coaches waited beyond the railings. Pibble decided to let the welter of visitors disappear before he looked for his police car, and when the coaches had sighed away he found that the stationmaster had changed his topper for a scruffy cap before collecting his ticket.

There was no police car, only a ridiculous museum piece of an open tourer with a graying blonde at the wheel. Pibble had taken a prima-donna-ish dislike to the stationmaster and was unwilling to return and ask him for advice, so he walked across toward this chariot to ask the woman the way to Herryngs, but before he realized they were in conversational earshot, she spoke; she did not need to raise her voice, for she commanded that curious, carrying, upper-class timbre which Yeats once called "hound voice"—the accent of people used to communing with dogs.

"Superintendent Pibble?"

"Yes. Are you from Herryngs?"

"They asked me to come and fetch you. My name's Anthea Singleton. Jump up. I'm sorry to come in this bloody old thing, but the General wants the Jag to go to Chichester and all the Land-Rovers are busy."

"I think it's beautiful," said Pibble. "What is it?"

"A 1914 Prince Henry Vauxhall. I think it's beautiful, too, actually. I'm glad you like it. Would you prefer to drive?"

"No, thank you," said Pibble, hoping the emphasis was not too noticeable. *Mrs.* Singleton, he remembered from the press cuttings, only daughter of Sir Ralph Clavering, married to one Harvey Singleton, who had had something to do with the Raid but was otherwise a gentleman of no antecedents that the gossip columnists had thought worth recording, and who was responsible for the growth of Herryngs into a dollar-spinning tourist trap.

Mrs. Singleton had large powder-blue eyes above Slavonic cheekbones. Her complexion had begun to rumple a little, the fine skin crinkling into innumerable tiny roughnesses like a once-used tissue, but that only increased her natural sexiness; a plum or pear tree, in the few years before it dies, fruits with overgenerous foison, and in the same way the appeal of certain women increases in the last few seasons before they pupate into old ladies.

Probably quite unconscious, thought Pibble. She may even be bored with the whole thing, but ten to one she has the men buzzing round her over the after-church Sunday sherry.

She wore a short-sleeved yellow cotton knit shirt and a tweedy skirt, and she drove beautifully, responding to the needs of the huge, slow-rotating engine with the same half-animal sympathy that enables a good show-jumper to respond to and get the best out of his horse. They sat several feet up, well above the tops of the hedgerows, and watched the tinted trees—elms and chestnuts and limes, their undersides shaved horizontal by browsing cows—amble backward.

"The General is always at me to put a modern engine into her," said Mrs. Singleton. "Automatic transmission and all. But luckily Harvey won't allow it because she's an appreciating asset as she is. A bookkeeping husband can sometimes be useful, though you wouldn't think it."

She laughed—a soft, syrupy chuckle.

"I don't know who I'll find to look after her now Deakin is dead," she went on. "There are plenty of other mechanics about, running Old England, but they'd all want to tamper with her; they can't tell the phony from the real, I suppose."

"Do you really call it Old England?" asked Pibble. "Among yourselves, I mean? I'd have thought you had some—some, well, nickname for it?"

She laughed again. (It really was a most engaging noise, mellow and autumnal, quite different from the commanding bark of her speaking voice.)

"D'you find it embarrassing?" she said. "It isn't really. The General calls it 'our bloody peep show,' but Harvey won't let anyone else call it anything except Old England— you soon get used to it. He got the idea from Disneyland— in California, you know—which is a sort of fairground on the grandest scale imaginable; you can ride in a stagecoach or go on a trip up the Amazon. Harvey's got a story about Disney giving orders for a three-hundred-foot model of Mont Blanc to be built from photographs, and then going off on a tour round Europe with his family and actually seeing Mont Blanc, so that when he got back and saw the Disneyland one he said 'Nothing like it—scrap it and start again.' Harvey says you've got to take it as seriously as that or the customers will sense that you're despising them, and that's as bad as swindling them. I married a very upright man, I now realize."

She chuckled, as though recalling some enjoyable error.

"Is Deakin the man who is thought to have killed himself?" said Pibble.

"Yes. He was Uncle Dick's coxswain for years and years, and came to Herryngs when Uncle Dick retired. You aren't really supposed to take your coxswain round from job to job, I think, but they don't pay much attention to that kind of rule—Uncle Dick and the General, I mean. It gives me the willies, what they expect to get away with—like sending for you, for instance."

"Why did they?" said Pibble. "The local police would be just as good at a thing like this. Better, if anything."

"That's what Harvey said, but they insisted that they had to go straight to the top, bonk, and then there wouldn't be any silly gossip about the bigwigs pulling a fast one over the locals. We have to be bloody careful, you know. Journalists are bastards, and the little provincial ones are the worst—they'd sell their souls for six lines in Charles Greville. It's a funny thing, being a Clavering, you know: in theory I could wangle almost anything I wanted—free flights to Bermuda, hols on Onassis's yacht, complimentary models of new cars—but you keep remembering that you've only got to step out of line somewhere and your name will be plastered across every headline in the country. So you don't do either—step out of line or take the giveaways. Harvey says it soon gets about that you can be bought once you've allowed yourself to be.

"Anyway, Deakin was a surly little gnome who loved us. What's more, I think he'd still have loved us if we hadn't been Claverings and St. Quentin had been canceled before a ship sailed. It was just like him, how tidily he hanged himself. Harvey heard the thump and went up and found him and tried to give him the kiss of life, but it wasn't any good."

The road ran beside a walled beechwood and took a right-angled bend; the gates of Herryngs lay in the crook of the wood thus formed, with a half moon of gravel before them. They were shut—wrought iron twenty feet high, with the spotted lion of Clavering rampant at the top of either gatepost. Mrs. Singleton pooped her bulb horn, and at once a sweet old biddy in a mob-cap and sprigged apron came out to open the gates, followed by a gangling colt of a girl similarly attired. The ankle-length skirt looked charming on the old woman but very rum indeed on the girl.

"I recognized your horn, Miss Anty," said the old woman as she undid the catch, "so I thought you wouldn't mind Claire coming out to practice."

"Quite right, Mrs. Chuck. Let's see what you make of it, Claire. At any rate it's a change from Bunsen burners."

The girl smiled sulkily and hauled her gate open. As the Prince Henry rolled between them, the women curtsied, the old one with an easy and becoming flourish, the younger rebelliously, like a boy who has to act the heroine in the school play. Mrs. Singleton stopped her car, and vaulted out.

"Oh dear, Claire," she said, "it isn't the end of the world—it's only a sort of game. If you really hate it, we can find you something else to do, but please have a shot at it for a week or two."

"I feel such a fool in this getup," said Claire.

"Just think how Simon must feel in his black tights and mask and nothing else."

"It's all right for a man," said Claire, with a deep, slow blush.

"Shame!" said Mrs. Singleton. "You'll never be a professor of chemistry if you start kowtowing to men like that. I'll put my arm round your waist and we'll try it together. Now. Down, up. Slower. Do-own, up. That's better. Down, up. You're getting it. Super. Down, up."

They practiced together, while Mrs. Chuck stood smiling by. Mrs. Singleton moved so easily, with such an unaffected dancerly sway, that before long she had coaxed Claire into her own mood. While they bobbed, she talked on.

"This is Superintendent Pibble, Mrs. Chuck, down, up, come down from London to investigate poor Deakin. Did you do all right out of that batch of visitors? Down, up. I think they were almost all Americans."

"Yes, Miss Anty, six pounds twelve and six. I've put it in the book. There'll be three more coaches on the two-fifteen, I do hear. My, Claire, but you *are* coming on; you'll be putting me to shame in a week, and I've been doing it these three years."

"Is that all?" said Pibble. "You manage to look as if you'd been doing it since you were a tot."

"Lawk-a-mussy, no, sir. Four years back I was working in the Sketchleys' in the town, when Miss Anty came and asked me to keep the gate here and I've never regretted it, though it does mean graying my hair. It's not really this color, sir—more a sort of pepper-and-salt."

"Whose idea is 'lawk-a-mussy'?" said Pibble.

"That's one of Harvey's," said Mrs. Singleton. "He compiled a sort of Old England vocabulary which everyone's supposed to use. Thank you, Mrs. Chuck. Give it a go for a few days, Claire, and then if you still don't fancy it come and see me on—let me see—Friday and we'll try and find something behind the scenes for you. I can't afford to lose Simon, not with that torso."

Claire blushed again, a sweet, delicate mantling that

would easily have dragged another shower of coins out of a coachload of tourists.

"Nice girl," said Mrs. Singleton as they drove on, "and brainy, too. She's going to marry our hangman as soon as she's finished her degree. She does it by post, somehow, but I don't understand that sort of thing, never having had an education."

She chuckled, pleased with the easy fruits of ignorance.

"Shall I have to dress up as a Bow Street runner?" said Pibble.

"Wrong period," said Mrs. Singleton. "We aim at a vaguely turn-of-the-century feeling, like the rustics in *Puck of Pook's Hill*. But in any case there's no need for you even to be seen in the public side; it's a bloody great place, and we keep the nicest parts for ourselves, though Harvey's got his eye on them for expansion. But you've got to have somewhere private to eat and sleep—and commit suicide, I suppose."

They rolled up the noble avenue, familiar from half a hundred beer advertisements. The Thetis fountain was squirting at full pressure at the end of it, and as the Prince Henry rounded the rumpled pool the last batch of tourists, guidebound at the top of the wide flight of entrance steps, fusilladed them with the whirr and click of shutters until the gravel took them around the corner of the central building. It was a huge mass of gold-gray stone, high Georgian, plonked down in the middle of the open fields by a Clavering who had come home with half the loot of India two centuries ago. John Wood had begun it, Robert Adam had finished it, and Lancelot Brown had marshaled regiments of laborers to melt the ungainly fields and lumpish hillocks into the swooping, tall-treed sward of the Englishman's dream. In front of them now lay another house, no larger than the average mansion, joined to the Main Block by a graceful curve of glassed-in colonnade.

"It doesn't look as though six pounds twelve and six would go far to maintain this lot," said Pibble.

"Bless you, my dear man, we send all that sort of thing to Oxfam. The visitors pay eight guineas a head, all in except the souvenirs. No *money* changes hands. The guide tells them beforehand that what they give to Mrs. Chuck is for charity. It was Harvey's idea—it puts them in an expensive mood, all guilt assuaged for half a crown."

She had brought the car to a standstill before she spoke the last sentence in her arrogant, penetrating voice; there was a man sitting in a deck chair on the sheltered nook of lawn to their left, and he looked up from his newspaper at the sound.

"You'll be late if you don't hurry, Mr. Waugh," said Mrs. Singleton a little chillily. "The last of them were going into the hall as we arrived."

"Oh, Christ!" said the man. "Who'd be a sodding butler? I've got a god-awful head this morning."

He looked as though he was used to it—a port or brandy man to judge by the deep flush of his complexion. He had been in shirtsleeves, but as he stood up he picked a black jacket from the stool beside him and slid into it. At once the mantle of the Ancestral Butler fell on him. Pibble noticed that the paper which he'd dropped was the *Stage*.

"Thank you for the information, Madam," said Mr. Waugh. "I will attend to the matter immediately."

He even contrived to hurry like a butler, with a curious sliding trot. In a moment they saw him ghosting down the colonnade toward the Main Block.

"He's come for four years now," said Mrs. Singleton, "and the drink gets worse into him every year. He usually gets a part in panto—the Dame or one of the Broker's Men—in the winter, but his ad's still appearing, so I don't think he's had any luck this time. Harvey won't like it if we have to put him up till spring, but we'd never get anyone half as good at the job. He gives them sherry off silver salvers in the Chinese Room and makes it worth the eight bob a glass they're paying. It's tea in the afternoon, of course. He does a marvelous act with one of the maids who has a minute smear of lipstick on her collar—I sometimes do her if we're short-staffed, and he always makes me feel that I'll never wear lipstick again."

"You must be quite close to the end of the season now," said Pibble.

"Yes, thank God. Two more weekends—and shorter days already, of course. At the height of the season, on Saturdays, we put three coachloads through every hour, from ten in the morning till seven at night—that's a thousand a day. Harvey's organized the timing so that it takes any given batch seventeen minutes to pass a particular point, and with a batch coming every twenty minutes there's only three minutes to cope if things go wrong. You have to book to come, you know—we can't have people rolling up on spec."

"It sounds terrifying," said Pibble.

"We have strong nerves, thank God," said Mrs. Singleton. "Even so, I can't think how we'd have coped if all this had happened a couple of months ago."

"Deakin was very important to the enterprise, then?" said Pibble.

"Deakin?" said Mrs. Singleton, with a tiny lilt of surprise. "He hated it. What makes you..."

"You said 'all this,'" said Pibble, "and it rather suggested..."

"Oh, I see what you mean. No, but it is terribly upsetting, of course, and it makes it difficult to keep a proper eye on things, and so on. Come and meet the General. We live in this bit. There were meant to be four, one at each corner of the Main Block, but they only built two, thank God. The other one's the old Kitchens, which Harvey's turned into a super sort of ye olde restaurant. This way. They'll be in the study, I should think."

She led him through a glass door into the colonnade. Through the arch opposite he could see the symmetrical colonnade curving away from the main building to where the symmetrical block stood, pretty and refined by distance, a beautifully judged piece of perspective. It was difficult to think that even now a roistering lunch was being prepared so that two coachloads of Americans could contribute to the tottering economy of the country. This colonnade was used as a greenhouse and was heavy with rich, dusty, vegetable odors, dominated by the muscat vine which reached across the corridor ten paces from where they had entered; there were a few clusters of grapes pendent from it. Mrs. Singleton led him in the other direction, into the Private Wing.

At first sniff and glance it was surprisingly like the inside of any other largish house. The stairs leading up from the hall were wood and not the expected marble, and the furniture was handsome but ordinary. The hall was really only a widening in a long passage that led straight ahead of him, with half a dozen doors on either side; it was dark enough for the lights to be on.

"Josiah built it for visiting orchestras and genealogists and people like that," said Mrs. Singleton, "people who weren't quite servants and weren't quite gentry. He had nightmares about a penniless Scotch flutist running off with one of his daughters, so he wanted to keep that kind of visitor separate, which makes it much more comfortable than the Main Block, by our standards. Let's try in here."

She opened the second door on the left, and for a moment the noise of a male voice, low, droning, persuasive, hung in the air. It stopped short. Mrs. Singleton went in, but stood aside so that Pibble could pass through.

"This is Superintendent Pibble," she said. "You'll have to watch your step, General, he's as quick as old Treacle. I'll go and see how the visitors are getting on—Mr. Waugh was still reading his paper when they came, Harvey. You'll have to watch your step, too, Mr. Pibble. The General likes telling lies. I hope I'll see you again at luncheon. Goodbye for now.'"

She was gone. Pibble, who had been trapped in the predicament of having to listen to somebody who was behind him without turning his back on the people he was being introduced to, moved properly into the room. There were two men there, both already standing, though he could see from their attitudes that they had just risen from a pair of long, chintz-covered, brokenspringed armchairs on either side of the fireplace. The older man walked across and held out his hand for Pibble to shake; it was dry, cold and rough-textured, like the skin of a grass snake. Pibble looked curiously at the famous face. He remembered his image of the chosen vulture. At close quarters this did not seem like a lion who was ready to have his carcass settled onto.

11:30 A.M.

"You mustn't worry about Anty," said the General. "She talks like that and expects everyone to follow because she never went to a proper school. Treacle was a Jack Russell—best ratter I ever owned. Let's have a look at you."

The words came with such authority in the high but husky voice that they were offenseless. Pibble suppressed an instinct to stand to attention and looked back at the General. Sir Ralph Clavering was a smallish man, not as small as a jockey, though there was something about his stance which gave that impression; and his clothes were definitely horsy— a flared russet jacket, scrambled-egg waistcoat, and narrow twill trousers. The white eyebrows probed forward like the horns of a stag beetle, and the brisk mustache repeated the note. There hadn't been any color photographs in the folder, so Pibble was surprised by the General's tan—an even fawn color like a starlet's legs, with only a faint suggestion of the mottlings of age beneath it. The eyes were a guileless blue, clear as a child's except for the red-laced whites.

"You a gentleman?" said the General abruptly.

"Not even in a technical sense," said Pibble.

"Excellent!" said the General, with an alto giggle. "Absolutely excellent!"

He crossed the room to the desk and flicked a button on a tape recorder.

"File this under test section," he said. "Asked policeman who came to see about Deakin the usual. Answer 'Not even in a technical sense.' No hesitation."

He flicked another button and turned back.

"Funny how few people have the nerve to say yes, straight out," he said. "This is my son-in-law, Harvey Singleton. He runs our sideshows. He'll explain why we got you down rather than letting in the local cops. Put it more glibly than me. Bloody lampreys! Sit down."

They all sat, Pibble on one of those many-cushioned sofas the slackness of whose upholstery precludes any posture except a lounging one. Mr. Singleton settled back into his chair and began to poke about at strawy wisps of tobacco in the bowl of an ugly great pipe, not as though he had any intention of smoking it but as though fiddling with it was a substitute for more vehement action. Pibble had hardly looked at him before he spoke, and had a vague feeling that he was unusually tall. Now he saw a pale, high-domed face, curly black hair, and an oddly straight mouth. When Mr. Singleton spoke, his lower jaw moved all of a piece, with a fluttering, but vaguely mechanical motion, like that of a TV puppet. The droning voice which their arrival had interrupted had been his.

"Not glibly," he said. "Plainly; the General tends not to mean precisely what he says. I do. Let me say at once, Superintendent, that we live an odd life here at Herryngs. I would not want you to think that we are proud of our ability to pull strings, such as the ones we pulled to get you down here. There are times when we are literally forced into actions of this sort. To put it bluntly, we have found the local police are too free with what they pass on to newspapermen. I don't know whether you know about journalists in an area like this—I have to, because we are so concerned with publicity—but most of them have some sort of connection with at least one of the national papers, and they can make a few quid by sending tidbits about Herryngs up to London.

"To be honest, we are usually glad of this arrangement, and from time to time we stage a newsworthy event, just to keep our name in the papers. But I spoke to one of them at a reception we gave and—I'm sorry to have to tell you this, and ought in fairness to add that he'd already drunk more than he could hold—he said that what he would really like from Herryngs was a nice juicy scandal. This may seem very shocking to you, Superintendent, but it is a fact we have to live with.

"Poor Deakin's death is not a scandal—by no means; I hope you won't think that. In fact it's a great sadness to us all, a great sadness, but journalists of the type I have described are distressingly willing to exaggerate a minor calamity of this sort into a major event, and to dress up their imaginings with irrelevant gossip. Now, from one or two things which have happened in the past year we have come to believe that there is at least one officer in the local force who is more than willing to abet these gentry in their efforts. We could, and I put it to you fairly, pull yet more strings and have the men posted elsewhere, but if we took that course and the facts leaked out, we would be running the risk of an even greater scandal; so for the most part we put up with them, and with the tiresome little insinuations about thefts and vandalism here of which they are the source. But in this case, to put it bluntly, we decided to circumvent them."

"Rang up the Chief Constable," broke in the General. "Bit of an ass, but not a bad chap. Know him well. Squared it with him."

"I hope you understand," said Mr. Singleton, leaning earnestly forward like a politician leaning toward a TV camera for a peroration. "You may feel that we have called you down here over a trivial matter, but I assure you it is not trivial to us, even at this stage of the season. May I take it that you concur?"

"Of course," muttered Pibble, shrinking further back into the bosomy cushions, half hypnotized by the dull, plangent voice. No point in telling them they were making a mistake: this, if anything, was the way to cause a stink, even if the Coroner was as tidily under their thumb as the Chief Constable seemed to be. And, Crippen, think if it had been Harry Brazzil! He'd have *arrived* with a carload of friends from Fleet Street.

"Doubtful?" said the General.

"It's only that routine procedures usually turn out to be least trouble in the end," said Pibble. "But you're stuck with me now, so there's no point in worrying about it."

"Sound fellow," said the General. "What would you like to do first?"

"Perhaps Mr. Singleton could tell me about finding the body; then I could ask any questions that occurred to me, and then we could look at the place where he died. I must see the body, and talk to the doctor who examined it—I suppose it's in Southampton. I ought also to talk to any of the local police who have already been involved; it would be madness, from your point of view, if I didn't."

"Quite right," said the General, springing from his chair. He picked an internal telephone off the desk and pressed one of the dozen buttons that lined its base.

"Judith? Arrange to get Dr. Kirtle out here at once, please. Ask him if he'd be kind enough to pick up Sergeant Maxwell on his way. Then ring up the police station and see that you talk to Roberts, not Flagstaff. Ask him to arrange for Maxwell to be free in ten minutes' time for about an hour, and say that Dr. Kirtle will pick him up. Got all that? Good lass."

"The body's still here," said Mr. Singleton. "We have a spare cold-storage room which we hardly use at this time of year, with the visitors tailing off; to be frank, they have nothing as suitable in town, and Southampton's a long way for you to drive over to. As for what happened, I never go to bed until three or four in the morning, and I have excellent hearing. There was a curious thud at about two, followed by a brief drumming, which I thought came from Uncle Dick's floor. I do not normally go up there, but I felt it was my duty to investigate. The light was on in Deakin's pantry, and the door was open. He was hanging by a rope from a pipe across the ceiling; his stool was lying on the floor; he was still swinging. I cut the rope with one of his chisels and lowered him to the floor to administer the kiss of life, a technique in which I have taken instruction. It was not efficacious. Indeed, Dr. Kirtle told me afterward that it could not have been, as Deakin had broken his neck."

"Hanged himself bloody neatly," said the General approvingly. "Deakin was always a thoroughly seamanlike fellow."

"Didn't Sir Richard hear any of this?" said Pibble.

"My brother's a bit deaf," said the General. "Sailors never learn; they will go standing too near those bloody great guns they affect. He's very cut up about it, particularly about not hearing, as a matter of fact. That's one reason why he's left it to us to cope with you."

"And the other reason?" said Pibble.

"He's an author," said the General, with his silly giggle, "and authors mustn't be bothered."

Mr. Singleton sighed, the despairing exhalation of the puritan confronted with frivolity.

"Let me be honest with you," he said. "The Claverings don't give a damn for anybody. I have reasoned with them, but they still insist on behaving with all the social irresponsibility of their grandparents."

The General leaned back in his chair, beaming as at a compliment.

"At the moment," said Mr. Singleton, "Uncle Dick is absorbed in writing a book about lions. We have some here, as you may be aware—indeed we make quite a feature of them. Uncle Dick has not interested himself much in the business side of the Herryngs enterprise, but a year ago he began to study the lions very seriously, very seriously indeed."

"He's had papers published in zoological journals," said the General with motherly pride. "He's got a theory that in a couple of generations there won't be any wild animals left; they'll all have to be kept in conditions like ours because pressure of human population will have squeezed them out of their habitats. Dick says these fellows who insist on studying them in the wild are all to cock, and will be out of date in a jiffy. Thing is to know as much as possible about them in captivity. Gets letters from dozens of zoos every day, you know. Costs us a fortune in stamps."

Harvey laughed suddenly, with the tolerant amusement of the expert.

"It hardly costs us a penny, General," he said. "Anything concerned with the welfare of the lions is an allowable expense. Be that as may be, Superintendent, Uncle Dick works at his book from nine to twelve-thirty every morning, and refuses to be disturbed. But there will be plenty to keep you occupied until luncheon, and then he can tell you all you need to know about Deakin's private life, which was, to be frank, negligible The General is going to Chichester shortly, so if you can think of anything you wish to ask him now, that would be convenient."

"I shall have to have a word with the Coroner at some point," said Pibble.

"Coming out this afternoon," said the General. "Always comes on the second and fourth Tuesdays of the month."

"He's one of our solicitors," explained Mr. Singleton, "and I have enough business with him to make a regular appointment worth while. You can see him before I do, and if you both agree that this matter is as straightforward as it appears to me, you will be able to catch the four-forty back to London."

"Almost all suicides are straightforward, in one sense," said Pibble. "Anybody except a complete bungler can kill himself if he really wants to, and leave no doubt about how he did it. But in another sense almost all suicides are mysterious, because we find it difficult to imagine ourselves reaching that pitch of desperation or resentment or whatever in which we'd take our own lives. However clear the time and method of Deakin's death may be, you'll find most people wondering why he did it—I think you'd have told me if he'd left a note."

"No note," said the General. "Too tidy and secretive for that—early pot training, I daresay. But Deakin was a randy little fellow, always hanging around after Harvey's serving wenches. You haven't seen him, but he was the hairiest little runt I ever clapped eyes on, and you know what they say about hairy runts. It's rubbish, of course—I'm a hairy runt myself, and I've always run neck and neck with Dick in the fornication stakes, and he's nothing like as hairy. Course, if I'd been a hairy runt *and* a sailor—"

He broke off with his bizarre giggle, suggesting in the aposiopesis whole littorals of dishonored womanhood. Mr. Singleton's implacable drone brought the conversation back to the coxswain in the cold-storage room.

"Our theory," he said, "is that Deakin was crossed in love. I am forced to employ a number of attractive girls and, though I have no wish to speak ill of the dead, he was in the habit of pestering them. He was, to put it bluntly, an unprepossessing specimen, and they used to lead him on and let him down. I must admit that tempers tend to wear thin by this stage of the season. By the way, General, I doubt if we can employ Waugh for another year—he was incapable again last night. I'm sorry, Superintendent, but there is so much to think of. I've told Mrs. Hurley, who is in general charge of the girls, to find out what she can, but she has not yet produced a solution."

"Fine," said Pibble. "That's all I can think of for the moment. What are you going to see in Chichester, sir?"

Social unease stalked into the room, like a ghost walking over a live man's grave. Pibble couldn't conceive what solecism he'd committed, as both the men stared at him in withdrawn surprise. Then the General giggled and the ghost was exorcised.

"What'll I see?" he sang, in a creaky countertenor, "I'll see the sea."

Mr. Singleton sighed again, the sigh which Pibble, after years of working with certain police colleagues, recognized as that of a man faced with a levity he has not the authority to reprimand.

"The General is going sailing," he said, "not to the theatre."

"God forbid," said the General. "I'm the last of the Philistines, Superintendent. I'll see you at the inquest, no doubt."

He left with a bouncy little strut, rising slightly onto the ball of his foot at each step. Mr. Singleton sighed for the third time as the door closed, but this time the sigh suggested that conversation would now be easier, without the monitoring presence from a dead generation. He rose and walked to the window. He really was unusually tall, at least six feet four. He stood for half a minute gazing through the glass, and then spoke without turning his head. There was a softer note in his robotlike utterance.

"This is the most marvelous view in the world, though I say it myself. I draw deep inspiration from it every day."

It would have been churlish not to go and share such a view, so Pibble weltered out of the sofa and crossed the room. His first reaction was that Mr. Singleton's source of inspiration was curiously dreamlike and escapist for so drearily pragmatic a man. They were looking at almost the same vista as the one he had glimpsed earlier from the colonnade, but the extra angle achieved by the jut of the Private Wing brought the Main Block into the picture, altering the whole perspective so that the further colonnade and the Kitchen Wing were no longer merely pretty in themselves, but became a necessary balance to the huge elegance of the central building. Down the first slope stood the famous lime tree, a solid fountain of yellowing leaf with a small herd of dappled deer grazing at its foot, and beyond that the traditional English landscape, at its most mistily genteel, rolled away into blueness.

As an extra touch to the artificiality of the scene, there was a scarlet blob in the foreground, like the red buoy Turner used to pop into the foreground of his seascapes on varnishing day, except that this was an E-Type Jaguar convertible standing on the gravel below them. It really was below them, as the slope of the ground left the Private Wing a story higher this side than the other. The car looked posed, as though for a color advertisement, but as they gazed over those leagues of plebs-concealing greenness a glass door in the colonnade opened and the General came prancing down the steps to the drive. His peculiar, dainty, arrogant gait reminded Pibble instantly of the movements of stags, such as those that grazed under the lime tree—something poised, limber, and fierce, but at the same time preserved (carefully and against the odds) into an alien age and climate.

Pibble knew at once that he wasn't going to Chichester to sail, either. There must be a woman there.

The General didn't actually leap into the car as though it were a saddle, but he settled into his seat like a man used to horses. The extending bonnet became an expression of his personality. He raised one hand in a theatrically romantic salute to their window and roared away, gravel spitting in twin arcs behind his half-spinning wheels.

"A very great man indeed," said Mr. Singleton plonkingly.

Before Pibble could answer, they were distracted by a new unreality in the panorama: out from behind one of the copses in the middle distance, crawling along a low embankment, came Stephenson's *Rocket;* slow puffs of purplish smoke whuffled from its ridiculous smokestack, and the monstrous cylinders on either side pumped like the legs of a grasshopper. Behind the engine came a dozen open trucks which carried about forty solemn citizens, wearing anachronistic bonnets and stovepipe hats. Only the incessant working of their limbs as they clicked, focused, panned, whirred, and hectically changed films showed that they were the same group of Americans that had shared Pibble's train.

"If an airliner exploded over here," he said, "you'd have a perfect record of the event. There'd be bound to be at least one cinecamera pointing skyward at any given moment."

"Couldn't happen," said Mr. Singleton. "I've had them all routed out of our air space. What would our visitors think of Old England if we allowed bloody great Boeings to come whining over during a peak moment like the execution? Excuse me."

He picked up the intercom.

"Judith? Yes, I know—we saw him go. Did he say anything important to you? No, I've got him here. O.K., fine, you've done very well. Now, look, will you get on to Fritz and tell him he's putting too much color into that damned smoke again—we don't want them all thinking their films have been wrongly developed. Good. When Kirtle and that policeman turn up, put them in the Zoffany Room. We'll be in Deakin's pantry for about ten minutes, and then over in the Kitchens, in the meat store. Right. Look after yourself."

Pibble had been half listening, vaguely aware of the sudden liveliness of tone, but really more interested by the way the *Rocket* disappeared into the next cutting—slowly, not with the rush and thump of a modern train slogging into a tunnel, but more like a millepede wriggling under a stone. There was something appealingly pathetic about it—such a weak, hopeless mutation of transport to have sired the snorting generations of the Iron Horse.

"That all right by you?" said Mr. Singleton. "If that train's on time, it is eleven-fifty-eight. You've time to see the pantry and the body, and then talk to the Doctor and Constable What's-His-Name, before luncheon. Spruheim, the Coroner, will be here soon after luncheon, and I trust we'll be able to put you on the four-forty with everything tidied up and ready for the inquest."

"That suits me very well," said Pibble. "You must pay a fantastic amount of attention to detail. I enjoyed Mrs. Chuck's 'lawk-a-mussy'—how did you choose the vocabulary?"

"I took a speed-reading course," said Mr. Singleton. "I confess I would have done that in any case—it seems to me essential in this day and age—but the first major project I used it for was to read all Thomas Hardy and all Mary Webb. This way."

Pibble could no longer protract his drowning in that dream landscape, for Mr. Singleton was already holding the door for him. The stairs were wide and soft-carpeted, their edges emitting a drowsy smell of floor polish. A pretty minidome, glassed like the colonnade, provided light for the square central well. On the first landing, through an open door, he saw a maid vacuuming the floor of a happily proportioned bedroom,

"One doesn't think of big houses having bits like this in them," he said, "where people can live a comfortable twentieth-century life."

He felt a fool the moment he said it, infected with the falsity of Herryngs, seduced into the suggestion that the Pibbles, too, dwelt habitually in marble, but in their case uncomfortable, halls, and maids vacuumed their bedroom. Singleton did not seem to notice the wrong note.

"Yes," he said as they started up the next flight, "but it is a wholly uneconomic arrangement. All this space could be...But I won't bother you with irrelevant details."

The speed at which he went upstairs seemed to Pibble to be also a wholly uneconomic arrangement, but it wasn't shortness of breath that had caused him to whisper. He approached the top landing with the reverence of a tourist who enters a two-star cathedral and finds a mass being sung.

"Uncle Dick's working in there," breathed Mr.

Singleton, pointing along the landing. (This landing was in fact a gallery running around all four sides of the stair well, with half a dozen doors opening off it. The door he pointed at had the barrel of a huge old key protruding half an inch through the keyhole.) "You can see he's locked himself in. That's his bathroom, that's a spare bathroom, that's Deakin's pantry, that's Deakin's room, the other two are spare rooms which we seldom use. This is the key of the pantry. Perhaps you would prefer to unlock it yourself."

The key was the size of a hatchet, but moved effortlessly in the lock of the big door. 'Pantry" turned out to be a curious name for what was more of a workshop, a small room smelling of oils and paints and fresh-cut timber. Most of the wall space was filled by cupboards, but a small workbench stood against the left-hand wall, and above it was fixed a large rectangle of pegboard, from whose hooks and clips hung a carefully ranged collection of excellent tools, all bearing that peculiar rich patina, on steel and wood, which comes from the endless rubbing of palms that have handled them often and properly. An upright chair stood by the sink under the window; there was a tiny cooker. On the bench was a finished but only half-painted model of a landing craft, about three feet long, and beside it a noose of rope cut off diagonally nine inches above the knot. The other piece of the rope was still hanging from a water pipe that crossed the ceiling. A kitchen stool lay diagonally across the linoleum.

"Did anyone think of putting a seal on the door?" said Pibble.

"The General wanted to," said Mr. Singleton, "but Sergeant Thing was shocked by the idea, and we had no wish to offend him. He did the fingerprinting and I took the photographs for him, which came out excellently though I say it myself. They were all mine and Deakin's. I have the proofs in my desk."

He was still whispering, though they must have been out of earshot of the lion-fancying Admiral; Pibble wondered whether it could have been a curious decency toward the dead which Mr. Singleton would never have manifested if the coxswain had been living, bowing, and scraping flesh. That, too, seemed improbable.

There was really nothing to look at: the cupboards were full of neatly arranged paints, glues, glass jars containing nails and screws, boxes of carefully sorted miscellanea, boxes of taps and dies, plugs and sockets, electric cords in various gauges, and so on. There was nothing conceivably personal, no reading matter or diary or family photographs, but there was a pad and pencil with which the suicide could have written his long farewell. Pibble held the pad sideways to the light and found the impression of the previous sheet still visible—a diagram and a set of figures, such as a man jots down when he is fitting a set of shelves into an alcove.

The noose on the workbench was as tidily made as the model beside it, with a proper hangman's knot to catch you under the corner of your jaw when your momentum—thirty-two feet per sec. per sec.—would jerk your head sideways and snap the vertebrae as finally as a chef breaking an egg. Pibble measured the distances with his eye: Deakin had been a little man, a runt; the stool was two feet six; he must have calculated things nicely to give himself the maximum drop, and finished with his toes a bare inch from the ground.

"You said something about a drumming noise," said Pibble.

"Yes," said Mr. Singleton. "I think he might have kicked out against that cupboard door, though that's only my own opinion."

Perhaps, but why worry? A suicide is a suicide, whatever noises he makes in his last six seconds.

Deakin's bedroom was even bleaker than his pantry; bed, upright chairs, chairs, satinwood cupboard, and chest of drawers full of carefully mended clothes of coarse quality, tin trunk containing much-mothballed uniforms, no books, no papers. Only on the small, bare table was there any sign of a personality, and that was not Deakin's: in a tooled blue morocco frame, almost three feet high, stood a signed photograph of Sir Richard Clavering riding in the Coronation procession. The old hero looked magnificent, small on his enormous horse, but as easy in his saddle as a border thief (he'd probably ridden to hounds since he was five, after all), withdrawn but assured, the embodiment of all that the Clavering myth meant to the English. The likeness between the brothers seemed much more noticeable in this picture than it had in the one in Pibble's file, despite the Admiral's clean-shaven lips and clipped eyebrows. But, subtly, the difference seemed stronger, too: here was none of the suggestion of the jockey, so noticeable in the General; the assuredness was far from breezy; Pibble was certain that the Admiral's walk would be entirely different from Sir Ralph's gazelle-like strut.

"Seen enough?" said Mr. Singleton sharply, from the door. "It will take us three and a half minutes to walk down to the Kitchen Wing and one and a half to come back. Kirtle should be here in ten minutes, which will leave you five to inspect the body. I have no wish to hurry you, of course."

They walked in silence down the stairs and along the colonnade under the scented muscats.

The Main Block was a different world, an air almost too grandiose to breathe: first a vast, chill salon, a perfect cube frilled with gilt plaster but mitigated by a deep-arched alcove which enshrined the scandalous Zoffany (nothing like as lubricious as Pibble had been led to expect); next the prodigious vaulted hall, which made the salon seem like a broom cupboard by its size, and out of which the marble stairs, frothing with statuary, swept upward. Here like a plump ghost with no one to haunt, mooned Mr. Waugh.

"All well?"' said Mr. Singleton.

"To the best of my knowledge, sir," said Mr. Waugh. "The foreign visitors seemed both impressed and satisfied."

"Good," said Mr. Singleton. "I will take Superintendent

Pibble down to the Kitchen Wing, and then I will come back and have a word with you."

Mr. Waugh bowed, a barely perceptible waggle of acquiescence, and they walked on across the furlong of polished oak. Mr. Singleton wore Hush Puppies which went squeak-squeak on the shiny surface, and Pibble's honest leather answered with a plebeian clack-clack. Beyond the hall, entered through a grape-swagged pair of fifteen-foot doors, was the Chinese Withdrawing Room, a double cube this time; in the remote corner the last knot of a batch of tourists was being sucked out of another pair of doors, slaves to Mr. Singleton's implacable schedule.

"The Americans must appreciate the warmth," said Pibble. "I don't see any radiators."

He looked around the monster collection of conversation bait: armor and weapons from every century; glass display cases full of documents and medals and curios; fine furniture enough to glut Sotheby's; and, gloaming down upon the bric-a-brac, the generations of Claverings, from the stiff yellow-and-black pre-Holbein portraits, through Vandyke and Reynolds and Romney and Sargent and Birley, to the General's practical-joke portrait by Dali and Epstein's genial bronze bust of the Admiral.

"We keep this room at seventy-two," said Mr. Singleton, not pausing in his stride. "I confess I was lucky in this case. Old Josiah had lived half his life in India and did not mind what he paid to be warm, so he installed a primitive hypocaust, which I simply adapted for oil. This way."

The other colonnade was also run as a greenhouse, but with a difference; the heavy smell, near to rottenness, of the muscats was missing, and so were the plants put out to wither; everything here was for display, and it must have needed another large greenhouse to keep this one stocked. An old man with a spade beard, his face hidden beneath a droop-brimmed hat, his trousers tied with string below the knee, was spraying an arrangement of ferns; he touched his hat as they passed, but did not look up. The doors at the far end led directly into the kitchen, a big plain room with deal tables and settles filling two-thirds of it. A big, plain woman was counting slabs of steak onto a butcher's block beside a bed of glowing charcoal.

"That looks good," said Pibble.

"It has to be," said Mr. Singleton. "Americans understand about meat."

There was a stone passage on the far side of the kitchen, with little round-topped doors opening off on the right every few feet; Mr. Singleton unlocked the fourth and Pibble followed him in. It was like stepping out of mellow October into black frost.

"There he is," said Mr. Singleton. "If you have finished before I come to fetch you, perhaps you would be kind enough to wait in the Chinese Room. The light switches are here. I will shut the door to keep the cold in. It opens from the inside."

"Fine," said Pibble. The door, thick as a strong-room hatch with insulation, swung shut with a breathy plup. He was entombed with the suicidal coxswain.

The light was garish. The dead man lay on a marble shelf, his eyes shut, the contours of his face (such of them as were visible through a Sealyham-like sprouting of white whiskers) relaxed into the strong lineaments of death. Pibble hated bodies; it wasn't squeamishness, but a sense of intrusion into a particularly bleak intimacy, and the facial changes always added to this feeling. With the disappearance of the shifting minute-by-minute animation of the moving blood, you saw the real, enduring character emerge in coarse lines like a caricature. The mouths harshened; the bones of the nose declared their nature; the intricate patterning of wrinkles resolved into a bold, interpretable ideogram.

Deakin's dogginess had resided not only in his whiskers; all his features were small and sharp, like a terrier's. The grisly process of hanging had even cocked his head inquiringly to one side, as though his last thought on earth had been a desire that someone should throw a stick for him. The contents of his pockets lay in a neat pile above his head, banal and uninformative. His shoes were old but glossy with ten thousand polishings. His hands were square and calloused, and in a cracked nail was a thread of what might have been hemp from the rope he used to hang himself.

Pibble stared at the waxy face and tried to imagine Mr. Singleton applying the kiss of life through all that hair. The chill made him feel detached, ruminative, just as the mild warmth through his carriage window had earlier that morning.

I am being conned, he thought. I am a tiny figure in some larger drama of theirs, simply here to be gulled and sent home, more momentary and peripheral even than loyal old Deakin. I must do my duty by God and the Claverings, certify this suicide, touch my cap, and depart. Anyway, it is a certifiable suicide, not quite unfakable but as near as makes no difference. You'd have to make him unconscious, lift him with the noose round his neck almost to the ceiling, drop him—it'd take at least two. Drugs would show in the autopsy, and so would the bruise of a knockout blow. Memo: see that stomach contents are analyzed.

Or you could hypnotize him—which is what they're doing to me, dangling their glittering life in front of me and letting it swing slowly to and fro, until I can only gasp, yes, yes. At the instant of arrival there is honeyish Mrs. Singleton in her dottily beautiful car, sent specially to meet me when they could easily have told the coaches to pick me up, and prattling away as if I were an old friend. Then Sir Ralph bowls me a dolly, watches me cart it for six, and records his admiration for posterity. Even Harvey Singleton, the rapid reader, for whom all time is composed of instants in which the profit motive can operate, tells me more than he need and stages a moment of soul-baring at the study window. "Stages" is the word. Memo: go and stand on the gravel and look whether a man driving away could actually see watchers behind glass a story higher.

What else? (He was now so cold that Deakin's whiskers took on the appearance of hoarfrost.) "I can't think how we'd have coped if *all this* had happened a couple of months ago." And then that leaky explanation about it being terribly upsetting, and making it difficult to keep a proper eye on things. What else had she been doing with Mrs. Chuck and Claire and Mr. Waugh, for heaven's sake? And then Mr. Singleton had claimed that Deakin's death was not trivial to *them, even at this stage of the season:* rum epitaph for a faithful servant. And the Singletons had told different tales about who'd insisted on calling in Scotland Yard, though Singleton himself might have said "we" for the sake of family solidarity. Memo: ask why Deakin was making a model landing craft. And why was Singleton whispering?

It wasn't much. (He sighed, and his breath hung mistily in the icy air.) Apart from the Claverings' assumption that the rules didn't apply to them—getting a wallah down from London, shoving the corpse in here, not allowing anyone to bother about an autopsy, freezing out the local police—there was only one genuinely odd thing: Singleton had heard a noise of drumming, but Deakin's neck had been broken clean, and his shoes and the cupboard door had been unmarked, though both were so polished that they looked as if a fly's footsteps would have scarred them. When a man hangs, he drums his heels—in literature; in fact he can only achieve that last tattoo if he's bungled the job and is strangling. But if you're inventing a story you put the drumming in because it feels right.

Not enough to bother a prosecutor with, or anyone else. Still, there was another rum thing about the wallah from London: that Tom Scott-Ellis and Harry Brazzil, the two most eager blue-blood suckers in Scotland Yard should have been joint favorites in the Herryngs Stakes—several other chaps had been far less busy. And then, with as much fuss as a big bank robbery would have warranted, it had been Pibble who'd been sent, quiet, easygoing Jimmy Pibble, whose main achievement in life had been to lever himself out of the upper-lower-middle class into the lower-middle-middle, despite the handicap of an overrefined wife—just the man to buy a social gold brick for its shiny outside, they'd thought. (No, not fair to the Ass. Com., who couldn't have known about the gold brick. It would just have been put to him, in grunts and half sentences, that an officer with some respect for his betters would be more welcome to the Claverings. They had chosen their own vulture, and specified one who didn't like the taste of lion.)

Crippen, I'm cold, he thought, but did nothing about it; stared at the blind face of the corpse and wondered why the Chichester Theatre had felt like a social gaffe. They ought to be used to gaffes, ride them as easily as a liner taking a ten-foot wave. Answer, he'd asked a question they hadn't prepared an answer for.

O.K., so he was being conned, and there was nothing to do about it. Make a fuss, ask tiresome questions, insist on formalities, and they'd all (including the Ass. Com. and Brazzil and Scott-Ellis) assume he was trying to spin the Herryngs paragraph in his book out into a Herryngs chapter. There was nothing to go on, except the drumming noise and the smell of being conned (sense of smell thanks to the exquisitely patient process of moving from upper-lower-middle to lower-middle-middle); so stay conned. Perhaps hint to the Ass. Com. of his unease (given the luck of catching him in the lift or something—no formal request for interview) and let *him* carry the ghostly load of responsibility. Otherwise let sleeping lions lie. A good policeman never has hunches, his first boss, Dick Foyle, used to say.

Gloomy with the foreknowledge of self-betrayal, Pibble turned to the door. His heart bounced in irrational panic as he walked toward its safe-like solidity: they'd locked him in

to die freezing, while eighty Americans chumped knowl-
edgeably through bleeding steaks not twenty yards away!

But the latch was on the other edge of the door, hidden
in a triangle of shadow, and the door opened smoothly. He
turned off the light, shut Deakin back into solitude, and
stood shuddering with cold in the flagged passage. Cold and
shock. He had believed them capable of it—they *were* capable of it, dammit.

O.K., he was going quietly. But let them stretch his conscience one notch further and the lion would feel the talons
of this vulture, blunt, bourgeois talons though they were.

12:25 P.M.

The Chinese Room was empty except for its trophies. Pibble mooned about, gazing halfheartedly at this and that: here a scrap of tarnished fabric from the Field of the Cloth of Gold; there a side drum which had been one of those not heard at the burial of Sir John Moore at Corunna; here an invitation to a soirée at the Hell-Fire Club; there fragments of birch twig rescued from the flesh of some previous Clavering after a thrashing at Eton.

He stopped, astonished and outraged, in front of a case of exhibits from the St. Quentin Raid—mainly weapons, all modern and apparently in good working order: the Sten which Sir Ralph himself had carried; the long-barreled Colt .45 with which "Dotty" Prosser, the Raid's posthumous V.C., had wiped out two nests of machine gunners guarding the submarine pens; a captured Skoda automatic; the famous but now dusty grenade which had failed to explode when it landed in the middle of the Raid's command group; Sir Ralph's sketches for one of his big booby traps; and so on. There must be a dozen gangs in London, not to mention several thousand semi-psychopaths up and down the country, to whom this lot would seem worth more than even the lovely Romney of Miss Hester Clavering which smiled with sweet eighteenth-century blankness immediately above the deadly collection. And deadly they looked, ready to go bang-bang or

rat-a-tat this instant and mow down the revolting plebs—
there was even a round of grayness where a drop of fresh oil
had fallen onto the typewritten label of the Colt, so carefully was everything maintained in its lethal perfection.

Ah, hell, what was the point in being outraged? It was
just typical Clavering, the assumption that pleas to hand
over weapons to the police didn't apply to *them*. To school
himself into the mood of going quietly, Pibble turned away
and walked across to inspect the bronze Epstein bust.

Seen close, it was a delicious piece of work. Pibble had
always associated an element of caricature with these portraits—shaggy Shaw rendered as an intellectual goat, saintly
Einstein haloed with his own hair. This time the artist
seemed to have chosen as Sir Richard's chief characteristic a
deliberate mildness, a balanced sweetness of mind, which he
had interpreted into bronze, treating the willing metal with
less than his usual fierceness so that the modeling of even
the ear lobes seemed to be part of a central douce harmony.

Curiously, the big-joke Dali above the bust shared some
of its qualities, for here, too, smoothness reigned, painstak-
ing and glossy. But beneath the sheer patina of varnish wal-
lowed all the Surrealist furies; Sir Ralph's face was purple
and twisted with Goya-like rage, and his scarlet uniform was
shown as a series of half-opened drawers full of corpses tumbled together like odd socks.

"Many of our visitors, especially the Germans, admire it
considerably, sir," said a voice at Pibble's elbow. Mr. Waugh
had glided in, silent on the moss-thick carpet, and now stood
in a beautifully calculated pose of haughty subservience.

"Can I get you anything, sir?" he added, and the disguise became marginally less complete: there was that in the
actor-butler's intonation which made it clear that the apparently limitless possibilities of "anything" began and ended
with a stiff drink.

"No, thanks," said Pibble. "Do you know if the Doctor
and Sergeant Maxwell have come?"

"I believe so, sir. Mr. Singleton is talking to them in the Zoffany Room."

"This time the faltering of tone was more marked. Pibble decided to risk a timid probe.

"Mr. Singleton must pay the most fantastic attention to detail," he said.

"Too sodding right he does," said Mr. Waugh rancorously. "Rings up Dick Looby at the Spotted Lion and asks him how much I had last night. Dick's a decent fellow, but he can't afford not to tell him. I tell you, that's the way to drive a man to secret drinking—I've seen it happen in long runs again and again—and Mr. Singleton thinks he can do it to *me*. Got me by the short hairs, he has; knows I'd never find another billet like this, any more than he'd find someone else to do the Beach bit—you read Wodehouse?"

"Yes," said Pibble. "Ice formed on the butler's upper slopes."

"Right," said Mr. Waugh. "I can do that, too: worth a guinea a visitor to Mr. Bleeding Singleton, I am. But he thinks he could scrabble along without me and he knows I couldn't do without him. He's got me by the knackers."

"I suppose nerves are always a big frayed by the end of the season," said Pibble cautiously.

"First time I've noticed it," said Mr. Waugh. "July, August, that's the time for tantrums, but by now everything ought to be slack and easy. Why, you heard how sharp Miss Anty spoke up to me this morning. 'Tisn't like her, Officer. Something's *up*."

Mr. Waugh's voice was now an urgent whisper. During the last short speech, layers of saloon-bar knowingness had peeled off his voice until he spoke with the direct appeal of the peasant, petitioning Authority (baffled, inadequate Pibble) to simplify the unfair mysteries of the universe. A faint bloom of sweat, a condensation of tiny globules, dewed the melon-structured tissues of his brow and jowls.

"Is it something to do with Deakin's death?" said Pibble. "I hear he was a bit of a womanizer, for instance."

"Him?" said Mr. Waugh, astonished back into the saloon bar. "Only woman old Deak would've taken an interest in was one made of knot-free deal, so he could've gone over her with his spokeshave. Anyway it started before that—everyone a bit nervy for about a fortnight, and then, whammo, something happens and we're all biting each other's head off, even Miss Anty, as I've always gotten on with particularly well. Three, four days of *that* and Deak hanged himself. Hanged himself *because* of it, if you ask me, and this, sir, is a document which many of our American visitors find most intriguing, being the then Sir Spenser Clavering's original letter to William Penn regretting as how a previous engagement made it impossible for Sir Spenser to come and help found Pennsylvania."

"Goodness me," said Pibble. How would a London detective behave after a history lesson from such a portentous domestic? He would tip him, with hesitation. Pibble found half a crown and said, "This has been the most interesting, dash it—" (Damn. A bit too much of the Woosters there.) "Thank you very much."

"Thank *you* very much, sir," said Mr. Waugh. "I endeavor to give satisfaction."

He wafted himself silently toward the door, yielding the floor to the watching Mr. Singleton.

"You've got an extraordinary collection here," said Pibble warmly.

"It's a disgraceful muddle, in my opinion," said Mr. Singleton. "Our German visitors, and I say this in confidence, are frequently disappointed by the inadequate exhibits on the Raid."

"Do you get many Germans?"

"An average of seven point two per cent increase in each of the last four years. The future of European tourism is in their hands."

"Ironic," said Pibble. "That landing craft Deakin was working on—was that his own idea, or part of some planned expansion?"

"Both, to be candid. Poor Deakin had got it into his head that I was going to build him a special display building for a panorama of the Raid, with himself in charge of it to talk a lot of unsubstantiated gossip about the Claverings at St. Quentin."

"Strip his sleeve and show his scars," said Pibble.

"It may seem to you statistically impossible, but only one man was wounded on Uncle Dick's ship, and he was hit while we were waiting to board. We were packed so tightly on deck that it took me a full minute to get a bar of chocolate out of my map pocket, and the sky was stiff with Stukas, but Uncle Dick brought us out. I don't need to tell you that it is not the kind of episode on which it is possible to calculate the odds, but they must be very high indeed."

"Fantastic," said Pibble, surprised as much by the sudden liveliness of tone as by the actual story.

"Yes. But we mustn't keep Kirtle waiting—he's a busy man. I expect you would prefer to interview them in private, so I will leave you."

With the demurest of footfalls they paced the vast hall. Mr. Singleton opened the door of the Zoffany Room but did not go in himself. It was lucky that Sergeant Maxwell was in uniform; otherwise Pibble would have been certain to commit the blunder of acknowledging them in the wrong social order, for it was Dr. Kirtle who had the slabby raw-beef face of the typical village bobby, whereas Maxwell was graying, harassed, wrinkled, humorous, tired—a good but overworked country G.P. to the life. Pibble shook hands with the Doctor and nodded to the Sergeant.

"I'm sorry to bring you out here like this," he said.

"Not at all, not at all," said the Doctor, in a strange half-whisper whose obsequiousness seemed to imply that the privilege of breathing the same air as the Claverings excused any inconvenience. Pibble felt stifled with all this insistent grandeur.

"Let's go outside," he said.

They both flashed him a sharp glance of surprise—in this sort of household one stayed where one was put until one was given permission to move. For a second Maxwell weighed the imponderables of two unlike disciplines, and then (no doubt in the comfortable knowledge that there was a senior officer to take the responsibility) made a vague half shuffle toward the door. The Doctor sensed himself outvoted, whispered "Oh, well," and moved in the same direction. Pibble led them out to the lawn where he had first seen Mr. Waugh sitting.

"Any bothers, Doctor?" he said. "Hanged himself all right, in your opinion?"

"Dear me, yes," said the Doctor, in his peculiar breathy whisper. Pibble now saw, in the full light of a sweet October noon, that his neck was puckered with the aftermath of a hideous wound. The flicker of shock in Pibble's eyes must have been very marked, or the Doctor peculiarly sensitive.

"I was on the Raid, too, you know," he breathed. "I bought it on the quay, just as we were getting ready for the final embarkation. Harvey Singleton carried me onto the boat and the General nursed me home, pumped me full of morphine, knew just what to do—astonishing man. But, yes, old Deak hanged himself, and I can't think why. I hear he was a bit too keen on the ladies, and it might have been something to do with that. He managed it very efficiently, too—clean break, dead in a second."

"No peculiar bruises, marks of that kind?"

The Doctor ceased pacing the bungey lawn and turned a chill eye on him.

"Great Scott, no!" he said. "You'll be asking me about stomach contents next."

"If you don't mind," said Pibble.

"I mind very much indeed," said the Doctor slowly.

"What sort of people do you think you're dealing with? The Claverings aren't here to provide you with your tuppeny-ha'penny sensation which you can peddle to your pals in Fleet Street. They're, they're...Old England!"

"Yes" said Pibble, "that's just why. Suppose the question came up at the inquest. Unlikely, but just suppose. Isn't it better for us to be able to say we looked, and there was nothing suspicious, than to say we wouldn't dream of doing so? I'd prefer to go the whole hog and see that the question *was* asked. I'd make it clear that the investigation had throughout been thorough, normally thorough. Anyway, I'm afraid I must insist on a proper analysis. Let me tell you, Dr. Kirtle, that there's far more nasty publicity in doubts and mysteries than there is in certainties."

"All right, all right," whispered the Doctor curtly. "You know more about this sort of thing than I do, I suppose. We're damned suspicious down here, you'll find. They'll have to do the job in Southampton, of course, but I'll lay it on. Anything else?"

"Well, it's a tiny point, but I'm bothered about Mr. Singleton trying to give him the kiss of life. He looked so very dead, and I'd have thought Mr. Singleton could have seen at a glance it was hopeless. You know him better than I do, but he doesn't seem to me the kind of man to make a mistake like that."

Winter glazed the Doctor's eye again.

"Harvey Singleton," he said, "had a good war. A very good war indeed. After the Raid he was parachuted into France three times. He was brave, clever, and a brilliant shot. No doubt he saw a lot of dead men, knifed, shot, blown up, garroted. But I doubt if he ever saw a man who'd had his neck broken by dropping three feet with a noose round his throat."

"No doubt you're right," said Pibble, stiff with the knowledge that his name was now chiseled deep into the Doctor's opinion as that of a complete tick. The Doctor's boneheaded reverence for great names comforted him not at all. "It's only that I'm paid to think of all the questions which anybody *might* ask."

"Well, let me tell you another thing. When Lady Clavering died, Herryngs near as a toucher went to pieces. I won't go into the details. But it was Harvey Singleton who held it together, put the Claverings back on their feet. He gave up a very promising job with a merchant bank in the City to come and do it, and he owed them nothing, nothing. He wasn't even married to Anty then. This place is *his* monument, almost as much as it is any of the Claverings'. Remember that."

"Thank you, Doctor. I will."

Pibble turned to Sergeant Maxwell, who had dropped a tactful few paces behind as they'd walked along the broad belt of sward between the wall of the house and the drive; they'd come now, in fact, right around the Private Wing to its south face. The Adam-the-Gardener figure, whom he'd last seen spraying the plants in the far colonnade, was now sweeping the edge of the turf with slow, thoughtful strokes where the General's E-Type had sprayed gravel onto the grass.

Sergeant Maxwell dithered unhappily forward to where Pibble waited. A nasty dilemma for a cap-touching local bobby, whether to side with the high-powered officer, who'd be gone back to London tomorrow, or with the Doctor, who had moved off asthmatic with contempt and anger and who would still be about, week after week, year after year, a witness of how Maxwell had borne himself in the hour of trial. Pibble tried to make things as easy as he could for the poor man.

"There's not much I want to ask you, really," he said. "But I'd better check that you've done all the proper things, just in case..."

Distant but unmistakable, the sound of two shots rang across the park, neither the crack of pistols nor the bark of rifles but a deeper, thudding boom. Pibble raised his eyebrows.

"It's the duel, sir," said the Sergeant. "Two of the tourists fight a duel with proper dueling pistols on the old Bowling Green. They use blanks, o'course, but they dress 'em up in old-fashioned clobber and proper lifelike it looks.'

"Sounds terrifying," said Pibble. "Don't they have a lot of wadding flying about, getting into people's eyes?"

"Old Deak fixed the guns so they'd fire very crooked indeed, he did tell me, sir."

"Oh," said Pibble, "did you know him well?"

"Well, sir, we played darts most Thursday and Monday evenings at the Clavering Arms."

"The point is," said Pibble, "that none of us have any real doubt that poor Deakin hanged himself, but he didn't leave a note and we can't say the thing's satisfactorily cleared up until we have some idea about a motive. When did you see him last?"

"Three nights gone, sir. Night afore he hanged himself."

"Did he seem any different from usual?"

Maxwell rubbed a toecap against his calf, like an embarrassed schoolboy. Ten yards away the Doctor coughed, a harsh, painful rasp.

"He seemed a bit sulky, like," said Maxwell. Then the hesitant voice changed gear into a quick, decisive monotone, as though he had nerved himself to get a painful experience over. "It's not right to speak against the dead, but he were a terrible one for the girls, always chasing and pestering after them and they wouldn't have him, and he went on and on about the Maureen Finnick as how she was leading him on, till I were proper fretted for him, sir."

"Did anyone else hear this conversation?"

"No, sir. We had the little bar all to ourselves, and he was mostly muttering, like."

"O.K.," said Pibble. "Well, see that you get the details as clear in your mind as you can remember. Now, about what

happened after the body was found—Mr. Singleton rang up
the police station, I take it."

"Yes, sir. Asked for me special."

Maxwell ran steadily through what he had done, which
had been everything necessary. When he had finished, Pibble
paced out into the drive, and looked up at the house.
Goodness, it was pretty, the precisely calculated frilliness of
balustrade and finial, the endearingly domestic pediment,
the generous swags of stone carving above the main windows—all subservient to the honest proportions of the basic
rectangle, and all blotchy with gold lichen.

Work, work, work. The first-floor windows mirrored
one bobbly cloudlet and a surround of sky; at this angle the
glass might just as well have been silvered—some monster or
vampire, the Curse of the Claverings, could have been staring hungrily down from behind it and a watcher on the gravel
would have seen neither tusk nor trunk. Pibble shifted about
on the drive, trying to find a point from which the looped
brocade curtains became visible, and his ghostly unease was
suddenly given solid flesh when the sash he was peering at
shot upward and Mrs. Singleton leaned out.

"Luncheon in ten minutes, if that suits you,
Superintendent," she said (no need to shout, with *her* voice).
"Just time for you to come and have a glass of hock, Fred.
There's beer for you, in the little kitchen if you want it,
Maxwell. Don't go into the big one—it'll be full of Yanks in
a couple of minutes and they'll think you're part of the act."

The sash slapped down, leaving none of the three a chance
to answer; the Clavering blood, however charmingly embod-
ied, was used to being obeyed. Dr. Kirtle, in fact, was already
mincing gloomily off toward his glass of hock, and that gave
Pibble the chance to satisfy a private inquisitiveness.

"Were you on the Raid, too, Maxwell?" he said.

"No, sir." The Sergeant's wilting melancholy deepened.

"What was Mr. Singleton talking about before he came
to fetch me?"

"Ah...er...sir...ah...something quite different, sir."

"Never mind. Anyway, the main point is that you've carried though the correct procedure, as far as you were allowed to, and that Deakin talked to you in a very depressed fashion about his sex life."

"Well...er...yes, sir."

"Never mind. Off you go for your beer. I should get some notes down about that conversation. If you think of anything else, you can just let me know direct at Scotland Yard. You don't *have* to tell them everything here, you know."

"Yes, sir. Thank you, sir."

Pibble stood still to give the Sergeant a decent start. More steaming intangibles, he thought: first Mr. Waugh's outburst and then a policeman who'd been hurriedly coached to lie. He walked off toward the Main Block, hoping that if he went the wrong way round the whole edifice he'd be too late for the hock. He didn't feel like standing there with a glass in his hand in the same room as the idiotic Doctor, who so openly despised him—at any rate not if Mrs. Singleton was in the room, too.

Roughly opposite the Main Block he came up with Adam the Gardener, still sweeping with the stolid stroke of a man rowing the Atlantic.

"Ah-hem!" said Pibble purposefully.

The man straightened up and touched the brim of his hat. Beneath its shade his visage—such of it as could be seen through the prodigious growth of beard—seemed preternaturally dark, as though he were on the verge of apoplexy.

"Did you know Mr. Deakin?" said Pibble.

Something in the man's attitude changed; he relaxed and ran a finger beneath the elastic of his beard, a gesture which revealed the true reason for the color of his face.

"No, suh," he said, in a booming Deep South voice. "I's a stranger in dese parts."

"Staying long?" said Pibble.

"You recknin' to run me out of town, Sheriff?" said the Negro, in a different voice, a John Wayne drawl.

"This burg ain't big enough for you and me, Black Jake," said Pibble.

The Negro laughed.

"Fuzz?" he said.

"Fraid so," said Pibble.

"Me, I'm a criminal back home," said the Negro, in what at last seemed to be his own voice.

"Burnt your draft card?" said Pibble.

"What makes you think that?"

"Sounds as if you'd rather talk with an English policeman than an American civilian."

"Maybe so."

"What do you make of this place?" asked Pibble, moving to a less tender subject.

"You know something, Sheriff?" said the Negro. "This setup is just about like all the stories 'bout Virginia 'fore the war—the kind of stories her gramma told my gramma."

"They've done that on purpose, of course," said Pibble.

"Yeah, but they done it too damn well, like they believed it."

"At least they've got something to believe."

"Yeah…but…but they believe it *all*," said the Negro, waving a hand to include the dream landscape, the exquisite house, and a noise of cheering, like far surf, which wafted from the concealed valley whence the shots had come. "Pardon me," he added, and resumed his monotonous sweeping.

Pibble walked on around the far wing, from which floated a cooking smell so appetizing that he decided it must be canned in aerosol sprays and vented to welcome the "visitors" back from their journey into the past. If so, something had gone amiss with Mr. Singleton's passionately precise timing, for the *Rocket* and its dollar-happy load were still invisible; so, he realized, was its track, but looking at the generous sweep of turf he saw a minute fold which might conceal a ha-ha. He strolled over and found himself on a tiny platform with Lilliputian-scale rails curving away to his right. *Three* rails; so the system was electrified, and those generous puffs of smoke and galvanically working cylinders had been as phony as...as Adam s beard.

His ten minutes about up, he walked back past the main frontage, and the now-stilled fountain. Dr. Kirtle was getting into his car by the colonnade entrance, but got out again and came toward Pibble.

"Must apologize," he whispered. "Daresay you thought me no end of an ass—quite unfit to do my job."

"Not at all," lied Pibble.

"Kind of you," said the Doctor. "Truth is I was talking to the Admiral about a month gone by—no, more like six weeks—and the subject of post-mortems came up. He told me—surprised me a bit—that the whole idea revolted him; he couldn't bear the thought of anyone he'd known being cut open. So when they called me in for Deakin I thought I'd try to spare him—England owes him a lot, you know. But I've just been talking to him and he seemed quite happy about the whole thing. Complete *volte-face.* He didn't seem very interested—didn't even look up from his paper, but I got the message all right. Course it's far better if we do the job properly. I'll put it in hand at once."

"Fine," said Pibble, embarrassed—he liked the Doctor, dammit. "Thank you very much," he added dimly. It seemed to be enough, for the Doctor minced back to his car and drove away.

Mrs. Singleton was waiting in the winy air of the colonnade, like an embodiment of all autumnal sweetness.

"You mustn't mind about Fred," she said. "His world begins and ends with us."

"All policemen expect to be resented," said Pibble. "It's part of the training. I hadn't realized how many of you were involved in the Raid. I bet if they make a film of it they'll find a place for *you* in a landing craft."

Mrs. Singleton laughed her ambrosial laugh.

"Actually they made two films," she said. "They turned Harvey into an American for one of them, and the actress who played me—Phyllis Calvert it was—was parachuted in to St. Quentin to join the Resistance and guide the ships in. It was awful nonsense, but the other one was very good and accurate—I'm surprised you didn't see it. Harvey arranged for us to have some sort of royalty, and it did terribly well, especially in the Commonwealth, and that's what gave him the capital to develop Herryngs the way he has. It pays for itself now, of course, but only just. Luncheon is ready and the Admiral's been ringing up your office to try and find out what you like to drink—your sergeant said beer, I hope that's all right."

"Lovely," said Pibble thankfully, but wondering what oubliettes lay beneath this lush expanse of red carpet.

As they went into the dimness of the hall, a small erect figure came forward, holding out his hand. The Admiral had none of his brother's exaggerated strut; he wore a quiet tweed suit; his voice was quiet, too, almost a murmur.

"Come along, Superintendent," he said, "you're just in time. Want a pee?"

"No, thank you.'

"Come in, then; we all help ourselves and are very informal."

He led the way into a room on the right-hand side of the passage. Really it was no more than a paneled nook left over from the construction of two shapelier rooms; a circular rosewood table nearly filled it. Mr. Singleton and a girl were talking over on the far side, by a crowded hot plate.

"That smells good," said the Admiral. "Pheasant stew. Waste of good meat to roast them, don't you agree, Superintendent?" He rubbed his pale hands together. His face was pale, too, with no tan to hide the lichenlike marks of old age; but apart from that and the absence of a mustache and the trimmer eyebrows, he really was astonishingly like his brother. Carried his head at a different angle, perhaps...

"I think you've met my nephew," he said. "Judith, this is Superintendent Pibble, who has come to sort us out; Superintendent, this is our secretary, Judith Scoplow."

Nothing special about her, really: a tall girl with a flat, pale face and hair that would probably have been mouse without the help of a copper rinse. She wore it lightly backcombed into a sort of half helmet, kept in place by a broad brown Alice band.

"How do you do," she said, and at once Pibble looked at her again. There *was* something special about her, once you had heard the voice; something happy, easy, confident, innocent; something dizzily out of keeping with this mansion of rich decay. Despite a couple of pimples below the corner of her wide mouth, she was beautiful, too. Pibble revised an earlier guess: the General's staglike strut down the steps had not meant he was on his way to visit a woman—it meant he had just been talking with one, had just seized an opportune half minute to sniff the deliriant bouquet of youth.

Queuing for his pheasant stew, Pibble struggled with the sense of having met someone like her in the past. (He struggled, too, with the knowledge that she was the kind of woman who would have that effect on men, a barely sophisticated variant of the urge to say "Haven't I met you before?") He was disconcerted out of both struggles by his encounter with the stewpot, which turned out to contain chunks of bird in a sauce heavy with cream and brandy; there was a little dish of fried diced apple by the side. Left to itself, his subconscious did the trick—that girl in the Salinski case! He was so pleased with himself that he took a double helping of creamed potatoes.

Anne something. And Salinski (fortyish, shiny-bald, dapper) had faked a brake failure and let his new Rover run over a cliff with his smart little wife in it, all on the strength of a barely more than nodding acquaintance with this Anne.

Again, it had been only when she'd answered Pibble's first question—there'd been a smell of collusion because Salinski had tried to use her as an element in his timetable alibi—that Pibble had realized that Salinski was perfectly sane. And in the end both counsels, for defense and prosecution, had outdone each other in courtesies, the judge had been a shade more than paternal, and several hard-nosed reporters had attempted to play down her role in their copy. Poor little pigeon, by the time she stepped down from the witness box she was the only person in the whole court who still didn't understand how Salinski could have done such a thing. And here was another of them. Well, well; no wonder the General had gone down toward his phallic car with the swagger of a hart at leaf fall.

"Come and sit here, my dear fellow, and tell me tall stories about life as a famous policeman." The Admiral was pulling out a chair on his right. Mrs. Singleton was already prodding a minute piece of bird on the other side of the gap.

"Your sergeant tells me that you know more about beer than anyone else in London," said the Admiral. "I'd value your opinion on this—we brew it ourselves. I believe it's a shade on the sweet side for the real purist, but we are trying to gratify the perverse palate of our American cousins."

Mr. Singleton butted in from the other side of the table.

"I commissioned a little firm in Chicago to market-research the American idea of what English beer ought to taste like."

"Courages at Alton were very nice to us," added the Admiral. "They sent a chap over to advise us how to get as near to Harvey's ideal as we could. I know a couple of chaps on the board, 'smatter of fact."

"I think it's horrible," said Mrs. Singleton, and sipped exaggeratedly from her glass of Burgundy.

Bodingly, Pibble lifted his tankard, and was surprised: true the beer was too sweet and a bit on the dark side; it was like one of those special brews which a few colleges in ancient universities specialize in, but it wasn't flat, as they tend to be; it had a creamy sparkle which suggested that the barrel must be in tiptop condition. He said so.

"I'm glad to hear you say that," said Mr. Singleton. "To be frank, I never let them keep anything left over. We throw away yesterday's barrel and start on a new one. Brewing's an extraordinarily cheap process, given the equipment."

"But are you sure that's what you want, Mr. Pibble?" said the Admiral solicitously. "There's some of Harvey's plonk if you prefer, or there ought to be another of these"— he pointed to his own half bottle of Pommery—"in the fridge, or you could have some of our excellent water, as dear Judith does."

"It's the nicest water I ever tasted," said Miss Scoplow. "A marvelous old man brings it up from the spring in two wooden buckets which he carries with a sort of yoke."

"I'm happy with this, thank you," said Pibble, wondering which level of the treasure house of police fantasy he should tap to please the Admiral's lust for gruesome tales. (Scotland Yard has an oral tradition rich enough to keep a college of Opies busy.) He needn't have bothered, for the old hero seemed set on talking about his lions, which he did with a mild but insistent volubility, often keeping hold of the conversation by simply repeating some tidbit which he had already rolled out. It was during one of these *da capos* that Pibble revised his opinion of Mrs. Adamson's lion books, which, when he'd read them, he'd thought had a too-good-to-be-true quality. She must have covered the ground pretty thoroughly, he now saw, since there was nothing in the Admiral's mellifluous monologue which he didn't already know. He seized a moment when the hero's mouth was full to ask him whether he'd enjoyed the books.

"What books?" said the Admiral, emphasizing his famous deafness by cupping a curiously lobeless ear.

"Elsa!" shouted Mrs. Singleton. It wasn't exactly a shout, though: she just notched her hound voice up another

intensity and produced a word which was still clearly spoken
but could have halted a marching regiment. Two more inten-
sities and the windowpanes would have fallen out.

"What's the matter with her?" said the Admiral. "You
are never satisfied with your food, Anty, not even in the nurs-
ery, I remember. Would you believe it, Superintendent—"

The door opposite him opened and a little old woman
with a crossly crimson face stood there.

"Did I hear you call, Miss Anty?" she said.

"Oh, I'm so sorry, Elsa," said Mrs. Singleton. "I didn't
mean you. We were talking about lions."

"Nasty heathenish things," snarled the cook. "It's all
very well for you to say they only eat black men, but who's
to know they won't acquire the taste and we'll all be gnawed
to pieces in our beds?"

The Admiral didn't even look in her direction, but
turned exaggeratedly toward Pibble.

"No, that's a very interesting aspect of lion psychology,"
he said. "Some of them do literally acquire a taste for man-
flesh, and can't be satisfied with anything else. There's not
been any research done on man-eating, though, for obvious…"

His soft voice was almost a whisper, but the cook
looked at him, put her hands over her ears, and rushed out.

"Now you've upset her," said Mr. Singleton to the room
in general. "Go and soothe her down, Anty."

Mrs. Singleton rose and left. Pibble sat in a daze. How
in holy hell had they thought they could get away with it?
Who had persuaded whom? And what in God's name were
they up to, to make it necessary? He pulled himself together
to listen to his host, who was murmuring again about lions,
but during the monologue he kept thinking of other little bits
of confirmation: the Epstein and the cook had started him
off; then there were the Adamson books; the General's stagy
departure; the locked door upstairs; Singleton's whispering—to emphasize the Admiral's presence behind it; the

mere necessity of having a policeman down from London for a case that didn't warrant it; the too-painstaking collusion in social hypnotism which he'd felt so strongly in the meat store; the *volte-face* over post-mortem...Oh, Crippen! And presumably Deakin had looked after the Admiral's shoes, hung up his clothes, taken his trays up, made his bed, even.

When Mrs. Singleton came back, she simply nodded to her husband and sat down. Pibble felt edgy now, but couldn't decide whether the others did, too, or whether he was attributing his own unease to them. Only Miss Scoplow seemed uninfected with this social itch; she talked little but listened to Mr. Singleton's jerky explanation of the economics of the wine trade with great animation; she had a pleasant trick of showing interest by opening her eyes absurdly wide, so that the white showed all around the iris. She gave the impression that she could have listened with intense delight to an account of a golf match between two moderate players on a featureless plain.

But Mr. Singleton's lecture seemed not to stimulate even himself; he had the tense air of an actor ad-libbing while he waits for a colleague to make a delayed entrance. Mrs. Singleton turned one fragment of meat over and over, as if it were the last piece of a jigsaw which was somehow the wrong shape for the last hole. And the old hero was now retailing complete myth as certified lion lore, even the false claw in the tail with which the beast is supposed to lash itself into a frenzy of rage, like some hack satirist.

"No pudding," said Mrs. Singleton suddenly, "and we've eaten the last of the nectarines. There's blue Cheshire and grapes and apples."

The shuffling to remove plates and queue (in charade-like parody of housewives at a greengrocer's) for muscats and pippins (not Cox or Ribston—something Pibble had never met before) broke the tension. As they settled again, Clavering turned to Miss Scoplow and told her all the legends he had just told Pibble, while she listened to each non-

sensical detail with astonished eyes. This left Pibble free for
the first time to enjoy Mrs. Singleton's presence; the contrast
with Miss Scoplow served to emphasize her musky, autumnal quality. You soon got used to the voice; it wasn't, after
all, loud, just penetrating. She must know what was up,
Pibble decided, but Miss Scoplow mightn't. If she thought of
Adam the Gardener as "a marvelous old man," she must be
either shortsighted or unobservant.

"You seem to take an enormous amount of trouble over
detail," he said. "Bringing your water up in buckets on a
yoke, I mean. There can't be much chance for tourists to
photograph that, however picturesque."

"Don't you believe it," said Mrs. Singleton, with her
liqueur-like chuckle. "Harvey sees to it that it's done while
there's a party going down the colonnade; Rastus walks up
just below those windows. Besides, we'd have the water
brought up from the spring anyway. As Judith says, it's much
nicer than the mains; there being a picturesque man to do it
is just luck."

"Is that the man I saw spraying ferns on the way to the
big Kitchen, dressed up like the gardener in those old
Express strip cartoons?"

"That's right—we call him Rastus. Do you follow the
strips? I always read them first."

They fell into a half-bantering discussion of the protag-
onists of the thought balloon, discovered a joint admiration
for the earliest Four-D Jones strips, and were discussing mid-
dle-period Garth plots when the grate of tires on the gravel
outside brought Mrs. Singleton to her feet (her hearing
seemed to be as keen as her voice).

"That's Carl Spruheim, Harvey," she said. "You go and
let him in while I fetch the coffee. We'll have it in my sitting
room."

Both Singletons left. Pibble allowed them twenty seconds before he rose, too.

"There's just something I ought to check on before I talk

to the Coroner," he said casually, moving as he spoke toward the door so that he was already through it before Clavering had a chance to answer. He ran across the hall and up the stairs; he was panting, more with nerves than exertion, before he reached the first landing. He plugged on.

The barrel of the big key still protruded through the lock of the Admiral's door, but the door didn't open—so there must be another entrance. He nipped into Deakin's pantry and took a pair of crocodile pliers from the pegboard, but he found that though he could grip the barrel with the pliers held sideways, the mahogany beading of the door panels prevented him from turning the key far enough, so he had to run back for a blunt-ended pair. Sweating now, he tried again; the serrations of the jaws slipped on the metal, making bright parallel gouges, then held. Contorting his body so that he did not have to take a fresh grip, he moved the key around until he heard the big wards click over. He dropped the pliers and turned the handle. The door opened.

But before he had moved it an inch, a weight thudded into it from the far side and slammed it shut. Pibble gripped the handle and twisted, throwing all his weight against the mahogany. A child? he wondered—there ought to be some Singleton kids about. Anyway, the door gave, and he jammed his foot into the opening and forced the gap wider, easily enough, with the leverage of knee and shoulder. Then the resistance ceased suddenly and only the inertia of the heavy mahogany saved him; if it had been a flimsy door, he would have fallen sprawling into the secret room. As it was, he entered with an ungainly stagger, to find Clavering, a little flushed and ruffled, facing him with chilly dignity. Who'd have thought the old man had so much agility in him, to race up here so fast and wrestle with the far side of the door?

"What the devil do you think you're up to?" said the old man with icy fierceness but in the wrong voice.

Pibble didn't answer but looked around the room. The hairy jacket, yellow waistcoat, and twill trousers were flung across the bed; not good enough—they might both have duds like that. Two Elsa books lay on the desk; nothing like good enough. One of a set of fitted cupboards in the right-hand wall was open, with the corner of a washbasin showing. Pibble walked across and found what he wanted, an uncleaned safety razor with a number of half-inch white bristles stuck in it, a tube of Helena Rubinstein "Tan in a Minute," a lot of tan-smeared tissues in the wastepaper basket, a pair of nail scissors, even a scattering of shorter, curving bristles on the carpet. As he was wrapping the razor and specimens of his other prizes in clean tissues from the box, Mrs. Singleton's voice came from the room.

"All right, General?"

The old hero answered with his wild giggle, more exaggerated than before—tension, or the strain of suppressing it for a couple of hours?

"Far from it, m'dear, far from it. You were right about Treacle—he even looks like him now. Down a rabbit hole, you remember?"

Pibble could imagine so, for he was on his knees collecting clippings of the famous eyebrows; he was aware that the seat of his trousers was shiny. From the room it must have looked as if he'd have been wagging his tail, if he'd had one. In fact he was both dismayed and miserable. How the hell could they have thought they'd get away with it?

"Oh, my aunt!" said Mrs. Singleton. "What on earth shall we do now? I thought he was such an agreeable little man."

2:00 P.M.

A false note, thought Pibble as he straightened up; a degree too Noel Cowardly, not quite right for her—or perhaps she's been acting, family-charade-playing, all morning and this is the real Miss Anty, the formic-acid one. More to avoid facing them than anything he started prying into the neighboring cupboards. The Admiral seemed to own few clothes but a formidable amount of shoes, each pair in its own special Deakin-built niche, and all the niches full. He nerved himself to turn and face the Claverings.

"I have to assume that there is some reason for this impersonation, Sir Ralph," he said. "Otherwise you would hardly have gone to the lengths of shaving off your mustache."

"Right," said the General. "Wish I hadn't now. Bloody fidgety it makes me feel—kept wanting to touch it all through luncheon—only thing stopped me was it would look as if I wanted to pick me nose. Bloody good stew, didn't you think? Wanted to say so at the time; only I couldn't express my appreciation with Dick's prim bloody vocabulary."

"Oh, General!" said Mrs. Singleton. "This is serious, and Carl Spruheim's waiting."

"Quite right, m'dear, but you might tell Elsa—wouldn't want her to think I didn't like it, eh? She spotted me right away, Superintendent. All your fault, Anty—you must learn to keep your voice down—it used to give your poor mother headaches, y'know."

Mrs. Singleton's face twitched for an instant into the haggard dimension of tragedy; then she recovered her smiling mask.

"How did you guess, Mr. Pibble?" she said.

"Sir Ralph's ears are not the same shape as the ones on the Epstein bust; besides, there were a lot of little things which made it look as if you were putting on a play for my benefit."

"My dear fellow," said the General with a sudden ferocity, "we've been putting on a bloody play for the last twenty years."

"I take it the Admiral is not in the house," said Pibble.

"Right," said the General.

"Can you tell me where he is?"

"No. He's gone missing. Disappeared completely. Bloody inconvenient."

"Since when?"

"Went the morning Deakin was found. Just walked away and hasn't come back. Done it before a couple of times, you know. First time when my wife died, 'smatter of fact."

"We're not frightfully worried about him," said Mrs. Singleton. "But you can just imagine what a hullabaloo there'd be if the papers got hold of it. That's why we couldn't have let the local police in; they'd have spotted the trick at once, and if we hadn't tried it they'd have raised a terrible hue and cry after Uncle Dick."

"Whose actual idea was it to get someone down from London?" said Pibble, inquisitive about the tiny discrepancy that had been worrying him.

"Harvey's," said the General.

"The General's," said Mrs. Singleton in the same breath, then glanced sharply at the old man.

"...as much as it was anyone's," he carried on, as though

there had been no full stop after Harvey's name, "but we all more or less hammered it out together. Anty's quite right, it'd be bloody chaos if this got out, but I won't blame you if you don't see it that way. Not that it affects Deakin's death, you realize. All that happened before."

"Do you mind if I go over it again?" said Pibble. "Everything was smooth and normal, except for Deakin's love life, and then he committed suicide. Sir Richard left next morning—yesterday morning. You decided he might be gone for a longish period, agreed between yourselves to get a policeman down from London, and rang up by lunchtime."

"I know it sounds terribly quick," said Mrs. Singleton, "but we do know Uncle Dick very well, and it was only just in case. If he'd come back, then everything would have been straightforward."

"I see," said Pibble. He hated it. It all sounded quite reasonable, according to their crazy, highhanded version of reason—very much the General's style of practical joke, in fact—and only sottish Mr. Waugh's sullen grumblings to set against it. And, by God, the caption to the funeral photograph among the press cuttings!

"How long was Sir Richard away the first time he disappeared?" he asked.

"About ten days," said Mrs. Singleton.

"Near enough," said the General, but there was a brooding flash of doubt below the shorn eyebrows, as though he sensed a pitfall; for the second time in five minutes Pibble was conscious of the lionlike past, the muscled majesty, moving wary through the ambushed scrub, who now lived moodily eccentric, the prime specimen behind the bars of Harvey Singleton's zoo. He liked the setup less than ever.

"All right," he said. "I don't see that there's any real need to tell the Coroner about Sir Richard's disappearance. The only snag I can see is that one of you would normally give evidence at the inquest, but now you've shaved I don't think that's possible, unless Sir Richard comes back in time. Either you or your husband could do the identification, Mrs. Singleton—he'll have to be there in any case, as he found the body. How deaf *is* Sir Richard, by the way?"

"Middling," said the General. "He's worst when he's bored. I found it bloody hard to hit it off right—you may have noticed."

"In any case," said Mrs. Singleton, "Uncle Dick took sleeping tablets."

"Neither of us used to need much sleep," said the General. "Now we're old we need it but can't get it. Most nights we sit up till about two, grunting at each other about this and that. Then we toddle upstairs and dope ourselves into dreamland."

"Well," said Pibble. "shall we go and settle the Coroner's worries? And Mr. Singleton's, too, I suppose."

The General allowed himself another of his happy cackles.

"You needn't fret about Harvey," he said. "Always makes his plans three layers deep—learnt it from me. D'you want this room locked up?"

Trap question. Pibble looked around the room slowly, the nape of his neck prickling. The little door through which the Claverings had come seemed to be at the top of a spiral stair in the thickness of the wall. They must have rummaged through the room already, but hadn't had time to clear up the detritus of the General's quick change act.

"No," he said, "unless you feel it is possible that something has happened to Sir Richard in his absence. In that case it might just be worth while making the room proof against interference. If it didn't mess up household arrangements, cleaning and so on, I'd advise you to lock both doors and keep the keys.'

"You lock up, General," said Mrs. Singleton, "and I'll take Mr. Pibble to see Carl. You'd better keep out of the way, I suppose."

The General grunted.

Down the stairs Pibble lagged, worried sick with syntax and shoes. Uncle Dick took sleeping tablets. There should have been an empty niche in the shoe cupboard. Took, took, took. Mrs. Singleton, two steps below him and to his right, moved down the gradient with the creamy suppleness of a skier in a slow-motion film. Took. Could she use the past tense, in that particular sentence, when everyone else was so painstakingly in the present? Yes, she could, but there hadn't been a gap for the shoes the Admiral ought to have been wearing when he walked away. Took. She was beautiful, sugary, irresistible, like a box of homemade fudge. But took was wrong, and the General had switched the tense back to the present very smoothly, and then had spoiled things by asking a question which demonstrated that he wanted to know how suspicious Pibble was. Took. Put it with Mr. Waugh's tirade and the shoes and the funeral photograph, and then there was a decent chance that the old hero was dead, the quiet one who had handled his boats so brilliantly. If he'd just disappeared, and had done so before, what cause was there for Deakin to hang himself? And it must have been that way round—three or four days, Waugh had said. But if he was dead, and they were trying to keep *that* from Fleet Street, then...Pibble remembered the photograph in Deakin's room, and Harvey Singleton's impatience with the coxswain's yen to be curator of a museum commemorating the Raid: perhaps the idea of missing the Admiral's funeral was enough to make life not worth living for such a man. Took. In that case, what the hell had they done with the body? Buried it under Capability Brown's smooth-flowing turf? Not their style.

"How do you do?" he found himself saying.

"Spruheim," said the blond man, holding out a robotic arm and hand for him to shake.

"I'll leave you to it," said Mrs. Singleton, and shut the door of the chintzy little room on the ground floor.

He was a caricature of a Prussian, with his yellow hair,

pale eyes, and angular jaw just shaped for the dueling scar which, mysteriously, did not adorn it.

"Don't tell me you were in the Raid, too?" said Pibble.

The Coroner made a noise which might have been a laugh or a clearing of the throat.

"Prisoner of war?" he said. "No, Superintendent, I left Germany in 1937. I used to practice law in Hamburg, but I am a Jew and by 1936 all my clients had found it wiser to consult an Aryan lawyer, so I came to England and found work as a baggage clerk. Fortunately your government interned me during the period of hostilities, which gave me time to explore the bizarre confusion which passes for law in these islands. So here I am, a respected solicitor in Southampton, trusted in great houses to deal adequately with the demise of servants. There is something fishy about this one, ha! or you would not be here."

Crippen, thought Pibble, here's another reason why they wanted me; they couldn't afford to have this unbluffable intelligence taking charge.

"I don't know," he said. "They're not the sort of people who need *reasons* for doing whatever they fancy. There are one or two little things which worry me, but I can't say how far they aren't just a reflection of the oddity of the whole setup. You find yourself hypnotized, you know."

"Who better? There is no doubt that Deakin hanged himself, Kirtle says."

"None, I think. I'd just like to clear up some aspects of the motive and leave the whole thing tidy. I've one witness who says he was crossed in love, and I hope to talk to another this afternoon, and that should leave everything shipshape. There will be some straightforward medical evidence, with no holes in it, and that ought to be that, with luck."

"The Claverings have always enjoyed excellent luck," said Mr. Spruheim. "Tuesday afternoon?"

"Fine."

"And there are no elements in the, ha! setup which you might wish to hint to me should be glossed over?"

"Not that I know of. Mrs. Singleton will give evidence of identity and Mr. Singleton will give evidence of finding the body. Sergeant Maxwell will give technical evidence. Dr. Kirtle will give medical evidence. Sergeant Maxwell, and perhaps a Miss Maureen Finnick, whom I haven't yet interviewed, will give evidence about the motive. That should be the lot."

"And neither Sir Ralph nor Sir Richard will attend," said Mr. Spruheim. "I suppose they are wise—at least it will mean fewer journalists cluttering up my little court. Good. That seems easy enough. You will let me know if there are any aspects which you feel require, ha! delicate handling, will you not, Superintendent?"

"Of course," said Pibble.

The Coroner scratched at the corner of his jaw with long, irritable strokes, like a cat clawing at a sofa leg. He was fixed, poor chap. He'd given Pibble every opportunity to voice the merest soupçon of a doubt and Pibble had refused, but still he knew that something was being kept back.

"So be it," he said, at last. "The last thing that any of us desires is a fuss—see how English I have become! Now I have business to conduct with Mr. Singleton—he does the conducting and I simply follow the baton to the best of my poor abilities—so I will wish you luck with your Miss Finnick. I believe I have had some dealing with her before, in some equally trivial matter. She has achieved a certain, ha! notoriety in this district, I understand."

He bowed like a doll hinged at the waist, but the expected click of heels did not follow.

"Superintendent, I am truly sorry that I have not been able to help you in your difficulties."

"Not at all," said Pibble, wondering whether there was something extra this odd man knew. No way of asking him, though—no natural way. Both men tried to open the door for each other, both to bow each other out first; Spruheim, with his longer reach and stronger formality, won each time. Harvey Singleton was in the hall, managing to look as if he had been on his way from X to Y when interrupted by this polite jostling.

"You've finished, then," he said heavily. "Carl, I have left a lot of notes which I have made about the planning application in the blue folder on the left-hand side of my desk. You'll find our new secretary, Judith Scoplow, in there."

"And she will not bite my head off?" said Mr. Spruheim.

"Far from it," said Mr. Singleton with an unexpected nuance of warmth. "While you look through the notes, I will conduct the Superintendent to wherever he wants to go next."

Ah, Crippen, thought Pibble, everywhere that Mary went, is it? I'll fix him. He tried to make a noise like an embarrassed cough.

"I really must disappear for a bit," he said, "if you'll show me where the toilet is—I'm sorry. And please don't wait. I ought to talk to someone called Maureen Finnick, but I'm sure I can find her myself if you'll just tell me which way to go."

Mr. Singleton studied his large, many-paneled wristwatch.

"Two-forty-three," he said. "You've just about got time if you aren't too long in the bog. The first of the afternoon coachloads is due to reach her stall at three-thirty-seven. But I'm afraid I have to insist that you must be accompanied on your way there because you will have to pass through the Lion Ground, and our insurers are—quite properly—very strict. I'll tell Anty to meet you here in ten minutes."

"Fine," lied Pibble, irritated at his failure to fix anything or anyone.

"The bog's the second on the left up there," said Mr. Singleton. "Maureen Finnick, eh?"

Mr. Spruheim glanced at him with a flicker of his pale

eyes. A telephone rang on the hall table, and Mr. Singleton picked it up.

"Of course not," Pibble heard him saying as he moved up the passage. "I don't care if he owns half Texas—let me talk to him. Hello, hello...Now, sir, I understand you wish to photograph our haunted Abbey by moonlight. Yes. I'm afraid, sir, that we have an absolute..."

The heavy mahogany of the cloakroom door cut him off. Pibble, having taken advantage of his immurement among the gray and peacock tiles, mooned about looking at brown photographs of groups of officers outside messes, others of polo teams posed under palm trees, and others which were barely more than enlarged snaps of nondescript scenes of military and naval activity. One large frame held nearly a dozen photographs with donnish captions and a label at the bottom saying that they were taken by the Signals officer at the St. Quentin Raid, who had nothing to do after his wirelesses had been temporarily put out of commission by friendly action. (Pibble remembered about that: the General had personally removed a selection of vital valves so that he was unable to receive what looked like becoming a series of pusillanimous messages from London.) *"Audis quo strepitu janua?"* said one caption: "Major Singleton in Horatian mood." It was difficult to make out what was actually going on in the doorway, and the central figure had his back to the camera, but once you realized that the figure was Singleton, the seemingly contextless flurry of action (there was another uniformed figure crouched at the far doorpost, apparently throwing something through a broken panel, as well as a corpse on the threshold) locked itself into a pattern of violence all centered on the muscled buttocks which were propelling the tall body—automatic weapon dangling low in the right hand, left shoulder hunched forward as a single-purpose projectile at the crack where the arched doors met.

Curious, thought Pibble. He ought to have a stammer or

something, with all that aggression locked away under the computer casing—or perhaps the sheer drabness of his speech style is an equivalent. And another thing: he's brainy, quick, self-confident but he keeps making elementary mistakes, such as not being surprised about Maureen Finnick, and then bringing her up with such belated emphasis that even the Coroner was bound to notice there was something a bit off. Or look at it another way: allow fantasy full rein and suppose they'd done away with the old Admiral (Lord knows why), then who's responsible for this loopy charade? Who'd agreed it would work? The General, probably, more out of pleasure in the absurdity of the melodrama than for down-to-earth practical reasons; Mrs. Singleton, perhaps, out of the inbred habit of getting away with the unforgivable; but sane, business-efficiency Harvey Singleton? *He* must have known what the odds against it were.

Or...ah, hell, leave it for the moment. Don't flush lav, because that's the signal Mrs. Singleton will be waiting for—sneak out and look for Elsa. He did so, conscious of the technical impossibility of tiptoeing around a house like this while trying to create the impression (if anyone should pop out of a door) that he'd lost his bearings.

He needn't have worried: Mrs. Singleton was in the kitchen, sitting on the cover of the Aga's cool plate. Elsa sat bolt upright in a wheel-back chair, her large raw-meat hands clenched so tightly into each other that the skin around the knuckles took on the whiteness of the underlying bone.

"Couldn't you make the waterworks waterwork?" said Mrs. Singleton. "They make an awful racket in here, don't they, Elsa?"

"Oh, Lord," said Pibble, and scuttered out.

"Don't be embarrassed," said Mrs. Singleton when he returned. "I'm always forgetting and it makes Harvey absolutely furious. The General's been reading pop psychology, and he says that's typical of both of us. Were you hoping to ask Elsa something?"

"Only the recipe of the pheasant we had for lunch."

"Super, wasn't it?" said Mrs. Singleton. "Elsa'll tell you about it while I go and find a gun—you don't want me to put on my jodhpurs and topee, as I do for the visitors, I hope."

Pibble made a deprecating cluck, thinking that a gun was about as much masculine gear as he could cope with on this honey woman if he wasn't to start actually slavering. Mrs. Singleton slid down from her perch and smoothed the back of her skirt with luxurious suppleness.

"I don't believe it gives you piles," she said, and left.

"Elizabeth David," said the cook. "*French Provincial Cooking*, page four hundred and nineteen. She calls it fezzon à la coshwaz. Your missus can get it out of the liberry, I dessay."

She spoke without looking at him, but with an astonishing active malevolence.

"Let me just write that down," said Pibble, getting out his notebook. "Page four hundred and…"

"Nineteen."

"Thanks. I'm afraid you must be missing Mr. Deakin."

"'Im."

"I mean, he must have been useful carrying trays up to the Admiral and things like that."

"Not 'im," said the cook. Her hands were now clenched so fiercely into each other that Pibble could see the blue-mauve crescent of skin where the nails bit in among the protruding veins at the back of each hand.

"Fine," said Pibble. "David, *French Provincial Cooking*, four one nine. Bet ours isn't as good as yours."

The cook didn't say anything.

"Ready?" said Mrs. Singleton, from the door. "It's about twelve minutes' walk."

She was carrying an ordinary .303 rifle under the crook of her right arm, as one carries a shotgun. She led him around by the front of the Main Block, where the Thetis fountain was once again lifting its ostrich plume of water against the background of yellowing limes—a distillation of the grand life whose pump could, presumably, be switched on and off for the benefit of "visitors," a horde of whom now frothed around the two coaches whose hunched lines and pop-art paintwork fought with the solemnity of the old stone. Pibble saw that you could tell that these were parting guests because they wore or carried an anachronistic collection of old English headgear, from Cavalier wide-awakes through Georgian three-cornereds up to Victorian stovepipes and deerstalkers.

Singleton was there, arguing with one of the leavers, a squat gentleman in purple whose stance implied a world of frustrated pleading. Singleton's gestures and manner were those of a very classy headwaiter dealing with a tipsy diner who has imagined some deficiency of service—deference concealing contempt.

"Is that the chap who wants to photograph the Abbey by moonlight?" said Pibble.

"I hadn't heard about that," said Mrs. Singleton. "These Americans can be tiresomely persistent, and some of them offer us fabulous wads of lolly to satisfy their whims. But Harvey says it does you no good in the long run if word gets out that you can be bought. He soaks the advertising people for all they're worth, for instance, but he puts a fantastic penalty clause in the contract so that they can't mention the name of Clavering or Herryngs in the copy. I suppose I mustn't ask what you want to see Maureen about."

Pibble shivered as a little flaw of wind drifted the ostrich plume in their direction, enveloping them in a momentary microclimate of Scotch mist. It made him realize how close winter actually was, how illusory the slant sun's warmth.

"I heard she might know something about Deakin's love life," he said.

"Oh dear," said Mrs. Singleton. "I'm afraid that's only too likely. Poor Deakin."

They walked on in a private two-minute silence for the dead man and his stilled lusts.

On the far side of the ha-ha, which they crossed by a pretty little Gothick bridge at a point where the railway lines had ceased, the parkland tilted away to form a wide hollow. The near slope was dotted with copses and thickets, so placed that though there seemed to be wide reaches of turf between them they completely screened the whole stretch of land that lay in the hollow. The path twisted through a clump of bamboo, and they reached a little gate in an enormously high fence of stout pig wire.

"We don't often bring visitors this way," said Mrs. Singleton. "The *Rocket* takes them all through the Lion Ground on a loop on their way back from Maureen's stall. It saves all the tiresome business of guides—white hunters they call them at Longleat. I'd better just load this thing."

She jerked the magazine off, fished half a dozen rounds out of the pocket of her tweed skirt, pressed them expertly in, and slapped the magazine home, working the bolt to send the first round into the breech.

"I won't offer to carry it," said Pibble, "because I suppose it would invalidate the insurance. Besides, you look as if you'd do better with it than I would."

"You're right about the insurance, anyway," she said, with her golden-syrup chuckle. "I'm afraid we keep the key under that stone there, and that's *not* in the insurance, but we simply couldn't find a sensible way of making sure it was available when anybody wanted it, because it always seemed to be in Uncle Dick's pocket on the other side of the park."

Pibble found the key and opened the gate.

"Hang it up on that little hook," said Mrs. Singleton, "so we can reach it on the way back. If a lion comes right up to you, stand still. They're very inquisitive, and if you start jumping about they think it's a game and I'm afraid they play very rough. Don't worry—it isn't likely."

They saw several lions in the next few hundred yards,

but none close except for a sleeping lioness who was draped across two low lime-tree branches beside the path, so floppy with indolence that she looked as if she were composed of some immensely viscous liquid. Two cubs scratched at another tree, leaving deep gouges in the bark, and around a fallen trunk a group of five or six adult lions had posed themselves in greenery-yallery attitudes. Two of them turned their heads to watch the passing humans with an amber, unblinking stare.

The lion enclosure did not seem to be very large, but now that Pibble's position relative to the screening copses had changed, he began to catch glimpses of chimneys and roofs beyond it. The basin through which they were walking itself sloped southward, and then dipped quite sharply. It was in this dip that the hitherto hidden building stood.

"Is that the old Abbey?" he said.

"It isn't really an abbey," said Mrs. Singleton, "except that parts of it came from an abbey they pulled down at Scambling at the dissolution of the monasteries. That's when my family started to come up in the world, you know—the early ones had a knack of backing the right kings. But have you ever noticed how they all seemed to build their houses in hollows, and it wasn't really till Queen Anne that people started building in places where you could see something from? The Abbey's the center of Old England now, with plastic ghosts popping out from behind panels, and tape-recorded clankings and wailings. But it really *is* old, and not at all phony, so it's always a wow with visitors."

"What else do they like?"

"They like everything. Harvey's very clever about that because he has this craze for authenticity. The duel always goes very well, because two of the visitors actually do the fighting and a couple of our people act as seconds and tell them, very po-faced, about all the etiquette that's expected of them; we do that on the Bowling Green, which has the most super echoes. Then there's a highwayman who robs a coach and they catch and hang him—it's terribly convincing... Hello, Maureen seems to be expecting us."

They had rounded a corner and another wire gate lay before them, but it was already open, held for them by a woman wearing the same mobcap and sprigged apron as Mrs. Chuck and Claire had at the main gate, but wearing them with a difference. Behind her rose four bizarrely foreshortened towers with onion-shaped roofs, as though a section of Brighton Pavilion or the Kremlin or the Taj Mahal had sunk, by some freak convulsion of the terrain, into the ground until only its topmost pinnacles were showing.

"Oh, Miss Anty," babbled the woman, "your hair appointment. Miss Whatnot, your new secretary, was speaking to me of it on the telephone."

"Bloody Hades!" said Mrs. Singleton. "When was it supposed to be for?"

"Three-thirty, she did be saying."

Mrs. Singleton looked at her watch.

"Oh, that's all right," she said. "I've just got time to talk to you about the inventory, if the Superintendent doesn't mind waiting, then I'll hare back. Mr. Pibble, do you mind if I get my job done first, and leave you? A girl comes to friz me up, and it doesn't seem fair to keep her hanging about. I'll send someone over to fetch you."

"Can't I get back round the outside of the fence?" said Pibble.

"Well, you could, if you don't mind walking a bit farther. And it's a bit overgrown, I'm afraid. Actually, it'd be a great help, because we'll all be busy giving the afternoon lot tea out of tiny little tinkling cups. It's much more of a nuisance than the sherry the morning ones get. I'll only keep Maureen for five minutes now, so perhaps it would amuse you to look at the old Tiger Pit—it's rather your sort of thing, I shouldn't wonder."

She waved, a gesture of seductive dismissal, toward the stunted minarets, and walked off with the woman in the mobcap toward a white thatched cottage which lay about thirty yards down the slope, under a superb sycamore.

"Fine," said Pibble, not even surprised that she hadn't waited for his assent.

PART II

THE LION GROUND

Once he lay in the mouth of a cave
And sunned his whiskers,
And lashed his tail slowly, slowly
Thinking of voluptuousness
Even of blood.

But later, in the sun of the afternoon,
Having tasted all there was to taste, and having slept his fill
He fell to frowning, as he lay with his head on his paws
And the sun coming in through the narrowest fibril of a slit
    in his eyes.

    —D. H. Lawrence, "The Beast of St. Mark"

3:10 P.M.

Pibble leaned over the parapet, and gasped: his first impression had been right—it *was* an Oriental building sunk two stories into the ground. He was looking down, as if from the rooftops, into an unpaved courtyard, fuzzy with scrub. The towers assumed their proper proportions now that their bases were visible, and between them ran a double series of cloisters, one above the other; the exaggeratedly ogive arches were frilled with a lacework of stone right down to the ground. The pit looked as if it were used—there were some mounds of what seemed to be dog's feces at the foot of one of the further towers—but nothing stirred in it. Presumably some of the lions from the enclosure were occasionally quartered here. There was a cage under one of the arches in the left-hand wall, with a gate which slid up and down like a portcullis; it was shut now.

To his left, at ground level, was a wooden notice on a post, of the kind used by local authorities to warn strangers of by-laws. It turned out to display an extract from a letter written in 1765 by Horace Walpole to George Montagu.

> I have sworn a vow on the bones of, oh, whatever saint you will (so be it not those of the fat ox of Smithfield, whom I know to be the only saint you and your rustick neighbours acknowledge) that I will speak nei-

ther good nor ill of Herryngs until three hundred more of our English summers have been grumbled away. Now 'tis but a pile, a raw new quarry turn'd inside-out. Let it become *mossy*, and then I will pronounce.

But one part I must tell you of, for it has quite ravished me with its absurdity. Josiah, that is the *Nabob* twin and not his stay-at-home toad of a brother who slops about still down at the Abbey (which I may tell you is ugly enough, for it is old and mean) is so prodigious rich that he has built a palace for his very animals. Two tygers which he brought from the Indies (being the only friends he made there, I doubt not) he has housed with true Nabobish phantasy in a great pit lined all around with Brahminical cloisters, enough to perambulate a whole templefull of monks, and all sunk below our honest English sward. Four towers squat at the corners which are copied from a ruin'd fort at *Calcutta*, but (since their foundations spring some fathoms below the horizontal) the effect is finely ridiculous. Mr. Clavering's first two friends were drowned by one of our little English *monsouns*, the pit filling with water, but he has undertaken prodigies of drainage and sent for two more. Their roarings will fright Hampshire, but less than it frights me to consider what a treasure house of thievery (for these *Nabobs*, you know, are nothing but land pirates) has been spent on the mere digging and ornamenting of a hole.

Pibble leaned again over the waist-high parapet and prepared to gaze with enjoyable melancholy at old Josiah's folly (as Mrs. Singleton had guessed, it was very much his kind of thing—Mrs. Pibble found him a difficult companion on holidays) when his half-arranged pose was stilted by a deep, breathy, thudding bark from enormous lungs. Islands of his skin, phobogenous zones, chilled—the voice was addressed to him. It came from the pit.

There was a lion down there, a large male with a heavy

black mane and a tuft of black fur at its tail tip. It was whisking its tail busily from side to side, but the rest of its body was entirely still and it was staring at Pibble—not the tired, dilettante stare with which the lions in the open ground had followed his passage, but an intent and focused gaze. Thus Galileo peered at the moons of Jupiter; thus a cat watches a wren; thus the chrysoberyl eyes looked at Pibble. Still unblinking, the animal raised its head and made its noise again, neither roar nor bark nor cough, so that Pibble could see the yellow teeth, reef-like, widely separated, useless for chewing but ideal for shearing off lumps of flesh to be swallowed whole. The pink tongue, wide but thin, curled up in a beckoning gesture before the jaws clicked shut.

"Scare the hell out of you, that one," said a voice at Pibble's elbow. He turned and saw the woman who had opened the gate for them. She bobbed him a curtsy, neither solemn like Mrs. Chuck's nor inept like Claire's, but joky and conspiratorial. Mrs. Singleton was already on the other side of the fence, walking fast with her gun under her arm. Pibble watched her for a few seconds, hoping that she might turn and wave, but she strode on. He looked at this other woman—Maureen Finnick, presumably—and saw that she had understood the meaning of his gaze over her shoulder. She was roundfaced, apple-cheeked, blue-eyed, plum-lipped, buxom, and sly. About twenty-five, perhaps, but watchful as an old hunter.

"You were wishful to talk with me, sir?' she said. What he had at first taken for a babble of urgency turned out to be her normal mode of speech, as though she had just run up three flights of stairs to impart fatal news.

"Don't you find that uniform a nuisance?" said Pibble. "I mean for instance making your hair look twentieth-century when you want to go out in the evening"

"Lor' love you, sir," said Miss Finnick, patting a russet ringlet into position, "there's little enough going out of an evening down in these parts, though, to be sure, if you was wishful to take me I would not disgrace you. Shall us go back down to my stall? There'll be visitors any minute, I do be thinking."

"You can talk twentieth-century if you prefer," said Pibble. "I'm afraid I'm only police, and I believe you may be able to help me clear up the problem why Mr. Deakin hanged himself."

Her watchfulness neither increased nor diminished.

"Ah," she said, "but even a clever City gentleman like yourself, sir, would find it a terrible thing to go chopping and changing your way of talking from sunup to cattle-calling time. No, sir, I'll bide by Mr. Harvey's manual, for the sake of the practice, and 'tis you must tell me if you think I might be overdoing it. Poor Arthur Deakin! And who'd have told you I might be knowing anything about him?"

"Nobody told me. The thing is this, Miss Finnick: I have no doubt at all that Deakin did hang himself, but he didn't leave a message. Suicides usually do, you know" *(You would, my girl, a message calculated to stir up the maximum possible misery; you're just that type)* "and it saves having everybody guessing stupid and embarrassing reasons if one can find out why he actually did it. Did you see much of him?"

"Arthur Deakin was seeing a deal more of me than ever I was of him," said Miss Finnick, with an exaggerated flounce. "Always hanging about in the shaw behind my stall, and peeking and prying—after you, sir. 'Tis more fitting."

She held the door of the cottage for him and he went in.

"Crippen," he said. "Is this another example of Mr. Singleton's passion for detail?"

"Indeed it is, though I haven't had time to arrange it proper orderly. They did be moving me down to the Abbey, and all my knickknacks, these three days past."

Her calling it a stall had misled him into thinking the room would be like a shop, with revolving stands of colored postcards and big polished counters cluttered with coarse

pottery souvenirs. Postcards there were, but in a casual-look-
ing line along the shelf above the crackling fire. A clutter of
souvenirs there was, too, but so spread out along dressers
and corner cupboards and old oak tables that the effect was
of a large cottage room, desperately overfurnished. Nor were
the souvenirs in the usual gnomeware style. Straight in front
of the entrance was a farmhouse dresser whose shelves held
a row of kitchen plates, blue and white, with the spotted lion
of the Claverings in the center; in front of these stood three
model gibbets complete with dangling bodies, a stagecoach
about five inches high, and a hay wain to the same scale.
Elsewhere in the room were lanthorns and pistols, antique
sickles and kitchen implements, and a number of old iron
gadgets (of the sort which people write to *Country Life*
about, asking what they are) used in the forgotten tech-
niques of a rustic economy. Apart from the models (another
dresser held several sizes of full-rigged ship), everything
looked cottagy and serviceable, and everything was stamped
or branded with the lion crest. No attempt had been made to
fake antiquity; all the ironwork looked as though the blacksmith had been hammering it yesterday. On the other hand
it also looked as if there had been a blacksmith who hammered it, instead of some million-copy mold in Birmingham.

"Do the gallows sell well?" said Pibble.

"Mortal well, sir. They visitors do be desperate astonished by the hanging down at the Abbey, and they often
fancy summat to mind them of it."

"Did Deakin ever make models for you?"

"Him!" said Miss Finnick, in a totally changed voice.
"Too bloody concerned with..."

"Never mind," said Pibble. "I think you *were* overdoing
it anyway. Are you on the stage, too, like Mr. Waugh?"

Miss Finnick put up a pretty little hand under her mob-
cap and scratched at her scalp in sighing perplexity. The
action unsettled both her cap and the russet curls, which
slipped downward in a fashion no live hair could possibly

achieve. She swore, mid-twentieth-century style, and pulled off cap and wig, revealing a sleek black Eton crop. Then she stood looking calculatingly at Pibble from under her long black lashes while she twiddled the cap around her index finger. At last she sighed again, like a sculptor rejecting a piece of unworkable marble, and turned to a wall mirror. As she adjusted her image back into the non-world of Herryngs, she talked in her other voice, which he'd heard for a moment up by the Tiger Pit and then again when she cursed the dead coxswain. It was quiet, sensible, a little hard.

"I am a schoolmaster's daughter, Mr. Pibble—that's the name, isn't it? I was all set to go to Sussex University and begin the long drift into matrimony when they came down here to film *The Ordeal of Richard Feverel.* I don't suppose you ever saw it—it was just after *Tom Jones* and they hoped to make the same sort of money by pulling the same sort of gags, but of course people were tired of that by then and they lost a packet. Anyway, I was an extra and the director gave me two or three words to speak, for reasons not wholly concerned with the aesthetics of celluloid. Of course they'd shot far more film than they could use—nine hours' worth or something ridiculous—and I think my three words must have been the very first things they cut. My director had got bored with me by then, but I went up to London and pestered him for another job—I didn't want *him* any more, he was a nasty little twit—and he wangled me another tiny part to get rid of me. We were about quits then, I reckoned—wangling parts isn't easy with Equity watching every credit line. But they cut that part, too, for the finished film, and a nice old biddy who I'd struck up with who makes a living by playing marchionesses in the background of ballroom scenes took me out to a lunch she couldn't afford just to tell me to go home, because I wasn't going to be any good—not even good enough for the background of ballroom scenes. I was always overdoing it, she said. Hetty, that's old Lady Clavering, the General's wife, was my godmother, and I was allowed to invite myself to Herryngs when I wanted to, although she had been dead for years, so I came here and gave the Admiral a bad weekend, telling him how harsh life was for someone who hadn't led his sheltered kind of existence."

"What was she like?" said Pibble.

"Hetty? She died before I had any idea what she was like—children have no idea, you know. Soft, easy, straightforward, beautiful, I think. Anty's the only one who will talk about her—she doted on her. There isn't a picture of her anywhere in the House, unless the Admiral's got one shut away in a drawer. Neither of them ever loved anyone else, I think."

She turned from the mirror, wig and cap prettily arranged, but face drawn into tired modern lines, like a debt-harassed mum helping out with charades.

"She was too good to live, Deakin once said," she added. "He had a knack of pronouncing some dreary old cliché as though it were all the law and the prophets. Where was I?"

"Pouring out your sorrows on the Admiral's shoulder."

"Truer than you know. I didn't realize what a cunning old sod he was. But he made Harvey give me a job—he was just starting up then. I was in the House at first, but Harvey decided I spoilt the atmosphere by hamming my part and moved me out here because I can do sums. He still gets sick at me for hamming, but he can't get rid of me without employing two other people—one to charm the visitors and one to keep the accounts. He doesn't have to worry anywhere else in Herryngs, because the rest of it's inclusive in the entrance fee. But here—well, look at those bloody little gallows, for instance: he bulk-bought the parts, and now he's decided that we've got to unload them by next June, latest, before some liberal busybody in Fleet Street hears about them and whips up a great fuss about their being bad for the image of England. So I've got to muck around with prices according to the feel and smell of every batch of tourists who come in clutching their hot little traveler's checks. I'll manage O.K., and Harvey knows it, but it drives him up the wall when he hears me ad-libbing his precious dialect. I'd go mad with boredom if I didn't; as it is, I don't say I'm miserable, I don't say I'm happy, and it's acting of a sort, I suppose, though Harvey swears there isn't a worse actress in all *Who's Who in the Theatre*. Oh, Christ, poor old Deakin. Look, Mr. Pibble, the visitors will be here any second. Twice seventeen is thirty-four, and say fifteen for the last batch, that makes fifty minutes. Could you come back in an hour and I'll have a chance to collect my wits and tell you what happened to old Deakin?"

"Fine," said Pibble, reflecting that that might make it possible for him to miss the four-forty and thus throw the whole dotty plot out of gear. "I only meant I thought you were overdoing the lingo, you know. Everything else works beautifully."

"Thankee kindly, zurr," said Miss Finnick, adding, with dismal relish in her modern voice as she came up from her flouncing curtsy, "I overdo *everything.*"

Pibble left her flicking moodily at the doll which dangled from the largest gallows. Already the monstrous purple puffs of the pseudo-*Rocket* were emerging above the reddening maples to his left, so he dodged around to the back of the cottage and found a little footpath leading under the sycamore and on through rank, tussocky grasses. It looked as if this ought to lead via the back of the Tiger Pit to the path around the outside of the enclosure. The other path ran beside the pit, and would have brought him into view of the visitors, damaging both the fake idyl and Miss Finnick's reputation. Besides, he was still absurdly unnerved by his interview with the big lion in the pit, by that sense of personal summons, and didn't feel like facing the creature again. Odd that Miss Finnick felt the same: she had said so, and in her modern accent.

The path deceived, curling away from the line he wanted toward a little wood. The rough grass was still wet with October dew, enough to discourage him from striking off across it in London shoes; he had nothing special to go back to the House for, and any little path would do for mooching an hour away on a prancing afternoon like this. He strode out, taking dutifully deep lungfuls of the historic oxygen.

To reward him, a set of crumbling crenelations began to appear behind the wood; when this building was sufficiently revealed to declare itself as a purpose-built folly, he could see a fragment of roof line, warty with crockets, rather nearer the wood. Just as he reached the edge of the trees, the path turned and dipped to an unsuspected ravine with a small stream muttering along the bottom; the folly, a single ivied tower, stood on the far side of the cleft, and a hyper-Gothick chapel on this side, fifty yards farther up. Pibble gazed curiously into the ravine, whose black and fern-hung walls seemed out of place in this chalk country—and quite right, too, he realized, studying the pattern of striations at his feet and discovering that the boulders were a thinnish facing of imported stone which kept the walls precipitous and the water aboveground. In places, he could still see where the blocks fitted together. Perhaps the whole group—folly and ravine and chapel—had been built under the inspiration of Horace Walpole's visit, but sited, so as not to spoil the landscape with a passing fad, in this unvisitable nook.

And the chapel seemed still in use; the door was open and a yellow light showed inside—and what are policemen for if not to nose around?

All he saw in the building was a vast old machine, made of enormous moldings of cast iron; hammers seemed to predominate, poised above a sloping trough. There were various meshes of sieve, too, a surprising collection of cogs and cams, and at the far end a big helical auger like the main shaft of a mincing machine; the drive came from an overhead axle. He went outside and walked around the building, to find that up the slope there was no ravine, but instead a fair-sized millpond feeding a lovely undershot wheel in the side of the chapel. He went back to continue his nosing, and found the General standing on the far side of the machine and letting a coarse white powder trickle through his hands.

"Thought it might be someone else," said the old man, "someone who wouldn't know what to make of me with me face hair shaved off, so I ducked down and had a peek at you as you left. Anty's got her hairdresser to botch me up some false whiskers. Going to find a clue in here, hey?"

"What on earth is it?" said Pibble.

"Bone meal. Engine keeps jamming, though. Now I'm getting old, I'm too impatient to leave the bones in the acid long enough or let 'em dry properly."

"Acid?"

"Sulfuric acid, in that tank there. Releases the phosphorus, or something—always hated chemistry. Trouble, is, we don't get enough bones these days, only what the lions can't crack up and a few from the House, but I like to keep things working. Hate to see a machine designed to do a job and just standing idle—too like home life, eh?"

"I suppose it's always been here," said Pibble.

"Since the place was built, nearabouts. Big landowner's household got through a fantastic lot of meat in those days— eighty or ninety in the House alone, not to mention the estate cottagers and the tigers and the foxhounds. Josiah put it in because he thought the local bone merchant was cheating him. Typical rich man, pouring out money like water and then fretting over a few shillings. Very big industry in those days, bone meal. D'you know, a fellow called Liebig—had a jar named after him, that one— accused England of buying up the bones of soldiers from European battlefields because we couldn't get enough animals. Didn't say anything about the Europeans who dug the things up and sold 'em—typical bloody foreigner, never see anyone's point of view but their own, hell to work with, you ask Harvey about his time with the Frogs after the Raid. Like to see it going?"

Without waiting for an answer he began to wind at a cast-iron wheel in the wall. Outside the sluices changed their note, and the mill wheel worked groaningly up to a monotone clack. The General flung his weight against what must have been the clutch lever, for the hammers began a slogging rustic dance above the sluice, iron feet rising and falling. The General picked a few bones out of a sack (a shoulder blade of mutton and some longer bones from a taller animal) and threw them into the top of the trough. The feet marked time on the bones, reducing them to splinters, to fragments, to powder. The sieves rattled between the feet with a cam-driven jigging which allowed only reduced particles of bone through to the next series of feet and tossed the unreduced back under the previous series. The trough itself vibrated, teasing the particles down, and at its end the huge screw, geared down to a hypnotically slow rotation, rammed the final produce through a pair of counter-rotating grids. The chapel clanged and boomed until, as the last few splinters were dropping into the auger, the whole contraption jammed and the driving axle started on a terrifying judder. The General, spry as a grasshopper, skipped across to the clutch lever and threw the machine out of gear. Only then did Pibble realize how skull-filling the noise of it had been.

"My fault," said the General. "Bones too damp. Be a good fellow and look outside and see if you can see that good-for-nothing Rastus coming."

"I's here, massa," said a voice at the door.

"Splendid," said the General, picking up a big wrench. "We can cope now, Superintendent."

"Can you tell me the way to the path round the back of the Lion Ground?" said Pibble.

"Rastus will show you," said the General. "It'll take me about five minutes to get this bloody casing off. Anything else you want to know?"

"What's so different about the lion in the pit?" said Pibble. "I mean why isn't he in with the others?"

"He's new," said the General. "We aren't insured for him yet."

"Oh, of course," said Pibble. He sensed the black gardener stiffen and relax beside him, and added, "Did you fly him in, like the cuckoos?"

The General straightened up from measuring the adjustment of the wrench against the big nuts on the top of the casing over the auger. Again Pibble saw the clown mask of old age quiver and dissolve, saw for a second the hero taut for action. But then the General giggled his strange, wild cry and said, "Just like the cuckoos. You've been doing your homework, hey?"

"Yes," said Pibble. "Incidentally, I didn't finish talking to Miss Finnick before the visitors came. I'd better get it all done today, so it doesn't look as if I'll be able to catch the four-forty."

"Stay as long as you like," said the General offhandedly, bending again to his wrench. "You've got a job to do, and Anty enjoys your company."

Outside the chapel stood a squat little tractor with a trailer, in which were a couple of shovels, a broom, a soft brush, and a plastic dustpan.

"You came to collect the bone meal, I suppose," said Pibble.

"Yeah," said the Negro. "He wants it dug into some new rose beds. This track—that leads no place. Funny about these grand old guys: they take a fancy to do something and it has to be done pronto—just like kids."

"Which of the grand old guys was that?" said Pibble, jerking his thumb back toward the chapel. They were walking along the footpath he had come by—or, rather, he was, while the Negro loped unconcerned through the rough grasses—but at his words his guide stopped and glowered at him.

"Massa, you no ask me trick questions. Massa Singleton he tell me you knows who dat be."

"All right," said Pibble, "let's change the subject. What *is* wrong about the lion?"

The Negro glowered at him again from under the absurd hat, grunted, and walked on without answering. The path forked right down an almost invisible track, which Pibble hadn't even noticed on the way up, and led around the Tiger Pit on the far side from the Horace Walpole letter. Pibble could see a group of visitors leaning over the opposite wall, cameras whining and churning. Suddenly out of the pit came that extraordinary coarse, yearning grunt; the line of visitors quivered like seaweed when the fringe of a wave slops into a rock pool; the Negro stopped again and gazed glumly at the four stunted minarets.

"They feel it, too," said Pibble.

"Yeah," said the Negro. "Like the boss says, he ain't insured. We Americans are surely sensitive to any breach of the capitalist system. You believe that?"

"No," said Pibble seriously, "and what's more if you know anything which might conceivably be relevant to Deakin's death, you have a duty to tell me."

"Duty," said the Negro fiercely. He pulled his beard down and forward, and then allowed the elastic to snap back up into his mouth; with a snort he blew the whole mass of artificial hair outward in staring derision. Then he walked on.

Pibble trudged behind him, boding, until they came to another fork and the Negro stood aside for him, pointing wordlessly to where the path led into a funnel made by the nearing fence on one side and the wood on the other.

"Thank you very much," said Pibble, and walked on without expecting an answer. The path between the fence and the wood turned out to be more overgrown that he had expected, and made possible only by the existence of an untended box hedge under the trees, which had mostly kept back the ranker growth of bramble, old-man's-beard, woody nightshade, and nameless protruding saplings. Every now

and then he had to pick his way gingerly through a gap, lifting the feelers of bramble out of his path carefully between
finger and thumb, as though they had been poisonous. It
made him realize by how fine a margin the whole enterprise
was kept trundling along: if there had been money to spare,
this would have been a handsome walk, full of incidental
delights.

At one point, where a beech tree spread its under-
growth-killing boughs wide enough to make the path easier
for a moment, he came on such a delight; a fair-sized lion
cub—a two-year-old, to judge by the photographs in the Elsa
books—was teasing its ear against one of the metal stan-
chions which supported the fencing. It stopped its rubbing
when it saw him and simply stayed leaning, like a drunk
against a lamppost, watching him with inquisitive yellow
eyes. Pibble walked carefully up to the fence, and, tense for
the first movement of snap or clawing, put his hand through
the pig wire and began to scratch between the animal's ears.
Hidden in the coarse, crew-cut fur he found a small mound
of bone, evidently put there by the Creator so that it would
one day be possible for a man to knead it and give the animal pleasure. The cub began to purr, a deep, confident
snore, and to try to get nearer the source of pleasure, almost
trapping Pibble's fingers between its own gristly weight and
the wire; but soon they reached a compromise position, suit-
ing each as well as circumstances permitted, with Pibble
scratching and the lion purring, as though both could have
gone on till teatime.

Then, without warning, the lion stopped halfway
through the downstroke of its purr and pranced off toward
the nearest cover, still looking over its shoulder. For a
moment Pibble thought that the noise he heard was an after-
echo, inside his skull, of all that purring, but then he realized
that it was wholly different in nature, not animal but
mechanical. It ceased as he wheeled around, but he was in
time to see a large purple object withdrawing behind the

trunk of the beech. The ground was pure moss and he was able to walk in almost perfect silence up to the tree; he edged around it and found himself facing a short, wide man in a purple blazer, festooned with photographic equipment—the American who had been arguing with Harvey Singleton when the coaches were due to leave.

"Goddam camera," said the American. "I have a silent one at my hotel, but not such a good lens, so I leave it behind the one day I want it."

"Bad luck," said Pibble. He felt irresponsibly friendly— here was the only other man in the whole country, for all he knew, who didn't take the Claverings at face value. "It's all right," he added. "I don't belong here, either."

"That so?" said the American flatly. "I'm relieved to hear it. Chanceley's the name, Calhoun Chanceley, from Dallas."

"How do you do, Mr. Chanceley. My name's James Pibble."

"Pleased to meet you," said Mr. Chanceley. "I take it you're not a fee-paying visitor, Mr. Pibble. You don't carry the kit."

He flapped his hands toward the several hundred quid worth of meters and lenses with which he was draped.

"No," said Pibble. "I came down here to do a job, and I got hung up, so I thought I'd nose around."

"You seen everything?" said Mr. Chanceley.

"Only the House and the lions so far, and the souvenir stall."

"That lion in the pit," said Mr. Chanceley. "You reckon it's true what they say, he's a man-eater?"

"Who told you that?"

"One of our party came before and she heard it then. Only the guide didn't mention it this time."

"I hear they're finding it difficult to insure that particular lion."

"That figures. Here's your pal come back—you reckon he'd let me scratch his ears while you photographed us?"

"Let's try," said Pibble. "You'll have to show me how your machine works. I haven't got one."

"You don't say?" said Mr. Chanceley, his voice wavering for the first time out of its *nil-admirari* flatness at this revelation of peasantlike non-affluence. "Well, all you got to do is aim at me through this window here, and when you got a good picture press this button here. Only secret is to keep cracking five times, as long as you think right. You got the shakes a mite, Mr. Pibble, so you better steady it against the tree. Nothing personal, sir—I had an uncle—but I'll tell you after."

Pibble steadied the camera against the chill green-streaked bark and kept it whirring while Mr. Chanceley clawed vigorously at the back of the cub's head. The cub, lost in its lust of irritation, did not seem to notice the different technique; every few seconds Mr. Chanceley turned with a ghastly naturalness to study an imaginary bird over Pibble's head, or a viper at his feet, so that the whole of his solemn countenance should be visible on the pattering celluloid. At last the camera made its terminal fizz and click, and Pibble released the button. Instant on his cue, Mr. Chanceley left the lion in mid-purr and came eagerly back toward the tree. The first thing Pibble looked for as he lowered the camera was to see whether the man's neck was as exceptionally thick as it had looked through the view finder. It was.

"How'd it go?" said Mr. Chanceley.

"O.K., I hope," said Pibble. "The tree hasn't got the shakes, and I kept going until the film ran out."

"I shouldn't have said that," said Mr. Chanceley. "My uncle, he was teetotal. He just had 'em natural."

"Forget it," said Pibble. "They come and go with me. I don't get them often."

"Glad to hear it," said Mr. Chanceley. "Here's my card. I'd like to send you a print of your scene, Mr. Pibble. You can borrow a projector, surely?"

"That's very kind of you," said Pibble. "I'm afraid I

haven't got a card, but I'll write my address down if you can wait."

He tore a page out of his notebook, and was pleased to find that his hand was quite steady as he printed in block capitals the number of his house and the name of his street in Ewell. The shakes did not come back until he was thirty yards on down the path and looked up from Mr. Chanceley's card (whose business in Dallas turned out, appropriately, to be Photographic Research) to see a full-grown lion watching him through the mesh. The gaze was again that of the bored aristocrat, but Pibble had to stand still and wait for his glands to stop squirting their panic additives into his bloodstream.

It gave Miss Finnick a chill, enough to make her talk twentieth-century. It lived alone in the pit. It made the visitors waver like seaweed. It was said to be difficult to insure. It had lusted, crazy-eyed, after Pibble's flesh. Add to that that they'd been telling visitors about it in the past, but not now. And that Miss Finnick's stall—the nearest place to the pit—had been shut for the last three days and her wares moved down to the Abbey. Not much, but suppose...

Suppose the Claverings had decided to win their argument with Lord Bath by flying in a genuine man-eater (as they'd done with with the cuckoos—and what about the General's reaction when he'd mentioned them?). And suppose they'd then hit the insurance reef ("Hello, Fred, I want cover for another lion." "Fine, usual terms?" "Well, that's what I wanted to talk to you about—this one's a man-eater." "I *say*, old boy! That's going to put the third-party rates up a bit. How'd you get hold of him?" "Asked Guffy Rickmansworth to look out for one—got that place in Kenya, yer know. Anaesthetic dart, crate him up, fly him in." "Is that legal?" "Well, er, Fred—" "Now, look here, old boy, how often have I told you you're not still cutting corners on that blasted Raid. This company..." Just the sort of crazy caper the Claverings might expect to get away with.) So they couldn't go to town on the publicity—though the guides had been telling the visitors; but not this time, not this time.

Then suppose the Admiral dies—no mention of sickness—has an accident, gets killed by the lion in the course of his researches, like as not; and for some reason (a fancy fiddle with death duties? Account for the impersonation bit, anyway) they want to keep quiet about it, then, could they, conceivably, have decided to feed the body to the lion? How much meat in a nine-stone human body? Say six stone of meat, a stone of small bones for roughage, four full meals for a hungry lion. If he had the craving for man-flesh which the General had talked of at luncheon—and there'd been a line about it in Mrs. Adamson's first book (bless you both Elsas, and all your six feet)—then he'd not have gorged himself on horse meat; he'd be hungry. A stomach which can digest zebra hide should be able to cope with Harris tweed. It would drag the body under cover, bury the stomach contents, and start by eating the guts. In four days there should be nothing left except the larger bones, which they could collect and...

He stopped again, chilly with recognition. Those long bones he'd seen rattling into the meal grinder—too long for sheep, too thin for beef. Deer, conceivably, but...Crippen, the old boy had a nerve, sending his brother's shins down the trough to be chomped up into fertilizer, and complaining that they weren't dry enough! And he'd a better reason for impatience than senility, too.

Pibble was surprised by how little he wanted to go through with the business; if ever there was a family entitled to indulge in the private eccentricity of feeding each other to lions, it was the Claverings; he was sure the Admiral wouldn't have wished him to interfere. And it would be simple enough to accept the proffered explanation, stamp Deakin's death with his seal of approval, and leave someone else (Carl Spruheim, like as not) to find out someday that it wouldn't wash.

Picking his way into the undergrowth to skirt an impenetrably fallen tree, putting his foot into a quaggy area which sent half a cupful of stinking inky ooze between shoe and sock, stopping to extract the thorns of a bramble tendril from his ear, emerging onto the path to find nests of big burs already deep-set into his trouser, legs, he decided to give up. He sat on a stump to pick the burs out, and decided that the odds against his being right were at least four to one. And if he was wrong, who would forgive his nosiness into the private griefs of the great? Not the Claverings, not the Ass. Com., not Mrs. Pibble. The burs were ripe enough to fall to bits as he pulled at them, leaving crumbs of embedded particles which had to be picked out piecemeal and brought shreds of precious blue pinstripe with them. All very well to say he was retiring soon and could afford to take a risk, but who wanted to go out in a blaze of infamy? So be it.

But as he trudged dispiritedly up the sward toward Herryngs, he realized that he would have to go on. If he'd been sure, either way, he could have dropped it; but living another twenty years and not knowing—knowing only that he'd been too scared to find out—what sort of calm old age would that be?

The first cloud of the day suddenly filched the sunlight, and the gold glow left the stone façade. The horizon seemed to close in, and the House to look as monstrous as it really was, an alien mass leaning its elbows on the landscape.

4:35 P.M.

Miss Scoplow was at the General's desk in the study, sorting papers out of a wire tray into a filing drawer. She looked up as Pibble came in.

"Gracious," she cooed, with a pretty little movement of her eyebrows which did service for a frown, "you know you've missed your train, don't you? They couldn't keep the coaches any longer. And where've you been? You look as though you'd been exploring darkest Africa!"

"Well," said Pibble, "there were a lot of lions."

She laughed—she seemed deliciously easy to amuse, like a child with no complexes.

"I can't *bear* them," she said, "but then I'm even frightened of cows. I adore Old England, though. Have you seen that yet?"

"Not yet," said Pibble.

"Oh, but you *must*, it's absolutely super. Of course, I've only been here a fortnight, so I haven't had time to get blasé, but it really is terribly well done. The Abbey's so terrifically gloomy and old, and that sets the tone for everything, you see. I nearly fainted the first time I watched the hanging, and I'm absolutely sure the building itself *is* haunted. Sir Ralph says so, and the Bowling Green *was* used as a dueling ground several times, so really it would be almost more surprising if you didn't sometimes hear shots in the middle of the night."

"And do you?" said Pibble.

"Well, it's difficult to be *sure* when you're not properly awake. Mr. Singleton teases me and says I hear what I want to hear, but I'm quite certain I heard something last week. Three bangs, but there's a terrific echo, you know, so it might only have been one and two echoes, but I remember it says in *Treasure Island* that ghosts don't make an echo."

"I thought Long John Silver invented that to cheer the pirates up. He can't have been scientifically sure, I'd say."

Miss Scoplow sat and stared at him with her round-eyed gaze.

"Goodness, how clever!" she said. "He must have been an extraordinary man to think of a trick like that when he only had one leg."

Pibble laughed, and she joined in.

"Oh, dear," she said, "I'm afraid I'm always saying things like that. What I *meant*"—and again the eyebrows rippled to denote concentration—"was that he must have been an extraordinary man to think of a trick like that in the middle of climbing up a sandy hill with only one leg."

"You've got a good memory," said Pibble.

"Yes, I have. I'm a first-class secretary, honestly. They pay me a London salary *and* they keep a horse for me, which is absolutely super. It's only that I *talk* like a ninny."

"Is it a full day's work?" said Pibble. "Do you have to type out bits of Sir Richard's book, and things like that?"

"Yes, Mr. Deakin brings—brought me down a great bundle of paper all written out in most beautiful copperplate every day."

"How's the book going?"

"It's all notes and quotations so far, and he seems to have got stuck for the last four days because there hasn't been anything. Do you know, lunch—luncheon today was the first real talk I've had with him since I've been here? Isn't he charming?"

"They're a very interesting family, all of them," said

Pibble. "Look, Miss Scoplow, I have to make a private call to London. Which telephone can I use?"

"Use this one. I've finished here, honestly. We're on direct dialing—shall I get the number for you?"

"No, please don't bother—I may have to chase my man around a bit. But could you apologize to anyone who was bothered by my keeping the coaches waiting? I've got about an hour's more work, so if someone will take me to another train in a couple of hours..."

"It'll have to be Southampton. I'll lay it on." She smiled a sweet, diffident goodbye and left. Pibble was pleased to know that she wasn't in the plot; she moved in a quaintly old-fashioned aura of innocence, which the diseased air of Herryngs seemed unable to infect. He sighed over the telephone.

His man was at the third hospital he'd been passed on to. A secretary answered.

"Is that you, Jane?" said Pibble. "I want to ask Professor Alstead a few questions. Jimmy Pibble here."

Mumble mumble went the telephone, click bonk.

"Could you ask me, Superintendent, and then I can shout the questions across to him and he can shout back? It'll save him washing his hands."

Ah, Crippen, thought Pibble, that the secrets of Herryngs should be bandied through the formaldehyde air, across the trolleys of half-unseamed corpses, and in and out of the ears of morose attendants.

"I'm afraid it's rather hot stuff," he said.

"Oh, all right, I expect he'd like a rest, actually."

Bump click mumble mumble click bonk.

"Jimmy, this had better be good. I'm busy."

"Sorry, Bill. I may be quite mad, but even if I am don't gossip about it or I'll be in really hot water."

Grunt.

"Look, Bill, if I fed my enemy to a man-eating lion, and ground up the bigger bones in a bone-meal machine I happened to have handy, what traces would be left?"

"You serious?"

"Yes."

"Blood and flesh traces, practically none. I've seen 'em eating in a game reserve, and they lick the bones damn clean—great rough tongues they've got—eat pretty well everything, too. Dig your bone meal into your cabbage patch—disperse it thoroughly—and you'd be safe there; it's only phosphate. Only thing I can think of is hair and bone splinters in the feces. You'd have to clean your bone-meal machine up damn thoroughly, though."

"Is that all? They bury the stomach contents, I've read."

"Useless, unless your enemy had been eating something peculiarly human and especially indigestible, O.K.?"

"Yes, thanks. I'll stand you a drink when I see you."

"Two drinks. One for interrupting me and one for asking tom-fool questions. Jimmy?"

"Yes."

"Take it easy, lad."

Click. Br-r-r-r-r.

Bad as that? thought Pibble, staring at the names on the internal system: he could ring up Finnick, he saw. He could chat with her over the phone, and never even interview the lion in the pit. No. Bucket, shovel, and bait. And string. Gun? There were levels of madness, and he wasn't yet obsessed enough to go down into the pit if he failed to lure the lion into its cage and shut it in. Suddenly he remembered the soft brush and dustpan in Rastus's trailer: why would they want that sort of houseproud kit out there if they weren't going to clean the machine to unnatural speckless-ness? These grand old guys: they take a fancy to do some-thing and it has to be done pronto—just like kids. He felt less mad again.

Elsa's kitchen was untenanted. He found a whole cold chicken in the fridge and put it into a yellow plastic bucket; it had been cooked in something peculiarly pungent. There was a ball of coarse brown string in a holder on the wall,

which he took. What would the implacable Elsa say if he also
made off with the handy little shovel for removing ash from
the bottom of the Aga? He went next door and fetched the
clumsier one from the dining-room fire irons.

Plastic is betraying stuff, more enduring than bronze
and a world less weatherable. As he worked his way through
the sparse cover of parkland trees toward the near side of the
avenue, he had a fantasy about nicking an old wooden bar-
row from an outhouse, improvising hat and beard, tying
string around his trousers, and trundling off on his adventure in disguise. As it was, the yellow bucket declared him
alien amid the brochure-like serenity. He scuttled across the
avenue and looked at his watch in the shelter of the further
trees; he was already late for his appointment with Miss
Finnick—he'd have to go across the Lion Ground instead of
working around by the overgrown path.

The key was under its stone, which meant that the
General must be back this side again. Presumably Miss
Finnick went home another way—or did she live in the
House? There had been an oddity about the way she'd
referred to Mr. Singleton as "Harvey"—quite proper in an
almost relation-in-law, but a little insistent, cozy...And why
had Singleton picked the worst actress in *Who's Who in the
Theatre* to bamboozle a professional detective? Memo: ask
Spruheim what her reputation was and what his dealings
with her had been.

The fresh outbreak of sun had not brought back the
warmth of noon; Pibble felt chilly as he plodded along the
path, wondering where the lions had got to. Slowly the chill
deepened into unease, into near panic. He swung around.
About fifteen lions, heads lowered, were following him
along the path.

They stopped when he stopped, and three more came
out of a thicket on his left to join the gang. They looked
solemn, but not really menacing, and while he watched them
they did not move. Pibble swallowed, turned around, and

walked on; now he could hear the silken swish-swish of their passage through the grass—it seemed to be getting nearer, so he swung around again. They would have made world-class players at Grandmother's Footsteps, those lions; only one abstracted animal at the rear was not still by the time he could see them, causing a tiny flurry of growling and cuffing among the lions it had bumped into.

They *were* nearer.

"Off you go," he said. "Good boys. Home."

They stared at him, three-dozen yellow eyes, with quiet surprise. Then one of them—it looked very like the cub he had made friends with half an hour ago—pranced forward with a happy, half-sideways movement, as if it were slightly shy, and put its nose eagerly into the bucket. Pibble had just time to snatch the thing into the air above his head; the fire shovel teetered and fell, but with a fluky snatch he caught it left-handed. The cub, more pleased than ever with this excellent game, sat back on its haunches for a spring at the bucket, but Pibble banged it sharply on the nose with his shovel just in time to unsettle its leap, so that it bounced straight up like a firecracker, clawing at air, and then ran whimpering around to the back of the pack.

He frowned at the other lions like a schoolmaster quelling an outbreak of pellet-flicking, turned and walked on, glad to know that cold chicken was the equivalent of lobworm when it came to choosing lion bait. Swish-swish went the grasses behind him. His right arm tired in less than a minute, so he changed hands, shovel flailing. His left arm tired even quicker. He lowered the bucket onto his head, merely steadying it with his hand, and walked on in the attitude of one of those bearers cartoonists used to portray following Blimpish explorers through imaginary Africas. The lions, perhaps appreciative of this more familiar posture, closed in again until he could feel (in imagination, anyway) their hot and heavy and carnivorous breath thick on the backs of his knees. But he strode on austere (no hope could have no fear) until a black-and-tawny patch on the very edge of his peripheral vision moved farther forward and became the maned head of a lion at less than arm's length. Then the thought came to him that really he must look, with his pompous escort, much less like the cartoonists' figure of fun than a minor character on the fringe of a school-of-Rubens "Bacchus and Ariadne," a nymph bearing a spare amphora for Silenus unperturbed by the welter of gamboling fauna. Carried away by the conceit, he reached out his right hand to place it on the lion's shoulder, but forgot that he was still brandishing the fire shovel. The lion, apparently impressed by the way Pibble had dispatched the too attentive lion cub, shied away, barging into what looked like the senior lion present. Pibble had turned his head for his abortive maneuver, and saw the enormous yellow fangs bare as the old lion snarled at his clumsy subordinate, which quite removed the savor from his joke. He returned to striding on austere.

When he reached the far gate, he was confronted with a hitch in the hitherto smooth logistics. He could see the stone under which the key must be kept, reachable from both sides of the fence, but he couldn't go and grovel for it without leaving his precious chicken prey to the lions. After a moment's thought he decided to tie it to the fence above the gate while he got the key out; he put the shovel in his mouth, reached into the bucket with his free hand for the ball of string, found the loose end, and, on tiptoe, knotted the handle clumsily to the wire at the extreme limit of his stretch. Just as he had made the knot fast, an enormous weight caught him between the shoulder blades, slamming him into the gate, accompanied by hideous pain; he stayed still and endured, unable even to drop the shovel from his mouth because it was jammed between his cheek and the wire. Something began to clatter above his head; he worked his neck backward until he could see the bucket bouncing to and ho under the blows of a fulvous paw—one of the lions had become bored with waking, and was using him as a convenient leaning post which might help it to get at the chicken.

There came a slight relaxation of the pressure and he squirmed sideways, unsettling the lion so that it dropped and he was able to back himself against the gate, snatching the shovel as he turned. He raised it like a householder stalking a bluebottle with a fly swatter, and the lions eyed it speculatively, as if they were working out the potentialities of the weapon. They backed away. He lowered the shovel and began to edge toward the stone. They closed in toward the bucket. He raised the shovel and returned to guard the chicken. They backed away. Impasse. His shovel arm ached through its whole length and his back sang with pain.

"Be you all right, zurr?" said a soft voice over his shoulder.

"Do I look it?" he snapped. "Unlock the gate but don't unlatch it and then go back to your stall and shut the door, in case I make a mess of getting out of here."

"I do be carrying a mortal gert firearm, zurr," said the voice. There was a pause and a click; then the gate began to move behind him. He hadn't realized how hard he'd been pressing against it.

"For God's sake, keep it shut until I've got this bloody thing untied," he said, and began to fumble above his head with the string, one-handed. But the knot now seemed higher than he could reach, and he had to get his penknife out, put the shovel between his teeth, and slash at the string. Then the gate gave and he tumbled through while Miss Finnick slapped it shut behind him. The lions had not stirred from their circle, but one of them now roared a mild protest at the brevity and inconclusiveness of his performance. It was answered by that hoarse bellow from the pit, and several of the lions looked inquisitively toward the minarets. Pibble found that he was shaking violently.

"Are you O.K.?" said Miss Finnick, in her modern voice. "Your back doesn't look too good. That was a silly

damn trick to try." She was still wearing her Herryngs uniform, but carried a Thompson submachine gun crooked
under her right arm.

"Where've you left your brown Bess?" said Pibble. His
voice came out shrill. He picked up the bucket.

"What the hell have you got there?" said Miss Finnick.

"You tell me about Deakin and I'll tell you about this,"
said Pibble. The firm step he took toward the stall melted in
mid-stride and he staggered. Miss Finnick switched the gun
to her other hand and put her right arm around him.

"You put yours over my shoulders," she said. "Go on.
It's all right. I'm as strong as a horse. I keep a first-aid kit
there—it's in the insurance, like the gun—I'll dress your
back while we gossip. Ah, come on. Just think, if this was a
film we'd have to do it forty or fifty times before they even
turned the cameras on us, and *then* they'd cut it. Wounded
scout staggers home to stockade. Take it easy—I don't
believe in heroes any more—*any* heroes."

Two of the model gallows had gone; the whole room
seemed a few degrees less cluttered; Pibble, as he bent forward on his milking stool to allow Miss Finnick to swab his
back with antiseptic and cotton wool, could read the label
attached to its leg, addressed in elegant script to Mrs. Ruth
Boleno, c/o Brown's Hotel, Dover St., W.I.

"Bean't wholly mortal, zurr," said Miss Finnick, "nobbut
her must hurt 'ee considerable. And thy poor jerkin be most
fearsome tattered."

"Oh, hell," said Pibble and reached to pick it up. There
were four half-inch tears in the blue cloth, two of them
stained with blood; they didn't look as though they would
mend very well. He hadn't calculated on buying a new suit
for another eighteen months.

"Tell me about Deakin," he said.

"O.K.," said Miss Finnick, "but you do understand that
if I'm asked about it in court I shall say something else. I
can't afford not to. There isn't honestly much to say about

him. He was a secret little man, and I didn't see much of him except that I did have a row with him once when I tried to get him to make models for the stall, which he could easily have done. I didn't even want him to turn the same thing out over and over again; I wanted things which I could tell visitors were unique and handcrafted—they'd have fetched an absolute packet. But all he was interested in was making models for his great panorama of the Raid, which Harvey's got his eye on. Anyway we had this rather chilly shindy, him very civil and me very *grande dame,* and neither of us enjoyed it a bit. It isn't *fun* being a bitch, you know, at least not in that sort of way to that sort of person. Am I hurting you?"

"No."

"Well, after that we were even more formal with each other than need be—not that we saw much of each other. In fact I didn't know he was dead until Harvey rang me up this morning and told me what he wanted. That's the best I can do. Your jacket's a bit damp where I've sponged it, but you might as well put your vest and shirt back on."

"And what was that?"

"Oh, that Deakin had been hanging around me and I'd let him think he was going to get somewhere and then let him fall flat on his face."

Pibble stood up and worked himself wincingly into his shirt.

"Why did Mr. Singleton choose you," he said, "if he was so scornful of your acting abilities?"

Miss Finnick sidled up to him and put her arm around his waist. Though she was barely shorter than he was, she managed to achieve a posture in which her head lay on his shoulder and she gazed up through long nylon lashes into his eyes.

"I be the type of poor ninny of a lass as heroes come home to," she said. "Menfolk, they reckon if they can trust 'ee for one thing they can trust 'ee for the rest. Thou bean't that mortal foolish, be 'ee, Mr. Pibble? Besides," she added, flitting irritatingly back into the present, "he knows I like money."

Pibble tucked his shirt in, thinking he might be that mortal foolish given the chance.

"Did he have any suggestions about your motives for behaving like that?" he said. "Or for letting me know that you had?"

"Christ! You don't think they believe that ordinary common people have *motives*. We are the stars' tennis balls, struck and bandied, except that they do the bandying."

"You may be right," said Pibble, "but perhaps they don't have what we'd understand as motives themselves. I don't know them well, but they give me a feeling of not really relating to each other at all, but each whirling on along his own chosen path, alone."

"They *have* been rather like that since Hetty died. They all related to each other through her—except Harvey, of course. He hardly knew her."

"It seems a rather unlikely marriage," said Pibble.

"Um. Harvey's...Ah, well...and it was a way of tying him to Herryngs, I expect."

"Anyway," said Pibble, "this isn't the kind of thing you're going to be asked about. We're much more likely to want to know the exact dates on which you had to move your stall down to the Abbey, and what reason was given you."

There was a long silence. Miss Finnick walked around the room rearranging knickknacks on the shelves to fill the gaps left by the marauding Americans. Finally she picked a bundle of tissue paper out of a dresser drawer, unwrapped some bits of wood and string and a little doll figure, and sat down at her table.

"Your turn," she said.

"The Admiral has disappeared," said Pibble, "and the General tried to impersonate him."

"I know." She took a tube of glue out of her apron pocket and fixed an upright into a little platform.

"When did you learn?"

"Harvey rang up after lunch."

"He didn't tell you when he rang up this morning about faking a motive?"

"No. But the second time he explained that this was why it was necessary to fake a motive."

"He told Rastus after lunch, too," said Pibble. "Elsa didn't know during lunch."

"Go on."

"Can you imagine a motive for Deakin hanging himself in the middle of painting a finished model for his panorama of the Raid?"

"You still seem to be asking all the questions," said Miss Finnick sulkily. She had assembled another bit of stick into an inverted L.

"All right. The Admiral hadn't sent any typing down to Judith Scoplow for four days. She heard some shots last week. None of his shoes are missing."

"La Scoplow hasn't been here long," said Miss Finnick. "They do that about once a month."

"Do what?"

"Go down to the Bowling Green and fight a duel. They use the pistols the tourists use, but they load them with proper ball to give themselves a bit of a thrill. The pistols are fixed to fire crooked, so it's not as terrifying as it sounds, but I bet you they were fighting over Scoplow, which is why they couldn't tell her."

"The General and the Admiral, you mean?"

"Who else? They still think of themselves as wild boys." She knotted a fine cord around the protruding arm of her structure.

"All right," said Pibble. "Who told you not to tell me that the lion in the pit was a man-eater?"

"Anty, this afternoon, and even so I damn near did

before I'd even started. She said they'd broken the law and you'd have to report it, which would be a bore. It still sounds reasonable."

"Yes. How often do they use the bone-meal machine?"

"The what?"

"The machine for grinding bones up in the fake chapel up by the folly."

"Oh, *that's* what it is—I've often wondered. You've a nasty mind for such a mild-looking man, Mr. Pibble. You really believe this, don't you?"

"I think it's sufficiently possible for me to have to try and look into it."

"Stern daughter of the voice of God," said Miss Finnick, settling the noose of her gallows around the doll's neck. "I never got further than that line—it didn't sound as if it was going to be my sort of poem. I think the odds are about twenty to one against your being right."

"You've forgotten about the shoes," said Pibble. "And Deakin's suicide—the motive for it, I mean. He had to have one, and you aren't it."

"Lawk-a-mussy, I do be main disrememberful. That brings it down to about two to one against."

"I'd back it at those odds," said Pibble.

"So would I," said Miss Finnick. "Oh, Mr. Pibble, don't 'ee go setting thyself up as a hero. I do be that mortal fixed against heroes, and I was just about beginning to fancy 'ee."

"I'm not going down unless I can shut it into its cage. That's what the chicken's for."

Miss Finnick went over to her mirror and straightened her cap and curls; then she read the label which was now tied to the mirror.

"Mrs. Rupert K. Grott, 2028 Main Street, Waxahachie, Texas. I've hung on to this for seven months, seen myself in it every day, and now it's going to Mrs. Grott, a squawking goose of a woman with a skin like raw veal. Give me five minutes to lock up, Mr. Pibble, and I'll just go clean away and pretend I never saw your bloody bucket. I keep the gun in the grandfather clock, whose key is in that snuffbox. That window's catch is the easiest one to force."

"Thank you," said Pibble.

"Don't mention it," said Miss Finnick. "Just tell me what you think about *her*. Tell me I'm not going off my rocker."

"Mrs. Singleton?"

"Scoplow."

"I think it's the context," he said judiciously. "People wouldn't pay much attention to her anywhere else, or at least not that much. But here, where everything's so rich, so spoilt—beautiful but mummified—old or phony or both—the most admirable the most corrupt—ah, they must find her like one of those dreams you have about being a child again, before anything went wrong, but with all your adult mind."

"Yes," said Miss Finnick, "that's probably it. Harvey, too, that's what shook me. So to think I'm becoming mummified. I must go away before I turn into another Mrs. Chuck—but if you're right I suppose the whole caboodle will come tumbling down before morning."

"You don't think it'd be an additional attraction?"

"The lion that ate the hero?"

"They wouldn't let you keep him, but you could double the pull of the Dueling Ground."

"Harvey could have him stuffed. Lord knows he could do with something like that—this place eats money, and the old boys still think they're rich as Croesus. And he'd be able to do all the things they won't let him. I'm off. Good luck, I suppose. You go, and I'll count fifty, then I shan't have seen which way you went. Don't start anything till you've heard my car, though."

"Goodbye," said Pibble. "I hope we meet again."

"Ah, what would a fine Lunnon gentleman be wanting with the likes of me? God go with 'ee, zurr, howsomever."

Pibble picked up his anachronistic bucket and left, wondering whether a slight wooziness, a sense that even the sycamore trunk was not as solid as it looked in the gloaming, was caused by delayed shock from his encounter with the lions or by the hallucinating effect of Miss Finnick's personality switches. Presumably one would tire of it, find oneself agreeing with Harvey that it was overdone, but for a while her joke Wardour Street English could serve most pleasantly as the language of love. Poor thing. Pibble remembered his earlier notion about her suicide note; not so remote a contingency, after all.

He found that he'd gone farther than he need along the path toward the folly; he stood and hesitated whether it was worth going to see how carefully the bone-meal machine had been cleaned, but decided that he hadn't the time. Down the slope, the sun already lay behind the minarets of the pit, making their stilted silhouettes black against the orange bars of fine-weather cloud. Somebody would realize he was missing soon and come and look for him. Miss Finnick might ring Singleton up—she wasn't exactly predictable, even to herself. Pibble realized that his unnecessary walk up the path, his hesitation, even the way he'd allowed the conversation in the cottage to trail down useless byways, all stemmed from dislike of what he was intending to do. He sighed and started to walk toward the pit, lifting his feet in exaggerated arcs to wade through the dew-dank grass.

There was a door in the northeast minaret, but it was padlocked with a very good self-locking Chubb and the key was in none of the possible hiding places. He went to the wall and leaned over; the lion was invisible under one of the arches, but the stone tracery down the inside of the tower was as he'd remembered it, almost as climbable as a ladder. He tied the shovel to the handle of the bucket and let the whole contraption down over the edge by the string, until it was just above the level of the lower balustrade; there he started it swinging, out and in, helping each swing with a twitch of his forearm until the pendulum effect carried it well into the archway beneath him and he could pay the string out with a rush. There was a clatter as the shovel clanged onto flagstones, but no movement in the pit.

Climbing down turned out nothing like as easy as it had looked. After about four feet he came to a bare-seeming place where he could neither see nor feel a foothold. He craned over his shoulder to study the neighboring tower, hoping that its symmetry would give him a guide about which way to reach, but the corner of his eye was attracted by a brownness at the bottom which hadn't been there before.

The lion had come silently out and was staring at him, the end of its tail flicking jerkily from side to side. Otherwise it was totally still.

It watched him with brooding passion while he clutched at a stone lotus as fiercely as if the tower had been a reeling mast; it was a minute before he could return to his study of the other tower and see that by working to his left he would reach a more ornamented section, and another two minutes before he could persuade his hands to let go of the lotus. Only when he was safely over the balustrade and hidden in the darkness of the upper cloister did the lion give a sign— that harsh, breathy, painful bellow which spoke its mad cravings so plainly.

Pibble had the shakes again, and his back was hurting— probably he'd just wrenched Miss Finnick's plasters out of position in his descent. He stood and gazed dimly at the inside wall, waiting for the shakes to go away and for his eyes to become used to the darkness: the lion must be a fairly recent importation, but the narrowness of the path to the upper door showed that visitors had not come down into the pit even when it had been untenanted. That probably meant the floors were unsafe, and he wanted to be sure of seeing any weakness which might hurtle him down to those yellow fangs and that sandpaper tongue.

But as his vision seeped back to him he saw that there was a different reason for keeping strangers out. A stone face grinned at him out of the wall; it wore a Johnsonian wig, but otherwise the figure was naked, and so was the stone beldame with whom he was coupling; and both were part of a jungle of writhing limbs, stretched bodies, faces strained into greedy masks or softened into peachy fulfillment. The obscene riot stretched all down this wall and around both corners, out of sight; it must be the longest pornographic frieze in Europe. No doubt old Josiah Clavering, during his nabob years, had seen some temple carvings like those at Ellora and translated the idea to his Tiger Pit; but these were not the perfect circular breasts, the double-jointed hips, the ingeniously varied attitudes of ecstasy of those hundred milkmaids whose eagerness Krishna satisfied simultaneously; still less was any face that rounded, Madonnalike softness in which the Indian sculptors had expressed the sanctities of lust. Here the coarse, vigorous chiselings into the soft stone had limned European bodies busy in the few basic postures of the unsophisticated imagination. And the faces were individual portraits. The carving was not good; it was peasant art of the kind that a few generations earlier had modeled the gargoyles; nowadays the nearest equivalent would be the dingy drawing found in horror comics. But it was a great oddity, scandalously publicizable, far more crowd-compelling than any hero-eating lion, stuffed, could ever be. Pibble was astonished that Mr. Singleton had made nothing of it.

The frieze continued all down the next side, where stood the mechanism which opened and shut the cage. A big handle drove a cast-iron cog whose teeth engaged with those of a thick vertical bar; this was fastened to the center of the gate, so that by turning the handle you could slide the whole frame upward; or you could disengage the cog from the bar with a crude clutch lever and let the gate fall. There was a circular hole in the middle of the paving through which you could inspect the inside of the cage. He turned the handle a couple of times, locked it into a cast-iron dog which was set in the framework of the mechanism for that purpose, and pulled the lever. The gate seemed to be counter-weighted, but it slid quickly and easily down.

Pibble unlocked the handle and began to turn steadily; the machine moved in complete silence, except for a solid knock each time the handle passed the locking-dog; it took him about thirty seconds to raise the gate high enough for a lion to pass underneath, and another minute to raise it to its full height, but it wasn't hard work. He locked the handle and went to the balustrade to see where the lion was.

He gazed straight down into the stretched jaws and yawning gullet, about six feet below him. It was standing on its hind legs beside the gate, scrabbling at the wall with great hooked pads; the claws were as long as a woman's fingers, and the brick and stone were already scored with deep gouges, as though the beast had reached up toward the unattainable meat many times before. Pibble picked the chicken out of his bucket and tore a leg off, and then broke the limb in two. He tied the string to the body of the chicken and let it down through the hole into the cage, swinging it to and fro until he could settle it well over toward the back wall; he fastened the top end of the string to the machine, picked up the bits of leg, and went to the balustrade again. The lion was still reaching up.

"Here, boy," said Pibble, his voice squeaky with fright. The lion stopped scratching and looked at him with melancholy scorn. Pibble held the drumstick up so that the lion could see it, then threw it down toward the entrance of the cage. With an incredibly quick scything movement of the huge head, the lion caught it in midair and swallowed it with the gulp of a man swallowing a bolus. Pibble held the thigh up, feinted to throw it the other way, then tossed it down to the entrance. The lion almost beat him again, but its jaws snicked shut a fraction late and it had to drop onto four feet to pick the morsel up. Gingerly Pibble jiggled his end of the string, so that the chicken twitched at the back of the cage.

The lion stiffened, paused, swished its tail, looked up toward Pibble's tempting living flesh, roared its great grumbling sigh, and stalked into its lair. Pibble pulled the lever and the gate slid down.

When he went, shivering, to look through the hole, the lion was already staring up at him, the chicken in its jaws. Pibble jerked the string, and the wing to which he had fastened it gave. The lion gnawed once, gulped once, and the bird was gone. Then it turned away and lay down, staring out through the bars of the gate. Pibble looped up the string and carried the bucket and shovel around to the farthest corner, where the feces were. He let the bucket over the edge and tied the other end of the string to the balustrade.

The fretted stone really was like a ladder here, a frill of oval openings just big enough for a toecap running down each side of the pillar. He picked up bucket and shovel and started to hunt for his nasty trove among the tussocks; there was more of it than he had realized, and it was difficult in the half light to pick out the freshest specimens. When the bucket was at the end of its tether, he put it down and searched farther afield, but there didn't seem to be anything there—the lion must be a creature of habit. On his way back he saw a specimen he had missed, with something shiny amid its involutions; wrinkling his nose, he bent closer and saw that it was the metal clip from a pair of braces. He did not feel at all triumphant as he scooped it up and put it in the top of the bucket.

He was looking around the scrubby floor, wondering whether there were carvings worth inspecting at this level, when he heard the noise. A solid, metallic tock. The handle going past the locking-dog.

The stone fretwork seemed less like a ladder on the way up, his climbing palsied, useless. Tock, tock, tock went the handle. He missed one of the oval holes with his right foot, got it in too high, couldn't exert any leverage with his leg bent like that, hauled himself up with his arms alone, reached the balustrade, and flung himself sideways over the edge as the lion hurtled into the stonework below. It had come as silent as frost, but now it roared its misery again and again. When Pibble hauled the bucket tremblingly up, it batted at it so that it swung wildly to and fro and the shovel clanged down. Pibble hauled the obscene cargo to safety.

"Visitors are requested not to tease the animals," said a voice at his elbow. It was the General.

6:10 P.M.

"DAMN SORRY, my dear fellow. Didn't spot you down there. I thought that moron Rastus had shut Bonzo in without water."

"General Clavering," said Pibble, "I have reason to suspect that your brother has been killed and that you have some knowledge of how this happened."

"I told Harvey it was bloody silly to get a real pro down," said the General. He put his hand into an inner pocket and Pibble stiffened to jump for a gun, but what the General drew forth was a small torch which he shone into the bucket, bending down to peer at its contents.

"Didn't think of that," he said as he straightened up. "What are you going to do?"

"Have it analyzed for hair. And there's something that looks like a braces clip. Meanwhile I'll apply for a search warrant. There's going to be a fuss, but you could save some of it by telling me what happened."

The General shone his torch on the back wall, where a tall English beauty with the popeyes so admired by the eighteenth century was entwined with an ecstatically grinning hunchback.

"Extraordinary fellow, Josiah," said the General. "That's Lady Feverfew, you know. He put all the neighbors in, but kept it for his own amusement. Didn't even let his brother down at the Abbey see it. Harvey wants us—I suppose I can say 'me' now— to open it to the visitors, but I don't see how we can. Not honorably. Silly word. That old chap"—he shone his torch farther down the wall—"was the Rector in Josiah's day, used to drink port with him after hunting, ancestor of Maureen Finnick's, as a matter of fact. Isn't the slightest evidence he was a pederast, and I don't see why a lot of salivating Yanks should be allowed to think so now, eh?"

"General Clavering," said Pibble, "will you please tell me how your brother died?"

"I am telling you, damn it," said the General sharply. "If you won't let me tell you my own way, you won't get a squeak out of me. You must be feeling bloody pleased with yourself, but you aren't home yet. Come here and listen. Going to take a long time, so we might as well be comfortable."

He leaned his hands on the balustrade, like a tripper admiring the view from Weymouth Pier. Pibble walked forward and settled warily beside him: there was something wrong, another oubliette being prepared in that subtle old mind—perhaps he'd brought Singleton with him and left him lurking in the shadows, ready to tiptoe in when Pibble was all set up and pitch him down to the disposal unit below. The disposal unit was in theatrical form, ravening to and fro with the stilted walk of a destroyer captain pacing his five-foot bridge; the long tail lashed against either flank; the mad eyes never stopped looking up to where there now stood, just out of reach, a double helping of Man.

"Going to be a cracking night," said the General. "Full moon, almost. We'll be having a frost in a week or two—I must remember to warn Rastus. That one might be Mars—we'd never see Venus from down here. You interested in astronomy?"

"Interested but ignorant," said Pibble, still tense for the Hush Puppy step on the flagstones behind him. The old man was keen to talk, to whatever end, and the sensible thing was to let him run on. They always tell you more than they mean to, the clever ones.

"Dick knew 'em all," said the General. "Show him a fiddling little patch of sky through cloud and he'd tell you the names of the stars in it. He had that sort of mind, which was why we brought the Raid off. I'll tell you something I haven't told anybody—funny what you're prepared to let them mumble over and then spit out again—writers, I mean. We decided early on that we'd always keep a bit back, so that the next chap could be offered a new crumb—you'd see if you read the books in order. The first ones had whole chapters about Dotty Prosser, most dangerous bloody bonehead I ever knew, wouldn't have made the slightest difference if he'd been wiped out in the landing. We let them run on, though, because he was part of our investment. The Raid was our capital. Where was I?"

"Why you brought the Raid off," said Pibble, unrelaxed.

"Course. Funny thing was *what* we chose to keep back, what seemed personal and private. Dick didn't mind about this, but to me it seemed so particularly him, so right for his nature...Well...shan't try to put it into words. Tried last night as a matter of fact, talking to Anty about him. She's very cut up about this business, much more than you'd think to talk to her. Never mind. You ever looked at a chart of the St. Quentin estuary?"

"Not closely."

"Well, I tell you it's absolutely bloody terrifying, a complete bloody pot-mess of shoals and channels, all different at different tides. Dick sat up with those charts night after night, and when he'd finished you could name a tide and wind direction and he could draw the whole estuary, bang, every depth right to six inches. He took us in and got us out along ways which even the fishermen hadn't thought of. War Office expected us to lose two-fifths of our boats before we'd even landed. Dick lost eight boats."

"Two-fifths!" said Pibble. "That's forty per cent! They didn't do worse than that at Dieppe!"

"Ha!" said the General. "You're going to learn a bit of history tonight, young man. You know why they mounted the Raid in the first place? *They wanted to prove that it couldn't be done.* Winston was roaring for action because Uncle Joe kept getting at him, but the others were a lot of yellowbellies who expected the Yanks and the R.A.F. to win the war for them. Winnie bellowed and prodded till they realized they'd have to arrange something; then they thought they might as well take the chance to get rid of a lot of nits and nuisances—bods like Dotty Prosser and me. Christ, they must have rubbed their hands when they thought of that one!"

"Did you realize this at the time?" said Pibble.

"Not in so many words; pal of mine told me, long after the war, when he'd had a couple of ports too many at some bloody function. But we *smelt* something at the time, Dick and me. Obvious, really. Why put *me* in charge if they wanted the Raid to be a wow? Daresay you've heard how some of them used to go on about Monty—that was nothing to what they said about me. Trouble was I had a brother in the Navy, very close to him all my life, so I knew what an absolute dog's dinner the Army was—even the clever chaps were sad-dled with a structure and a tradition so bloody inefficient that they were damned lucky if they got a quarter of their force into the right place at the right time. I used to say so, and I was too good at my job for them to sack me, so they must absolutely have pissed themselves silly with giggles when they thought of putting me in charge of the Raid. And it wasn't only me. Prosser was just about typical of the sort of officer they landed me with."

"And Mr. Singleton, and Dr. Kirtle?" said Pibble.

"Oh, for God's sake, you couldn't expect them to pick out individually tiresome M.O.s—Fred just got detailed. Same with other ranks; they were mostly just stray units who happened to be messing up some desk wallah's paper work, and St. Quentin was a heaven-sent opportunity to tidy them away, a great big bloody W.P.B. But Harvey was in the same sort of mess as I was, only lower down the ladder; he'd made himself unpopular with his regiment, one of those toffee-nosed lots—the Halberdiers, as a matter of fact. He'd got just as riled at the damned stupid inefficiency of the Army as I had, though more in a profit-and-loss way, seeing he's Harvey. Luckily there were quite a lot like him, to balance the Prossers, and between us we brought the thing off. Couldn't have done it without Dick, though. He was in Western Approaches, but he wangled himself off, just to come with me. That mean anything to you?"

"I think so," said Pibble.

"They were a bloody good crowd—they wouldn't have changed jobs until they were dead, given the option. But Dick pulled strings, and there we were."

"I see," said Pibble, watching the lion pause in its pac-ing and stretch up the fretted stonework toward them, remeasuring its height against the unshrinkable distance. He heard a rustling in the gallery behind him and swung sud-denly around, but though it was almost pitch dark now under the vaulted ceiling, he could see that no enemy stood there; it must have been a mouse, or even a leaf.

"Nervy?" said the General. "Not surprised—nasty great brute and he bloody nearly got you. To be fair, Dick was always a small-boat man at heart, lost in those damn great ships; all seemed to be run by pursers, he told me. So we sat down together and decided to trust no one. Had to do every-one's homework for them: Army's perfectly capable of send-ing two shiploads of boots somewhere, left boots all in one boat, right boots all in the other; then they can't understand why the whole bloody lot's useless when one of the ships gets sunk. Harvey was bloody good at sorting that sort of pot-mess out, and I had my pals. After all, Winnie had set his heart on the Raid, so we always had one bloody great string to pull when all our anti-tank guns were sent to lie rusting at Arbroath Station. Same with Intelligence—talk about wish fulfillment! Anything they want to be true is true. Journalists are the worst, archaeologists the best—I got journalists. So we just said, 'Yes, yes, how bloody clever you are,' and went off and asked elsewhere. I got more usable gen in the bar of the Travellers' than I did out of the whole of my I Section.

"Huns knew we were coming, of course, but we insisted on a full rehearsal, week early, and Dick and I went in on the rehearsal. Nobody thought we could do it; tides quite wrong, they said. Dick knew better. Caught the Hun bending. Caught 'em bending at the Air Ministry, too, but I knew old Rufus McGoggin couldn't afford to pull out without letting the Bomber Command boys have everything their own way in future. Always hated my guts, but he had to put on a show for me. Hello, your pal's getting ideas above his station."

He watched with mild interest as the lion, maddened beyond bearing by the noise of this garrulous meal above its head in the darkness, compressed itself back onto its haunches and sprang for the balustrade; its claws scrabbled at the brickwork a couple of feet below where they stood; then, still flailing, it fell thudding on hard earth. Pibble could hear the wind whoosh out of its lungs. It lay gasping for several seconds before it rose painfully to its feet and stalked off through the gloaming.

The General talked on; his short sentences, clipped of articles and pronouns like early Auden verse, were a fitting vehicle for the brutal story. Much of his argument was mathematical: how many men had it been worth sacrificing in the feint toward the double submarine pen on the chance of reaching the single pen? What were the odds that they'd get mauled to bits during the sudden switch from the Western Harbour to the Eastern? How long would the Resistance manage to delay the panzers coming up from the south? And, finally, how many deaths was it worth to last out how many days before the Admiral could get them off?

The lion came back, discouraged, and stared up into the cloister, its tail twitching slightly. The moon rose, full and regal, into a cloudless night. Pibble grew cold, listening to the old man with half his mind, glancing unconvincingly around from time to time (as Mr. Chanceley had glanced while he teased the lion cub's ears) but never seeing an attacker; he knew he was being set up for something, being lulled into a sense of trust and friendship, but he couldn't tell why. And, dammit, when would an ex-upper-lower-middle-class detective again get the chance to stand in the grounds of one of the greatest houses in England and listen to the bearer of one of his country's proudest names telling the secret history of the greatest single feat of arms in the Second World War? You could set that in G.C.E. as an example of a rhetorical question.

"I'd lost a stone and a quarter," said the General, "but they rang the City bells for us. And that was that."

"You mean you never got another command?"

"Unemployable. You've got to remember St. Quentin was a *defeat*. Lost two-thirds of my men, four-fifths of my equipment, only destroyed one submarine pen. The Boche had the other two working again three weeks after we left. They had to sell it as a victory, but the professionals knew what it was worth. A few heads rolled when Winnie found out what had been going on, but he couldn't do much, considering that it had all been his idea and then he'd been the first to get cold feet. You've heard about me smashing my wirelesses? Those signals were coming from him. Wouldn't have done it if I'd known. But the others didn't care how much of a bloody shambles it became—they were proving their point about raids.

"Dick sailored on for a bit, but his heart wasn't in it. I went lecturing in the States—never liked the Yanks since then. There was a bit of a move to put me in command at Arnhem but Monty wasn't too joyous about the idea.

"Nor was I. I'd had enough. You spend your life training for one thing, you give every second of your time to your profession, you sacrifice your wife and daughter to it, you're there, coiled, ready—and they launch you off on a bloody abortion of an enterprise like St. Quentin. I gave up. I'd done my best for my country and my service; Herryngs and the Claverings were the limits of my horizon now. I told you earlier that Dick and I thought of the Raid as our capital; I just sat down to nurse it. Even on the boat coming back I was thinking along those lines—hadn't got it worked out clearly, of course—but chose the bods for the decorations strictly according to what would look good in the papers. Had to fake the record a bit with Prosser, you know; we'd got at those gunners with a couple of rooftop Brens before he did his death-or-glory bit, but he was just right for a V.C., handsome, dashing, good family, dead. Couldn't have a live V.C. stealing any of the limelight. Chap who should have got it was a Signals corporal called Martin. He was working his wireless in a house by the quay when the room caught fire just as the signals were coming through from Dick about taking us off. He stuck it out. Never seen a man so burnt. Wouldn't have looked good in the papers, not at all. I did put him on the list for an M.M., but some civilian desk wallah decided I'd had my ration and crossed him off."

The General stared at the rising moon. Only the gleam of reflection from his cornea showed that he wasn't stone, or perhaps a wax model propped there until it should be needed for some puppetlike re-enactment of the heroic story. The lion lay down still watching them. Pibble shivered and listened to the silences behind him.

"It was a mistake," said the General, the thin tongue licking between the thinner lips.

"The Admiral's death?" slid Pibble.

"No. Yes. No," said the General impatiently. "I mean that was a mistake, too, dammit, but the mistake I was talking about was shutting up shop. You remember what I said about being trained, being coiled and ready, and then going off at half cock? Your mind's a machine, and it can't take that sort of treatment. It goes sick, and the only cure is work. Work. Work. Slog away at the job you were bred for. But we packed it in, settled down to be heroes. Nothing to do but let the adulation roll in. Bad mistake.

"We *were* heroes, mark you. We'd done everything between us, saved everybody's bacon, given Englishmen something to be proud of. I know, as well as I know that I'm talking to Superintendent James Pibble, that if Dick and I hadn't been there it would have been an absolute bloody shambles. They might have lost a few less lives, but they wouldn't have got anything done, and then they'd have surrendered. We didn't win the bloody war, but if we hadn't done what we did at St. Quentin we might have lost it: we bucked people up, strengthened Winnie's hand a bit, lopped out a few useless bastards in high places, shook the Boche— he had nineteen men to my one there by the end, you know—we felt we'd done our stuff, but we trapped ourselves. Twenty-five years we've sat here, doing nothing to spoil our investment. We could have done anything, absolutely any bloody thing, Dick and I, but we stored ourselves away like apples in a loft, and lay on our shelves, waiting for the soft brown patches to appear. We got a bit mad, like your pal down there. Daresay you noticed it."

"Do you think he's mad?" said Pibble.

"Course I do. Hasn't got rabies, but you've only got to look at his eyes. I'll be honest with you: he reminds me of Dotty Prosser. Dotty was a killer—he'd have been in Broadmoor if there hadn't been a war—very nasty type indeed. Your pal has just the same sort of look about his eyes. All lions are a bit loopy, you know: comes of being the strongest animal around, like Captains R.N. *They* go out on those shapeless great seas in their little tin ships, nobody of their own rank to talk to, so they go potty, start believing they're the lost ten tribes, learn Tamil, think they're going to retire and make money out of dairy farming, that sort of thing. Lions are the same—dangerous clowns. But your pal's not dotty—he's *mad*. Aren't you, boy?"

The lion sensed that a communication was being made to it and raised its sullen head. It looked completely black by now in, the moonlight, but as it opened its jaws the thin rays caught its teeth so that they glistened for a moment, like remote stars. The roar came late, bored, ghastly.

"I see what you mean," said Pibble.

"Come along here and I'll show you something else."

Pibble, poised for a trap, followed half behind the old man's shoulder, almost on tiptoe, like a tennis player readied for a fast serve, peering into the thick but moving shadows for the inevitable ambush. The General had his torch out and was shining it along the obscene frieze, making the stone limbs quake in slow-motion simulations of the ecstasies of flesh.

"Here we are," he said, and allowed the beam to pick out a particular character, hold it for a moment, and then move on to a handsome couple who were engaged in Nature's trade in a fashion which, for once in all that extraordinary carving, did not seem corrupt or perverse. The sculptor had taken more trouble over them, rounding the splayed limbs with real affection, giving the pair, in his own crude terms, an innocence and beauty wholly different from the Swiftian frenzy of the rest of the work.

The torch moved up and to the side a little, and Pibble saw that this section had been separated from the rest of the riot; there was a lull, a clearing in the jungle of limbs, a blank space in which stood three shocks of corn. The beam moved back to the first figure and Pibble saw that it was fully clothed: an elderly, austere man with a high-buttoned frock coat, and a small wig above a thin face and a hooky nose, gazed down at the busy pair.

"That's Josiah," said the General. "That's his mistress, girl called Mercy Plum. And that's her lover, horse coper called Simon—nobody knows his other name. Josiah framed him and had him transported, and Mercy hanged herself in the old man's bedroom. All this"—he waved his torch up and down the frieze—"is their monument. Rum sort of fellow, Josiah, don't you think?"

"Yes," said Pibble, realizing with a jerk that he'd let his defenses drop, fascinated by the abrupt Arcadian tone which the unknown sculptor had achieved. He looked over his shoulder and saw nothing but the arched darkness, then back to the sad, cruel face held in the beam of the torch.

"That's what happened to us," said the General, "in a manner of speaking. Haven't got to that stage physically yet, thank God. We became remote, 'outsiders' is the fashionable jargon, I think. We just stared at the world as if it didn't concern us. But we knew it did, same way that Mercy and Simon concerned *him*. We soured. We rotted. The brown patches came. I was worse than Dick, maybe, but not much. He could be a terror in private. I used to break out a bit in public, to show the world what I thought of it."

"I read about the cuckoos," said Pibble, "and the Epstein at Framplingfield."

"Poor old George," said the General. "Absolutely bloody awful artist. Typical of the sort of people they wished on me for the Raid. But I really did that to get at Blight. You know he cut down a row of limes my mother had planted, in Richmond, just in order to put up a filthy great block of offices?"

"Tell me about the duel," said Pibble.

"Ha! Didn't realize you'd sorted it out that far. Suppose we'd better get on to that. What's your pal up to?"

Pibble moved well away from the old man, just in case of attack, and leaned over the balustrade to scan the moonlit floor. He couldn't see the lion anywhere.

"Gone away to think," said the General. "Better keep an eye open. Madmen might try anything, once they've thought about it a bit."

"The duel," said Pibble.

"Coming to that," said the General. "You met our Judith?"

"Yes," said Pibble.

"Funny face she's got," said the General. "Noticed how it slopes backward, all the way up, like an orangutan's? Not so much, but quite marked once you've spotted it. Flat face, big mouth, little nose, everything tilted a bit backward. Ape woman—Eve must have been like that in Eden, Dick used to say."

"You talked about her a lot?" asked Pibble.

"Nothing else, during the fortnight she was here. Not much else for two old men to talk about, really: not when they haven't had a proper job for over twenty years, and they find themselves taking stairs in ones which they always used to take in twos. Rotting's a slow process, and you think about it all the time. I tell you, I've found myself in bed with a woman, everything gone like a house on fire, she's feeling all soft and mumbly, but what I've been thinking about is whether I'll ever be able to do it again. Takes the edge off your pleasure, that sort of thing. Last few years Dick and I've been tending to egg each other on, if you see what I mean. Just talk, fantasy, but a sort of challenge at the same time—like when we were kids and used to dare each other to climb trees. And the same with horses, later."

He paused, looking up at the minareted skyline. Pibble saw that the lion had come back and was sniffing one of the pillars farther along the arcade—the one he himself had climbed down and up by, most likely. He felt bewildered by all this self-revelation; there seemed to be too much of it for it to be just bait to lull him into unwariness. Probably it was no more than repressed shock, the old boy having played the Spartan over his brother's death but now being betrayed by the second shock of being found out.

"Plenty of women in these parts, of course," said the General, "happy to oblige a rich old hero. Then there are fancier campaigns which keep you occupied for a bit: Dick spent eight months maneuvering to cuckold old Blight after he'd cut down my mother's trees—brought it off, too. Pretty girl, been a model, got that expensive leather look, very good, Dick said. But every now and then you come across a girl (and they get younger as you get older) who really cuts you up. You begin to think that having her is the most important thing in the whole bloody world—tell yourself that after her you'll die happy. Funny thing, those are the ones you never make, more often than not. These last years Dick and I managed to steer clear of each other's obsessions until Judith turned up.

"Anty chose her, and still can't see what all the cheering's about. But Dick and I developed a lot of needle over her. Started to get jealous of each other's dirty minds, even. Didn't stop us talking about her, of course, but there was no best-man-win nonsense about it. We'd sit up into the small hours jeering at each other and drinking too much. Couldn't sail straight in and start seducing her the day she arrived, naturally. Got to give her the chance to feel like one of the family first. But the time was coming, and we both wanted to make a start before the other one. Trouble was we both thought we'd seen her first and the other one ought to do the decent thing and lay off. *Two* rich old heroes scratching on her door in the small hours and she'd have packed up and gone home to Mum.

"Four nights ago, one o'clock in the morning, we decided to have a duel. Both pretty tight by then. Deakin made the dueling pistols they use at the Abbey—made 'em to throw low and to the left, so that nobody gets bits of wadding in their eye and sues us. We've often loaded them up and pooped off at each other. Silly game, but made the old blood run quicker for a few minutes. No chance of hitting, provided you aimed straight.

"But this time I meant to hit him, and I knew he meant the same. Partly whiskey, partly jealousy. We both fell over a couple of times on the way down to the Abbey, and didn't help each other up. I thought we weren't going to be able to do it after all, it took such a time to load those damn pistols, black powder everywhere, both of us swearing like fishwives at the other one's clumsiness. But we managed. Night like this, almost bright as day, heavy shadows.

"Dick said, 'Feed me to Bonzo, Ralph.' That's Bonzo down there. He'd often said it before, much obsessed by death, so I knew he meant it. Can't remember what I said. We stood back to back and paced apart, both counting aloud, turned round at ten, aimed. You're allowed to fire as soon as you've turned, but there's no point in it. Thing is to take a steady aim. I could see Dick's pistol pointing high and to his right. Mine was, too. We fired just about together and I felt his ball going past my ear. Couldn't hear it, because of the echoes. Then I saw I'd got him. He'd keeled over before in duels, just for the hell of it, but we weren't in the mood this time.

"I walked across and saw I'd got his heart. Bloody fine shot. Serve you right, you randy old bastard, I thought. Then I went and fetched Rastus's tractor and levered him onto the trailer and brought him up here and pitched him over. Took his shoes off, first—kicking myself now for not realizing Deakin would clean 'em and put 'em back. Spotted that, didn't you? I was pretty sure Bonzo would drag him under cover, and he did. Told Harvey what had happened next morning, Harvey told Anty. We didn't tell anyone else, but Deakin seems to have sorted it out. That's why he hanged himself. Elsa knows now, and I've a sort of feeling some of the others have guessed something's up. Rastus was acting up in the bone house, too. Did you say anything to him?"

"I asked him about the lion," said Pibble. "He didn't tell me anything. Now, this is an important point, Sir Ralph. Would you have done the same thing if you'd been sober?"

"Wouldn't have tried to hit him if I'd been sober, if that's what you mean. Least, I don't think so. Difficult to tell:

we were both considerably touched about that girl. Wouldn't kill him again, of course, now that I know what it's like living without him. But if you mean would I have fed him to Bonzo if I'd been sober—yes, I would. That's what he wanted, and what the hell bloody business is it of anyone else's?"

Pibble sighed, and the lion, who had come back to pace below the arch at their feet, answered with its enormous breathy roar.

"I'll just go and get my bucket," he said, "and then we can go to the house and ask one of the local policemen up to hear you make a formal statement."

"He's going to be disappointed," said the General. "You don't believe I'm going to spout that lot out in front of a witness, do you? Just because I felt the urge to get it off my chest to you? You've got a long furrow to plow yet, my boy."

Pibble sighed again, but this time the lion did not answer.

"It won't make a lot of difference, I'm afraid," he said, and started to walk back down the arcading. He didn't mind any more. What the General had told him about the Raid—particularly about the Signals corporal and Dotty Prosser—had dealt with the Clavering myth as a first frost deals with dahlias, turning all their green sappiness to blackened withering. He saw that the old boy was mad, probably always had been mad. No definition of sanity covered people who believed they could treat the world they lived in, the citizens they lived among, with such brutal, insolent...Why, the man was as mad and—

Something banged bonily into his rib cage behind his left elbow, hustling him half sprawling against the balustrade. His ankle was gripped and wrenched upward, twisting him further over, so that for a second he was almost on his back on top of the stonework, with no handhold to prevent his being pitched down below like a hay bale tossed from a barn loft; but as his left arm flailed outward above his head its knuckles banged against stonework—the next pillar.

His right arm was already flailing, but he steered it in a panicky sweep in that direction and grabbed. Magically his fist was full of clean, unmoving stone. Suddenly he was in control of his body, which an instant before had been whirling mindlessly about like a tangle of snapped hawser. He let the attacker waste his attack on forcing his legs over the balustrade while he jerked himself upward with his right arm.

He was already in a sitting position when the next rush came. He leaned inward and pushed it away. His assailant was so light, so weak, so old.

"Worth trying," panted the General. "Five years ago and I could have done it easy. Judith listened to a bit of your talk with your sawbones pal, you know. Told us about it at tea. Haven't a clue what it meant."

Pibble didn't say anything. He stood down onto the flagstones and was about to move toward his bucket when he heard a new noise, a rattling scrape just outside the balustrade. He took a firm hold of the pillar and looked over, straight down into the lion's mask. Either the animal had done its thinking or it had been stimulated to a fresh idea by the sound of the fracas above it, and now it was working its way up the ladder of fretted stone which Pibble had used. The oval holes were not quite large enough for the big pads, but as Pibble stared it forced its right paw into another rung and the mask followed in a jerking six-inch rush. Pibble thought for a wild second of trying to shove the creature back; he might have done it if he'd still had his shovel, but that lay hopelessly down at the bottom of the pit.

The General was leaning over the balustrade beside him.

"Told you he'd think it out," he said coolly. "We'd better be off."

For an old man he achieved a lively scamper. Pibble ran for his bucket but saw as he came back that the extra few yards might now be fatal. A hairy blackness was scrabbling at the top of the stone, the moonlight striking a faint gleam off its claws. He ran desperately and caught up with the General just around the corner. Inexplicably the old man had slowed to a walk.

"Quick!" panted Pibble as he rushed past him. "He's almost there!"

And they'd been running the wrong way. The General, for all his apparent coolness, had led him in the direction which involved running almost three sides of the pit instead of one and a bit. He looked wildly over his shoulder across the diagonal of the courtyard and saw that the lion had vanished. It must be already under the arcading and leaping after them. He was balancing his run, awkward because of the wallowing bucket, for the final corner when a hand caught his back-flung shoe and wrenched him off balance. As he went down, he glimpsed amid the whirling shadows the General prancing past him. The old boy had led him around the long way on purpose, slowed on purpose to be overtaken.

Pibble let the twisting momentum of his fall roll him sideways into the blackness under the frieze. Against the arcaded sky he saw a jagged shadow whirl past him, heard the quick flutter of big pads taking the corner, then silence, then a brief barking cry which was not the cry of the lion, a thud, and then silence again.

PART III

THE DUELING GROUND

The ceremony he was in a hurry to have over: he was stopped at the gallows by the vast crowd, but got out of his coach as soon as he could, and was but seven minutes on the scaffold, which was hung with black, and prepared by the undertaker of his family at their expense. There was a new contrivance for sinking the stage under him, which did not play well; and he suffered a little by the delay, but was dead in four minutes. The mob was decent, and admired him, and almost pitied him...

—Horace Walpole
On the execution of Lord Ferrers, May 6, 1760

7:00 P.M.

The tower proved easier to climb up than it had down, even in darkness. From the arcading across the diagonal, Pibble could hear a busy snuffling, as of a terrier rootling in a compost heap. Intermittently the noise paused for a purring growl.

His heart was working with a dangerous bubbling beat as he stumbled through the tussocky grass around to the minaret with the door in it. The door was open, and the same snuffling and growling came up the black stairwell. Pibble shut it and slipped the hasp of the padlock through the latch, then allowed his tired legs to take him in a reeling career down the thin path to Miss Finnick's cottage. He cut the corner toward the forceable window, walking the last few paces to give his limbs a chance to work efficiently. A light glared at him from the black shadows of the porch.

"Something the matter?" said a man's voice.

"The lion's caught Sir Ralph," said Pibble. "At the foot of the stairs. On the first story. I climbed one of the towers. There's a gun in here. I think it's too late. This is the easiest window to force."

"Good God!" said Mr. Singleton, moving his gangling shape into the moonlight. "Don't waste time with the window—I keep a key."

Electric light shone cozily from carriage lanterns and

adapted paraffin lamps, twinkling off the polished brass of innumerable knickknacks.

"She keeps it in the grandfather clock," said Pibble. "The key's in this snuffbox." The barely suppressed panic of the last ten minutes was nudging his voice into hysteria now that he had someone else to carry the responsibilities, a job which Mr. Singleton seemed to have assumed without hesitation. For someone so clumsily put together, he moved very fast and neatly; already he was checking the gun over, and trying a couple of grips which would allow him to point the torch along the gun barrel.

"I'll come and hold the light," said Pibble.

"The door doesn't shut on the inside, so I think it would be best if you remained at the top to latch it behind me, in case I mishandle the business. I trust you didn't lock it."

"No," said Pibble.

Mr. Singleton went up the path at an enormously fast controlled lope, which looked as if he would be breathing no faster by the time he reached the pit. Pibble followed at a weak-kneed trot. He was still sure that the General had been waiting for reinforcements during his long monologue. And how did Singleton know he had shut the door? Miss Finnick's porch seemed an odd place for him to be, too; she'd been long gone.

The door was ajar when he reached it; he stood and listened. The silence stretched out from seconds to minutes, to a desert-wide agony of tense and suspicious boredom. His sweat- and dew-drenched trousers chilled against his legs. He watched a star vanish behind the black ridge of trees to the west. He felt cold, ill, the feverish aftermath of shock and action.

Suddenly a noise came up through the chilly blackness of the stairwell: gulping and whuffling and purring, all mixed together. Crippen, could the lion have finished with Singleton before Pibble had even reached the pit? Surely not. More likely, Singleton had disturbed the animal by opening the door, and since then they had been conducting a long duel of waiting. And what steps did you take, Superintendent Pibble, to rescue this great man from the creature that attacked him? You heard him cry out and assumed that he was already dead, so you ran away? You did not go to look? Thank you, Superintendent.

The whuffling modulated to a giant roar. The stairway bellowed with indescribable noise, the gun slamming its bullets out in a confined space. In the whining silence the roar came again, but strangled and gurgling. There was one last deep cough, then the thud of a falling weight. Another short silence before the gun clattered again, not quite so loud (further from the foot of the stairs, maybe) but a longer burst. Pibble felt his way carefully down into blackness.

Singleton was a tall shadow leaning in the first archway, his torch still burning, his attitude a little relaxed from its busy tautness.

"Are you all right?" said Pibble.

"I apologize for the delay, but he heard me coming down the stairs, and I had to wait him out. I must admit he damn near got me, even so. I advise you not to look at the General. The best thing would be for us both to go back to the house for a drink and then you can explain what has occurred."

"Lend me your torch a minute."

The door at the bottom of the stairs was held by three wrist-thick bolts, and when Pibble opened it he found it was four inches thick, studded with iron; no one had known, presumably, how strong a door had to be to keep a tiger in. He picked up his shovel in the far corner of the pit and, to save time, climbed the stone ladder he had used before. The bucket had spilt its nauseous contents in his fall, but he scooped up what he could find and walked on toward the stairs.

He came to the General first. The body lay on its back, its head flattened out of perspective like a plum which someone has trodden on. The lion had begun, just as Mrs. Adamson had described Elsa as doing, at the belly, treating the twill trousers and canary waistcoat like so much hide. It looked as if the body had been hit in the midriff by a small explosive shell.

The lion lay only a yard or two from the stair, its long flank stitched by a regular double series of bullet holes which did not seem to have bled at all; but the giant mask was a crimson tangle. There had been two bursts of firing—the first must have killed it, then Singleton, driven by some urge of violence, had sprayed the second burst along the animal's length.

"What's that?" said Singleton, from the shadows.

"Some evidence. How many keys are there to this place?"

"Two. The General had Uncle Dick's on him, and I suppose he has still, but I would prefer not to investigate his pockets. The other one is in my safe."

"I'll leave this here, then. We can click the lock to and the lab team can pick it up when they come for the bodies."

"Bodies?"

"With a bit of luck they'll be able to prove that the lion ate Sir Richard by finding human bone fragments in its intestines. The pistol ball may still be there, too."

"It appears that you know all about our affairs," said Mr. Singleton slowly.

"I've still got a fair amount of checking up, but first I must do some telephoning. And you will want to tell Mrs. Singleton what's happened."

"Anty? Oh, yes, I suppose so. Naturally."

They locked the door and Singleton led Pibble down the path toward the cottage, past it, and on toward the screen of trees.

"Where are we going?" said Pibble.

"I left my car in the car park; I consider it unsafe to go through the Lion Ground after dark."

"What brought you out here?"

"I thought it my duty to look for the General. We have been perturbed, I do not mind confessing, by his behavior since Uncle Dick died. Anty, who has a vivid turn of phrase, observed to me that he seemed no more put out than he would have if a strong wind had stripped the tiles off the stables. It was she who asked me to come and investigate his whereabouts, and it seemed possible that he might be down at the Dueling Ground. But when I stopped my car I heard Bonzo roaring, and decided that I had better investigate."

Pibble was silent, his scalp prickling with wariness as they dipped into the blackness under the trees. Judith told us, the General had said, and "us" must have included one of the Singletons. Suppose she'd told the General and Mrs. Singleton, and the General had come out to see what he could do alone, leaving a message for Singleton to follow. That would explain the long, bravura piece of spellbinding. But perhaps Singleton, though happy to camouflage the occasional murder inside the family circle, was not sufficiently imbued with the Clavering ethos to help in the obliteration of inconvenient strangers.

"Did Sir Ralph seem his normal self at tea?" said Pibble.

"I do not take tea."

The car park was a small square of gravel, entirely screened by trees. It held the General's E-Type, open, and a Land-Rover.

"Do you feel capable of driving one of these?" said Mr. Singleton.

"I'd rather not. I'm pretty shaken. He tried to kill me three times."

"In that case it would be advisable to put the Jaguar's roof up. This type of machine depreciates quite fast enough, without allowing the upholstery to be wet through."

Pibble held the torch while Singleton flicked the roof into position; then they both climbed into the Land-Rover. Singleton drove in an odd, bolt-upright attitude, like an elderly lady at a tea party, but banged the car through corners on the very verge of skidding, so that Pibble lurched and grabbed. The lion-flanked gates were open—perhaps they were only shut when visitors were expected, so that Mrs. Chuck could scutter out and curtsy and collect, like Danaë, her shower of half crowns. Mr. Singleton stopped the car halfway up the avenue and switched off the headlights.

"I hope you will forgive what must appear unwarranted inquisitiveness," he said, "but who were you proposing to telephone?"

"I ought to ring your Chief Constable," said Pibble, "to keep him in the picture. He'll have to arrange for all the technicians—lab men and photographers, and so on—to come out tomorrow. I must ring my wife. I must telephone my own boss and tell him what's up. I must have at least one assistant—Sergeant Maxwell would do—up here tonight. That's the lot. Oh, no, I must telephone the local pub for a room."

"Good Lord," said Mr. Singleton with surprising warmth—no, not warmth, emphasis—"you must stay with us. As for the other matters, I wonder if you could be persuaded to leave contacting the local police until tomorrow morning. I ask because we will need time to organize our defenses against a horde of journalists. You must take my word for it, but they are bound to descend on us in swarms, and it is my duty to arrange my staff work so that everybody knows how they are to be handled. You may not be aware of it, but tomorrow is a busy day for us. *Queen Elizabeth's* in, and that involves four coaches in the morning and six in the afternoon."

"Queen Elizabeth?"

"The boat, man!"

"Oh, of course."

Um, nyum. Pibble stared through the windscreen. The lights of the Private Wing glowed warm and friendly between the tree trunks, but the rest of Herryngs brooded under the moon like a sullen fortress. Reasonable request, in a sort of way—tell a policeman any dirt, and it's all over Fleet Street in half an hour, like muck across plowland. Besides...besides...Pibble was not content with the solution presented him. It made sense, but it had been shoved at him. Why had Singleton selected two such spectacularly bad liars as Maxwell and Miss Finnick to prop up the General's ramshackle structure of deceit? And there were Miss Scoplow's three shots, when he'd heard only two during the duels while the Americans had been going through the mill; echoes, most likely, but it ought to be nosed into. And there was something else, something round and gray, nagging at a corner of his mind. Get the official machinery grinding and everything would suddenly become fixed in its present posture, like a bunch of kids playing musical statues.

And what had Singleton been doing, hiding on Miss Finnick's porch?

"I must certainly ring my boss," he said, "but I'll ring him at home. He's very stuffy about journalists. I must ring my wife, too; but she doesn't know any. I'll ask my boss's permission to delay informing your local police till the morning, and I think he'll agree. That only leaves the problem of an assistant. Isn't there a member of the local force you can ring at his home, and—"

"Mr. Waugh," interrupted Mr. Singleton. "He was a special constable, I believe. I am certain he would be more than willing to do his duty as a citizen by assisting you."

"Well..." began Pibble. But why not? So many rules broken so far, what does one more matter? But give in and they'd think he was taking matters easy, accepting the solution which had been shoved at him. Only wanted a chap for a couple of things, nothing Waugh couldn't do.

"All right," he said, "let's try him."

"I am most grateful," said Mr. Singleton, and drove on.

Mrs. Singleton was pushing a trolley of drinks along the hall as they came in.

"Just in time," she said. "How'd...Oh, it's you, Mr. Pibble. Where's the General?"

"Perhaps you'd take the drinks into the study, Pibble," said Mr. Singleton. "I'm sure you'll excuse us for a minute."

He took his wife by the elbow and turned her around to walk her down the hall. Pibble wheeled the trolley into the study, where Miss Scoplow was sitting reading *Nova* with that tiny derangement of the eyebrows which showed she was concentrating on something a bit beyond her.

"Oh, I'm so glad you've come," she said. "I expect you know a lot of Lesbians—being a policeman, I mean. Do *you* think Queen Elizabeth the First was one?"

"I was always taught she was really a man," said Pibble. There seemed to be three sorts of whiskey, so he chose the palest.

"Oh, you mustn't put water in *that!*" said Miss Scoplow. "The General will throw a fit. Are you all right, Mr. Pibble?"

"No," said Pibble. He poured water into his drink and took two big mouthfuls. Normally he didn't like whiskey, but this was delicious. Miss Scoplow was watching him with her exaggerated wide-eyed stare.

"I do think you'd be better off with aspirin," she said.

"No, I'm better with this, thank you. What can I get you?"

"I don't drink, thank you very much."

"I think you should, this time."

She looked at him again, a quite different gaze, remote and for once self-concerned.

"Something sweet, then," she said.

Pibble mixed vodka with Italian vermouth and put a lump of ice into it. Miss Scoplow took several small sips.

"Who's dead now?" she said, at last.

"You knew about Sir Richard?"

"The Admiral? No, for heaven's sake. He was all right at lunch—luncheon, I mean."

"That was the General pretending to be Sir Richard."

"Are you *sure* you're all right, Mr. Pibble?"

"How did what he told you about lions tie up with what you'd been typing?"

"Well, it was a bit funny, because sometimes he said the exact opposite of his notes. I just thought he wasn't thinking what he was saying—men are often like that."

Bet they are with you around, thought Pibble.

"I'm afraid they're both dead now," he said. "The Admiral was killed four nights ago by the General in a mock duel—I believe you heard the shots. Now the lion in the Tiger Pit, the one they call Bonzo, has caught the General and killed him."

"Mr. Pibble," said Miss Scoplow with great earnestness, "will you promise you aren't teasing me? This is exactly Sir Ralph's idea of a joke, and it isn't fair on people like me who have no sense of humor."

"I promise," said Pibble. "It isn't my idea of a joke, either. You heard me talking to a doctor in London about it."

"Oh, poor Anty!" cried Miss Scoplow, her face puckering like a child's at the death of a goldfish.

"I'm all right," said Mrs. Singleton, from the door. "They were a couple of silly old buffers, and really they'd have liked the idea of going out in a great blaze of nonsense like this. Mr. Pibble, I hope you'll stay to supper. I don't know what it'll be, because Elsa's in a tantrum about someone pinching one of her buckets and her ball of string."

"I'm afraid that was me," said Pibble.

"Christ!" said Mrs. Singleton. "Thank God I didn't know!"

"And I took a boiled chicken out of the fridge."

"A boiled...Oh, it doesn't matter about *that*." Mrs. Singleton produced her mellow giggle as easily as if no frost had come to blacken the honeyed hours of autumn. "You *must* have been hungry. That was Uncle Dick's lion bait for getting Bonzo back into his cage: he used to marinate it in aniseed. Mr. Pibble, I hope you will accept my apologies for the General's—my father's behavior. I can't think what came over him, trying to kill you like that. He had such extremely strict ideas about the duties of hospitality."

Now *this* was play-acting, from fluttering eyelashes to pleading palms. Pibble looked at the wide cheekbones under the Wedgwood eyes and noticed for the first time the pretty little mounds of muscle, product of much smiling, bunched on them like an elf's biceps. Callousness did not appear to be a recessive strain in her heredity.

"Perhaps he didn't think of me as a guest," he said sourly. "I came down here to do a job."

"Of *course,*" said Mrs. Singleton. It is a characteristic of noble families that their honor can be satisfied with great facility, when it suits them. She sniffed the inside of the cocktail shaker, ladled ice into it, and added careless splashes from half a dozen bottles, talking while she did so.

"Judith, I'm afraid you're going to find this very unsettling. I promise you no one will think any the worse of you whatever you decide to do, but Harvey and I would both like you to stay if you can bear it. In any case we're going to have to put a bit of overtime on you, getting ready for the bloodsucking scribblers who're bound to come flocking in tomorrow. Harvey's making a list of what he wants at the moment."

She shook the shaker with great dash and poured out two tumblers of milky fluid.

"So we're all going to have a working evening," she said. "Superintendent, Harvey said something about your wanting Mr. Waugh to help you."

"If possible" said Pibble.

"Can you arrange that, Judith?" said Mrs. Singleton. "Get him up here at once—he'll be at the Spotted Lion, not the Clavering Arms. Talk to the landlord—his name's Mr. Looby—and ask him to get one of his customers to drive Mr.

Waugh up here. Say it's for me, and it's urgent, but don't say what it's about. Can you manage that?"

"I think so," said Miss Scoplow, in a shaky whisper. Pibble could see a line of white-and-purple markings just below her lip, where her upper teeth had been biting. She walked out with desperate steadiness. Mrs. Singleton relaxed.

"Poor little squit," she said. "She cheered up the old boys' lives a lot, you know—and Harvey's very struck with her. But we ruin everything we touch sooner or later, everything. My mother...Never mind. Work is the only cure. I believe you want to do some telephoning; you can use this one as soon as Judith's off the line. You're being very gentle with us, Superintendent, considering. Thank you very much. Supper will be at eight, with luck. Elsa's rages don't last long."

She smiled a we-understand-each-other smile, picked up her tumblers, and swayed out. Am I mad? thought Pibble. *Nobody* can really behave like that. What's done is done: no hint yet of what's done cannot be undone. Even supposing she was putting on a show to help Miss Scoplow feel less weepy, could she have produced that laugh? Of course no one has to like and admire her own dad—what had the General said about sacrificing his wife and daughter?—or her own uncle. But there was something about the quick rattle of command, the sure grip on the scepter, which seemed to accord ill with a deep dynastic wound. And Mr. Singleton: Pibble had been fretted by his manner even when they were walking down to the car park—an odd charged confidence, like a cricketer batting on a horrible wicket but dead on form—was it only the residual euphoria of action? Certainly the photograph in the lavatory implied that violence, aimed explosions of destruction, had once been a necessary part of his nature; perhaps he could switch it on but not switch it off again without a few flashes of shorting blueness and charred electrodes. At least that would account for the double shooting of the lion.

Pibble picked up the telephone; a hoarse voice was saying, 'Tm sure someone will be glad to bring him up, Miss Cyril! Be a gent and run Mr. Waugh up to the House—it's for Miss Anty. Yes, that's all right, Miss, he'll be with you in five minutes." Click.

Mrs. Pibble had a comedy show on, to judge by the surflike ebb and return of laughter.

"Hello, pigeon, I've got bad news, I'm afraid...No, not really, but I shan't get home tonight. I'm stuck down at Herryngs...No...Yes, but not quite like that—there are excitements and excitements...No, it's just more complicated than anyone had thought, but I ought to get it sorted out tomorrow. I'll tell you all about it then...Can't you put them off?...Oh, all right, at least it'll move you up a couple of rungs in your coffee circle...No, of course I didn't mean that, and anyway *I'm* a snob. Forget it. D'you want me to bring you a toy gallows?...Yes, really, apparently they sell like hot cakes...No, in the House...I'm sorry, I *am* a bit tired, darling, that's why. What about you?...Oh Crippen, but I told them in my letter...Well, they'll just have to take it back and try again. I'm sorry—how infuriating for you...Good. Go to bed early...Yes, I'll try to. Bye, pigeon. I love you...Bye."

Extraordinary the emollient aura of great names—she'd even sounded rather pleased that he'd been cornered into spending a night under that myth-reverberating roof; odds were if he rang up again the line would be engaged. Twenty to eight: the Ass. Com. should be back in his flat in five minutes. Wonder who she'd tell first?

Pibble turned at a stagy throat-clearing from the doorway; Mr. Waugh was there, still in his overcoat and heavy fawn muffler. "I understand you required my services, sir," he said.

"Yes, please," said Pibble. "Take off your coat and sit down and I'll tell you what I want. Drink? Whiskey?"

"Daren't touch it, sir. A couple of glasses lay me clean out." Mr. Waugh suddenly decided to discard the obsequious style. "Fact is I've overdone the booze all my life and now my bleeding system won't stand it. Saw me this morning, din'cher? Know what got me to that state? Three half pints of bitter and a couple of piddling little ports. I'll have a dry vermouth with a lump of ice in it. What's up?"

"Sir Ralph's had an accident," said Pibble. "It's vaguely connected with Deakin's death, and also with what you were telling me this morning."

He found that he'd dropped his voice and was trying to watch the crack at the hinges of the door out of his peripheral vision.

"I read a lot of spy stories," said Mr. Waugh. "They usually put 'The Ride of the Valkyries' on."

He shoved his bulk out of his armchair and shut the door. Then he came to sit beside Pibble on the over-welcoming sofa.

"I played Watson for eight months on a northern tour," he said, "but I don't recall Holmes mentioning Wagner."

"Perhaps he just scraped away at his violin when he wanted to hold private conversations," said Pibble. "The problem is this, Mr. Waugh: I've reached a stage where normally I'd get another policeman to help, but the Singletons have suggested that I ask you to stand in, so that we don't have Fleet Street crawling all over the place before they're ready for them. If you don't mind—"

"Dead, is he?" interrupted Mr. Waugh. "What about the Admiral?"

"He's dead, too, I'm afraid."

"Jesus Ker-riced!" said Mr. Waugh with great solemnity. "What the hell are you playing at, telling *me*? You know I've only got to give one of my pals on the Street a tinkle—and I still send Christmas cards to half a dozen of 'em—and I'd earn meself a juicy five hundred quid. More maybe. *And* I'm under notice here, good as. My fanny, but you're a bleeding innocent if ever I met one."

Pibble felt his face go chill and sweat start from his

palms. Of course an old heavy like Mr. Waugh would know a nasty clutch of gossip columnists. What now? Offer him, vicariously, a three-year contract? Threaten him with continuous police chivying hereafter? (It had been done.) Get Mr. Singleton...

"You're all right, as it happens," Mr. Waugh went on. "I owe you nothing, and I owe Mr. Harvey Singleton less than nothing. Anty's a nice enough lass, but not five hundred nicker nice. But I'm not the one to set a pack of news hounds scratching away at the Claverings' graves like dogs on a rubbish dump—I know I couldn't live with myself afterward. I was playing an Air-Raid Warden in *The Morning Star,* Emlyn Williams, when the news of the Raid came through. Not in the West End—Cardiff, as a matter of fact—but it was on the wireless that morning. Never seen an audience like it. They cheered every line, almost, despite they were a lot of bleeding Welshmen. Made me proud to be in uniform. Sorry, better not have any more of this. I'm a bit pissed already. What do you want me to do?"

"The first thing might be a little tricky," said Pibble. "I want to ring up my boss and I don't want anyone listening on extensions—that means the Singletons or Miss Scoplow. I'm not trying to keep any nasty secrets from them, but I want to be able to say what I feel like without worrying whether I'm upsetting somebody. I've had one call overheard already today, and that made a considerable mess of things."

"Mate," said Mr. Waugh, "I feel for you. The whole of the Main Block is bugged so that Mr. Harvey Singleton can listen to the visitors saying 'Ooh' and 'Aah' and check on whether his staff are doing what he tells 'em without moving his bleeding arse from his desk chair. Right little electronic genius, he is. How do I set about *that,* then? I've played my share of police sergeants, but I haven't the authority here, if you see what I mean."

"Yes, you have," said Pibble. "I say so. All you need do is nose around; if they aren't all in one room, ask where the other one is. If they are, ask how often Bonzo was fed and who fed him. Take as much time about it as you can. Write it all down, slowly."

"Bonzo?"

"The big lion in the Tiger Pit."

"Christ! Did *he* get one of them?"

"Both."

"Christ!"

"Think you can manage that? All you have to do is make it impossible for them to use the extension continuously. If they keep picking it up and putting it down, I shall hear them. Let's see if it's free."

There were voices in the receiver. Miss Scoplow was saying, "So if you could be here at nine o'clock, Harvey will be telling everyone about the special arrangements for tomorrow. He'll explain what it's all about then." "Sure and easy," said Miss Finnick's voice, "I'm just about trustworthy to be there betimes. And please, Miss Judith, if 'ee have any tidings of that funny liddle Lunnon gentleman as was quizzing me this afternoon, I'd be grateful of hearing 'em." "Oh, *he's* all right," said Miss Scoplow. "Is that all, Maureen? I've a lot of telephoning to do." "Aye, that be all. God be with 'ee." Click.

Pibble put his receiver down, counted five, and picked it up again. The earpiece was full of the rhythmic chicker of dialing.

"Wait a moment, Miss Scoplow," he said.

The chicker stopped.

"Who's that?"

"Pibble. May I have the phone for five minutes? My boss should be in his flat now, but he might go out again later. I've taken quite a bit more responsibility than I'm entitled to, and I'll be in a real mess if I don't get him to O.K. what I'm doing."

A brief deadness—her hand must be over the speaker. So Singleton was with her. Then she said, "Of course that's all right. Harvey and I can go over to the Kitchen Wing—there's another line there."

"Oh, in that case I could just as easily go over."

The deadness again, rather longer, then a rustling and Mr. Singleton's voice.

"Pibble? Best if we go over, as a matter of fact. I have someone I must see over there, so you may stay where you are."

"OK, fine." Click.

But who? The Kitchen Wing had looked as black as a slab of slate in a Welsh churchyard when they were talking in the drive.

"That makes life easier, Mr. Waugh," said Pibble. "If you could just check that Mr. Singleton and Miss Scoplow do go over to the other wing...D'you happen to know if the telephone over there is on a different line?"

"That is correct, sir."

"Then all you've got to do is go and make small talk to Mrs. Singleton."

"Will she be in the mood for small talk, sir?"

Interesting point. Pibble looked at him. The big oval face seemed uncommon white.

"Yes," he said, "I think she will. She was very matter-of-fact about her father's death when I talked to her ten minutes back. But in any case you don't have to say anything; just see she's not listening in. There they go, by the sound of it."

Mr. Waugh crossed to the door as the voices outside lost their volume. The erect butlerine stance seemed to have wilted, but he edged the door quietly open and peeked through the cranny. Then he nodded and went out.

The Ass. Cam. was in his bath, his man said.

"Get him out," barked Pibble edgily. "Tell him it's Pibble."

Clunk, and then silence.

At the prospect of saddling someone else with his load

of guilt and doubt, Pibble began to breathe like a man in a fever, quick and shallow. In effect he had killed—he, Pibble, personally—the last English hero. Now he was busy grubbing up trifles to show how far the legend had sickened, how much the whole of Herryngs smelt of the sweetish odor of decaying timber. He needed horribly to be told that he had done, was doing, right. And there was the way he'd completely shoveled aside all standard police procedure: it'd been his original brief, but not in any words he could use to justify himself, just hints and…

"You in trouble, Jimmy?" said the thin, tired voice. "It's damn cold out here in the hall."

"Sorry, sir, but it really couldn't wait till tomorrow, you'll agree when I tell you." Pibble realized he was gabbling but couldn't stop. "The whole thing has turned out the most horrible mess, they're both dead and he tried to kill me three times, and—"

"James! Pull yourself together, man. Who's dead beside the servant who committed suicide?"

"Sorry, sir. Both the Claverings are dead. A lion ate them."

"Jimmy, are you sure you're all right? If I didn't know you better, I'd say you'd been on the bottle."

"I've had one whiskey, sir."

"Carry on, then. A lion has eaten both Sir Ralph and Sir Richard Clavering. Not at one sitting, I take it."

"No, sir. Sir Ralph killed Sir Richard in a duel four days ago and fed him to the man-eating lion they keep here because that was his last wish, he told me they were both drunk at the time—"

"Slower, Jimmy. Sir Ralph told you this?"

"Yes, sir. I had a hunch something was wrong with Deakin's suicide, that's the coxswain I came down to see about, and the lion had something to do with it, so I went to look for evidence in the pit where they keep the lion and Sir Ralph followed me and let the lion out but I managed to climb up to a sort of balcony where Sir Ralph was and he pretended he hadn't known I was there." (Pull yourself together. Talk in short sentences, slowly. Drown the squeak of hysteria with deep, manly tones. Try.) "He told me all about the Raid, sir, and then about the duel. It was over a girl. He was trying to catch me off my guard, sir, and he did and near as dammit threw me over again, and then the lion climbed up to the balcony and we ran away and he tripped me up but the lion ran past and got him instead, and—"

"Dear me. What a comfort I didn't send Harry down. What next?"

"Then Mr. Singleton, that's the son-in-law, killed the lion, and then he asked me not to set the police machine going until tomorrow morning, which would give them time to prepare for an invasion of journalists. Apparently the force down here has a permanent line to William Hickey direct. I said yes, because there's a couple of things I want to check on before the whole situation sets hard, and—"

"What things?"

"I don't know, sir."

"James!"

"Nothing tangible, sir, I mean. Except for some noises which somebody heard in the middle of the night, that is, and she's not the world's best witness. But there's several things I feel don't really fit in..."

A longish silence, and then the tired sigh.

"I hope I don't have to tell you, Jimmy, what you're asking me. I can't believe that a few oddities of behavior are remotely exceptional in the milieu of Herryngs. Will you please assure me that you are in full possession of your senses, not suffering from shock, not seeing murderers under the bed? You realize that if you put a foot wrong you are liable to release a most unrewarding stink."

"I've put all my feet wrong already, sir." The hysterical squeak was back and Pibble tried to modulate into his lower register—it didn't sound good. "I mean if I'd gone quietly this morning and just sniffed at the evidence that was shown me and said yes, yes, I could have come away by now with nothing but the suicide of a whiskery old coxswain to show for it, but they'd have been getting away with...I mean I felt uneasy this morning and I feel the same again now. First time there was something in it, and there may be again. But I'll take it very carefully, sir. Only I wish to Christ I hadn't killed the General."

"From what you told me just now, it sounded as though he was entirely responsible for his own demise."

"I suppose so, sir."

"All right, Jimmy. The position is this: you have found one very gruesome skeleton in the Herryngs cupboard and think there may be another. The family want a lull, so that they can stand by to repel Fleet Street. You are asking me to sanction that lull while you look for your second skeleton. I hereby do so. Presumably you didn't ring me up at the office because your local bobbies aren't the only ones with a direct line to Hickey, so if anything more comes up you'd better ring me here. I'm going out to see my first blue opera, but I'll be back soon after eleven. You can ring me then."

"Right, sir."

"Take it easy, Jimmy. I trust you will forgive my saying so, but you must recognize that if half of what you say is true you have been under a considerable strain. What I said about shock just now was not intended as a joke."

"No, sir."

"You do understand me, don't you? I have to trust you, Jimmy, because you're the only one there, but if I'd the slightest chance I'd take you off and put someone else on— even Harry Brazzil."

The voice was deliberate, bloodless, cruel. It was as though the Ass. Com. had taken a bucket of icy water and sloshed it into the receiver, forcing it along the wires so that it should gush chillingly out over poor Pibble, driving him out of his self-pity, back into sanity and responsibility.

"I quite understand, sir. I'll play it down the middle."

"Good. If anything really urgent comes up, I'll be at the Cruelty Theatre, Seat D8, but I don't fancy being paged while Donna Whatnot's being raped in top C. Try and ring me here at half past eleven, even if nothing's happened."

"Right, sir. I hope you enjoy your evening."

"The things I do for Art."

Click.

Another small whiskey would be excusable. It really tasted like five quid a bottle—probably was, too. However hard Singleton had wrestled with the finances, the General had still talked of himself as rich, a rich old hero. With his glass in his hand Pibble went out to look for Mr. Waugh and, led by the resonance of a woman's voice, found him in a pretty little sitting room, a bit *Voguey* with its persimmon walls, two doors down the corridor. Mr. Waugh was cradling an empty glass and looking very somber while Mrs. Singleton, spilt lissomely across the arm of a chaise longue, told him a tale about grooms dead before the war; she did the rustic accents with great accuracy but managed all the time to underpin them with the subliminal presence of her own expensive vowels. She nodded at Pibble as he came in, and carried on to the end of her story. Mr. Waugh smiled gamely, drowned in his own puddle of misery.

"I'm afraid I've made a bloomer, Mr. Pibble," she said when she'd finished. "I didn't realize you hadn't told Mr. Waugh everything that had happened, so I waded right in as if he knew, and then I *had* to tell him—I hope that's all right. Since then we've been talking small talk."

"I should have told him," said Pibble. "I'm sorry, Mr. Waugh. I'm afraid it's a very shocking business."

"Too right, too right," muttered Mr. Waugh.

"Why don't you have another drink, Mr. Waugh?" said Mrs. Singleton. "It's ten minutes till supper still. Mr. Waugh's going to dine with us, Superintendent, supposing there's anything to eat. Elsa's in a record tantrum, banging her pans down as if she wanted to crack the Aga. I do wish you could have found a different bucket and a different bail of string."

"I'm sorry," said Pibble. "Would it help if I went and apologized?"

"Good God, man, she'd *eat* you," said Mrs. Singleton. "Oh, hell, isn't it frightful how one can't keep off a subject once it's sensitive, like sitting with someone everybody knows is dying and all the conversation seems to be about shrouds. Mr. Waugh, do go and get yourself another, really."

"Thank you," said Mr. Waugh, rising. "Perhaps it would be appropriate."

He went out slowly, missing the handle of the door at his first attempt.

"Poor Mr. Waugh," said Mrs. Singleton. "He's such a very sentimental man at heart, and just as loyal as if he really were an old family retainer. Old family retainers are the worst, actually. Elsa's a most frightful pest, even if she does cook like a dream, but we'll be able to pension her off now. Funny how he uses his butler act as a sort of spiritual truss; you feel he'd melt and run all over the floor without it."

"And Deakin?" asked Pibble.

"Oh, he was an old sweetie, willing to do anything anyone asked—any of *us* asked, I mean. I'm sorry we had to tell such frightful lies about him. But really he belonged to Uncle Dick. Here's Harvey back."

The euphoria of action had not worn off the tall man; as he held the door for Miss Scoplow and then chivied Mr. Waugh into taking a guest's precedence, every gawky angle of his body seemed to throb with a subdued pleasure, though his face retained its puppetlike stolidity.

"All is now satisfactorily arranged," he said. "Can we do anything for you before supper, Superintendent?"

"I want to go down and look at the Dueling Ground by moonlight, but that can wait until after supper. While I'm there, I'd like to take a look at the dueling pistols, if you can tell me how they work. I'll need Mr. Waugh to come with me."

"I would prefer it if Waugh stayed and listened to the briefing I shall be giving to all senior members of the staff."

"Would it be possible to brief him separately?" said Pibble.

"Harvey," said Mrs. Singleton, "Mr. Pibble has already bent his police conscience for us as far as it will go. It's our turn now."

"Of course, of course," said Mr. Singleton, in his walking-dead voice. "I apologize, Superintendent—I confess I have much on my mind. Judith, would you be so kind as to fetch one of those duplicated maps out of the third drawer on the left-hand side of my desk, and the big ring of keys from my safe?"

She looked as miserable as Mr. Waugh, but she nodded and scuttled out.

"The dueling pistols," said Mr. Singleton, "are kept in the old icehouse, which I will mark on the map for you. I can assure you that the actual well where they stored the ice has been filled in, so you need have no apprehension of falling down it. All the equipment is there, but there is no electricity, so you will need to take a torch, which I will provide. The pistols will have been cleaned after today's duels. You will find a small vise screwed to the bench, into which you fit one of the pistols muzzle upward. The powder flask will have been refilled, so all that is necessary is to unscrew the cap, fit the nozzle into the muzzle of the pistol, pull out the flange on the side of the flask's neck, count three, push it back, and count another three."

"It works just like one of those gin-dispenser doofers in a pub," said Mrs. Singleton.

"Exactly," said Mr. Singleton. "It is a measure. Next you insert a wad with the ramrod. Provided you get it in level, it will go down level. Finally you take a ball from the box on the shelf above the bench and insert that. The ball is an oblate spheroid—"

"Not quite round, on purpose, he means," said Mrs. Singleton.

"Precisely," said Mr. Singleton. "That is to say, it will only fit into the barrel along one axis. You push it down with the ramrod, which you then rap smartly on the end with the mallet provided. This has the effect of reshaping the ball into a round, and at the same time forcing it against the sides of the barrel, so that it cannot fall out if the pistol is held pointing below the horizontal."

"I've always wondered how they did that," said Pibble.

"Why do you want to know all this?" said Mrs. Singleton.

"I'd like to see the place by moonlight," said Pibble. "The General told me it was a night very like this. And if I can see how difficult it is to load the pistols it will help me to estimate how drunk they were, which may well be important."

"Nobody told me they were drunk!" said Miss Scoplow, in a sobbing wail behind him.

"Of course they were, darling," said Mrs. Singleton. "If you think about it you'll see it makes it *much* better. Come and sit here and we'll talk about something else; I've just been telling Mr. Waugh about the terrible old rustic who taught me to ride."

"Thank you, Judith," said Mr. Singleton, taking a sheet of paper and a great bangle of keys out of her wavering hand. "Perhaps it would be best if you were to sit down and Waugh fetched you a drink. Now, Pibble, in my opinion the optimum way for a stranger is to walk down the railway line—here—where you will discover a pair of gates, to which this is the key. Immediately beyond the gates, you must strike left along a small path through the yew grove, which will lead you down to the Bowling Green. This is the icehouse, which I will mark with an 'X,' and this key must be turned twice in the lock. Do you wish me to repeat that?"

"No, thanks," said Pibble. "That's fine. I think I've got it."

"Harvey," said Mrs. Singleton, "you've forgotten to tell him how to prime the pistol."

"You interrupted me, darling," said Mr. Singleton, an irritable grate in his voice which seemed out of keeping with so small an annoyance. "When you have inserted the ball and rammed it home, you rotate the pistol in the vise until the barrel is horizontal. On the right-hand side you will observe the steel against which the flint strikes when firing. You push this forward, and the action opens the priming pan, which you fill with a pinch of black powder from the flask. Close the pan. To fire the pistol, you cock the flint and pull the trigger. I think you will find it very simple."

"Dinner is served, Madam!" screamed a furious voice in the passage. All conversation died, and in the silence they could hear Elsa's booted feet stumping back to her kitchen. A fresh agony of hysteria started to well up inside Pibble, like seasickness; the extra load of guilt—the bucket and the string, on top of the hero's dreadful dying—was more than he could bear. His mouth was open to make a noise, any noise, a high mad laughter, when he felt the flesh above his elbow gripped in that curious hold that salesmen use when they wish to demonstrate that you can trust them. The laughter stifled into a gawp and Harvey Singleton led him out after the ladies. Mr. Waugh came last of all.

Mrs. Singleton was smiling inside the small dining room.

"It's all right," she said, "she's done us proud. She's like Beethoven, sort of—all temper and beastliness, and then producing this marvelous thing. Help yourself, Judith; it's pâté, and then roast mutton. Harvey, she seems to have decanted some claret."

Elsa and Mrs. Singleton rescued that meal, Elsa by her miraculous ability to persuade you that anything she cooked, even a boiled potato, had been treated in such a way that the very essence of its nature was made manifest. Pibble remembered a journalist, a music critic who doubled in crime, telling him about an interview with an aging diva who was making a comeback in her home town, Vienna: the journalist had found the lady sitting on her bed in her hotel beside an old 78-rpm gramophone, which was tilted off the level by the folds of the eiderdown; she was playing records of her own arias, shoving the pickup arm across to where she knew the good bits were; every time the music came to a high note she would grin, lift a minatory finger as the true young voice winged out, and shout *"Geschlossen!"* Elsa's cooking was like that, bang on the note, so that you had to enjoy it however miserable you felt.

Mrs. Singleton's performance was different, full of false notes but carrying everybody along by the almost rumbustious quality of her animal attractiveness and high spirits. In that mood she could have wished gaiety on a convocation of decimal coinists. Mr. Waugh was caught up and began bandying Creeveyish anecdotes about theatrical knights. Miss Scoplow, though she relapsed occasionally into crumpled despair, laughed a little and talked a little and did her eye-opening trick several times. Pibble, too, felt the clamminess of shock seeping away from him. Only Mr. Singleton seemed detached, holding his wine up to the light, tilting his glass to look at the color of the meniscus, sloshing the liquid around inside the glass so that it would release its secreted odors, and then taking a great gulp and, rattling it to and fro between his molars like a man rinsing his teeth at the dentist's. It was a hulking, muscular wine, tasting of old cavalry boots, but Mr. Singleton seemed determined to show it who was master.

"Is it all right, Harvey?" said Mrs. Singleton suddenly.

"Too young still, a trifle too young."

Pibble shivered, clammy again. He realized all at once what echo Mrs. Singleton's behavior had been rousing: Lady Macbeth. What's done is done. First at the discovery of the murder, and now at the banquet. While Harvey had been lost in his trance, she had kept the chatter moving, and now she was cajoling him to do his duty by his guests, for all the world as if the blood-boltered General—no, it would have to be the blood-boltered Admiral, unless it was just the blood-boltered Bonzo—haunting him around the inside of his glass. Like Macbeth, his response to the cajoling was fitful.

Mrs. Singleton rapidly rethawed the frozen conversation and forced it to tinkle on down the long slope of the evening.

9:00 P.M.

Mr. Waugh, swathed to the great white gills in borrowed mufflers, waited in the shadow of the Private Wing. Pibble plodded away from him across the moon-blanched lawn, lowered himself clumsily into the ha-ha, and began the tedious walk along sleepers which were spaced exactly wrong for any comfortable stride. Three shots, Miss Scoplow had said. Couldn't hear it because of the echoes, the General had said. Two old soaks, drunk enough to fall twice on their way down, drunk enough to make a hash of loading the pistols, but not too drunk For A to hit B and feel B's ball fanning past his cheek. Good shooting for drunks—and Pibble had heard no echoes in the morning, just the two shots of the Americans burning powder. Nothing in it, probably; sounds are always different at night; best wait and see what Waugh heard.

Well, then, what about the worst actress in *Who's Who in the Theatre* (worst supporting actors, Sergeant Maxwell and loyal Dr. Kirtle)? A rum trio to pick, except in the hope of betrayal. What about the double shooting of the lion? And what about that gray blob, gray and spreading, like a cell under a microscope, off key, wrong? What the hell had it been? How big? Pibble could see it on his inner retina, as large as a baby's head and pulsing slightly, changing color now—ah, Crippen, it hadn't been like that. No use trying to

167

force it up: that never works, the summoning of apparitions from the Endor inside the skull. They come when it suits them.

Anyway suppose, if only for the sake of the Macbeth fantasy, that Harvey Singleton had hidden behind the General and shot the Admiral. That would account for both the death and the General's feeling a bullet pass, but what other machinery would be needed? He'd been a brilliant shot, Dr. Kirtle had said. He went to bed late, he'd said himself, and had very good hearing, so he might have listened to the quarrel. Could he have relied on the General tipping the body over for Bonzo? Probably—the Admiral had often asked to go that way—or he could have appeared as if wakened by the shots and suggested it. That would be one old hero out of the way, and a fair chance of having the other one locked up for murder.

But why? They don't believe ordinary common folk have motives, Miss Finnick had said. Policemen do, though. Why would business-efficiency Singleton knock off a couple of dotty old heroes? The old boys still think they're as rich as Croesus, she'd said. The General had talked about Harvey's sideshows. They wouldn't let him show the dirty frieze. He gave up a very promising job with a merchant bank to put the Claverings back on their feet, and here he was, after all those striving years, running sideshows. Forty-nine, say—last possible age to decide between blazing success and gray mediocrity. And all that fizzing action bottled up inside him. Not surprising if the cork popped.

The cork popped, then. Four days of intrigue, and somebody had argued somebody else into sending for a chap from London. Never mind who now, but it was an oddity. No, we're overrunning; Deakin had died in those four days. Could he have killed him, or was it just a lucky chance to set the General careering down his crazy slalom of deception, so sure to fail taking a curve too fast, relying on the lost reflexes of youth? Then all he'd had to do was nudge the plot nearer to discovery. Then Scoplow had told them about the telephone call, and he'd hung around at the top of the Tiger Pit while the General waited for him to come and ambush this intrusive Londoner—what would he have said if the hero had emerged triumphant, like Rikki-Tikki-Tavi out of the king cobras' hole, covered with dirt, licking his whiskers? Perhaps the General would have been so cock-a-hoop at managing it alone that any excuse would have done.

But they'd both waited for each other, the General and his son-in-law, and Singleton had waited longer. Pibble had seen it happen again—or heard it, rather—when Singleton, motionless in the blackness of the stair well, had outwaited the lion. What had he felt like during that first waiting, when the General might have babbled anything to the detective? Or perhaps he'd spent the whole history lesson leaning on the parapet above them, listening with his very good hearing. Then the fracas, then the last fearsome bark of the hero as the huge claws caught him. Then down the path to the cottage while Pibble was fastening the door; the victor, Pibble or General, would be sure to go there. He'd known the door was shut, too.

Action next, killing the lion. Twice. Yes, of course. If the Admiral had really been killed by a pistol ball, it might still be in the lion's two-fathom of guts, and the police might slice the beast up to look for it, and they'd find a modern bullet. Hide it; spray the long body with modern bullets, same size and caliber; a rimless .45 wasn't it?

Ah, hell, the whole thing was pure supposition; Pibble decided he believed some of it some of the time, like the Nicene Creed.

But Singleton had "forgotten" to explain how to prime the pistols.

He had been walking toward a belt of trees and was almost into their black shadows when he saw amid their upper branches two spike-topped helmets with flat brims, such as Sidney's men might have worn at Zutphen. No, two towers with helmet-shaped roofs on the far side of the trees, enormous—why couldn't you see them from the house? He shone his torch at them and found that they were on the near side of the trees, a small pastiche of the Tower of London, into which the railway gate was set.

The key turned easily. Beyond the gates Pibble could see the glint of moonlight striking off the rails where they curved out from under the trees. There were mossy steps in the low embankment to his left, and then the path plunged steeply down. This must be another section of the ravine by which the bone-meal chapel stood. The path twisted between shrouding yews; logs were set across it to form crude steps at the steepest places. He came around a hairpin corner, shone his torch in front of him, and felt his heart bounce with panic as the beam fell on a very old man, on his knees, rapt, in front of a rough-hewn crucifix. The panic lasted only half a second before he realized that the figure, however priestly its attitude, was lay. Nicely done, though, with real sackcloth on the plaster limbs, and the cell behind clean with a bed of fresh bracken in the corner. There was even a charming hollow in the rock where a spring oozed out between small ferns to fill a natural basin—or perhaps an unnatural one, scooped here at the whim of some long-dead Clavering to provide drink for a living, breathing, wage-earning hermit. Odd world they'd lived in, those great Whig gentry—odd uses which they'd thought it proper to put their fellow men to. Still did. A jink in his train of thought made Pibble wonder who the next heir was, after Mrs. Singleton, and whether he'd inherited the same arrogance.

Another mini-folly stood untenanted beside the path a few yards farther down; then the slope eased and the path widened to a mossy walk, and there was the Bowling Green. It wasn't at all as he'd imagined it, not a lawn below formal terraces, fringed with heraldic topiary. This was a deep romantic chasm, with the Abbey roofs invisible and only the claustrophobic crags, shaggy with trees, surrounding the level turf. The space was a little larger than a tennis court, and when Pibble crossed it to look at the stream, which licked quietly along below the further cliff, he found that the crevice opened to his right so that he could now see what looked like the pitch of an outbuilding roof, and beyond it a star-obliterating line of blackness, the far crest of the valley.

The icehouse was Gothick, flint-built, crenelated. Pibble opened the door and laid his torch on a shelf. The pistols were in a polished mahogany box lined with blue satin; they were larger than he'd expected, but nice to hold. Once you knew about it, it was easy to spot how crookedly the barrels were set, though Deakin had taken full advantage of the asymmetry of the flintlock on one side and sweated a tapering sleeve of steel down the other, covering its surface with fine chasing.

Loading should have been straightforward enough but Pibble was trapped by his instinctive distrust of all contrivances, however primitive, and couldn't believe that the measuring device at the neck of the flask would work; so he unclamped his pistol from the vise and tipped the barrel out onto the shelf. A nasty little pile of black granules mocked him—it *had* worked. But how do you extract a ball and wad from a pistol which has no powder in it to shove them out? There must be a method; it must have happened often enough in genuine flintlock days; but it's not the sort of question a chance-come detective cares to ask at a great house after bungling an attempt to incriminate his host.

He tried again, resolutely trusting all the antique gadgets, bonking the ramrod down onto the ball with manful precision. Nothing rattled when he turned the weapon horizontal, but he couldn't bring himself to point it downward for fear of seeing the whole tiresome cargo cascade out on the floor. He shoved the steel forward and poured some of his spillage into the pan. Snapping the lid shut, he inspected the whole contrivance with wonder: the little flint was held in a miniature vise at the end of an arm on a spring; you pulled it back with your thumb to cock it, and then when you pulled the trigger it shot forward, bashing into the vertical steel to produce its minute meteor shower; the impact also shoved the steel forward, opening the lid of the pan because they were all one piece, thus letting the meteors sprinkle down into the saltspoonful of gunpowder, which then flared—flared enough to send a gout of flame down the pin-sized hole in the barrel, igniting the main charge.

He stared at the gadget, humming, struck by the rum collection of ingenuities which man will assemble to achieve his peculiar ends. There is a town in remote Guatemala called El Progreso, whose sole industry is the cultivation of a single crop; a mountain railway has been built over fantastic canyons in order that this crop may be exported to another part of Guatemala; the crop is the staple diet of the cochineal beetle, which is in turn harvested and pulped so that its juices may be re-exported to enhance the color of European blancmanges without affecting their taste. Never was a town better named: it is by fitting together processes such as these that man heaved himself up from simian innocence to the point where he could assemble iron and carbon into a steel tube, add a flint, a mixture of niter and saltpeter and charcoal, and a lump of lead, and use the resulting contrivance to kill his brother.

Pibble stalked out into the moonlight, pointed the results of Progress at the further cliff, and pulled the trigger.

There was a fractional instant after the click, in which he could begin to think he had loaded wrongly, begin to loosen his grip on the butt. Then the thing went off with a noise louder and lower than a modern pistol, a true bark, not a yap. The butt bucked in his hand, up and to the left. The echoes lasted for several seconds, distinct but fading booms. Pibble counted five of them volleying between the two cliffs. Then he put the gun back in the icehouse, picked up his torch, locked up, and began to climb the path past the plaster hermit, brooding as he went.

What was the best thing to do if he was wrong about
Singleton—pragmatically best? They couldn't have been all
that drunk if they'd managed the complex process of loading (though the General had said it took a bit of time, and
they'd had a lot of practice) and then shot accurately
enough to produce one hit and one near miss. But need anyone know about the duel? Wouldn't all England be happier
if the evidence was faked so that they both appeared to have
been killed by the lion? There could be a grand state funeral of the unconsumed portions, and the world could enjoy
its big, soft weep. Say the lion had caught the Admiral, and
the General was trying to rescue his brother and got nob-
bled, too? A good death—both original and heroic. Deakin
would have to be fitted in somewhere: say he'd usually
helped the Admiral feed Bonzo and his death induced the
Admiral to try and do it alone. Rastus could be shipped
home; five years in jug would keep him quiet. Everyone else
would play. Yes. Better than two soured old soaks squabbling over a woman two generations younger than themselves.

He went through the gate and locked it.

Except that that would leave Singleton in honorable
command of Herryngs, ready to shift the last of the
Claverings out of the Private Wing, ready to expose the non-
pederastic Rector to the view of salivating Yanks, ready to
extinguish the last spark of genuine life in the House amid
the neon glare of a dollar-earning fun fair. Well, good luck to
him, provided he hadn't murdered one old hero and possibly
one whiskery coxswain for the sake of transforming his non-
profit concern into a tourist blue-chip.

And how could you prove that, one way or t'other?
Check with Mr. Waugh on how many shots/echoes he'd
heard; take him to witness a statement from Miss Scoplow
about how many she'd heard; have Bonzo sliced up and the
bullets counted and inspected; search the Tiger Pit for the
odd slug out; search the undergrowth round the Bowling

Green for a place of ambush where Singleton had waited. That bullet, it would have to look roughly the same as one from the tommy gun (he wouldn't have had time to get across to the stall and fetch that). A .45, then, and...

He missed the next sleeper, stumbled sideways, banged his shin on the railway line and sprawled onto the bank of the cutting. As he climbed angrily back to his feet, his brain did one of those extraordinary linkages which the mind can sometimes achieve if you don't force it—the gray blob which had been fretting him swam into his mind's eye, fluttered for a second, and diminished with a rush of perspective to a dirty mark about a quarter of an inch across marring the white smoothness of the label under Dotty Prosser's Colt—a long-barreled .45.

And the grenade beside it had been dusty.

Mr. Waugh was fast asleep on the dank lawn in the shadow of the Private Wing. His breath came loudly, but in the nasty gulps of the dead drunk. Fine witness to the number of bangs audible he'd be. Pibble shone his torch around and spotted a small tumbler which he picked up with his handkerchief and smelled. Neat whiskey. So some friendly spirit had brought out a warming toddy to comfort the poor old actor on his chilly vigil—someone who knew that in his shocked and dismal loneliness he would risk a sip and then a swig and then keel ponderously over.

Pibble hid the tumbler in a tuft of long grass in the corner of the wall, where no mower could reach. The evidence would be barely useful, but he was angry and he wanted to know who'd actually carried the liquor.

He couldn't think of a method of getting Mr. Waugh indoors, off the rheumatism-breeding turf, without asking Singleton for help. Ah, well, five minutes wouldn't make all that difference. First things first, and with a bit of luck the lit windows of the Kitchen Wing meant that the briefing was still in progress and everyone out of his way. The door to the colonnade was unlocked; dim bulbs shone amid the vines;

but the Main Block was dark, and Pibble picked his way by torchlight across the Zoffany Room and into the enormous hall. The wetness of his shoes deadened their clacking on the resounding wood; at a real flat-foot's pace he crept sound-lessly into the Chinese Room, rapt in a charade of stealth, and tiptoed across the carpet toward the case of weapons.

The label had been changed since the morning; and the dusty grenade had been cleaned and polished.

Now he was certain, though there was no way of prov-ing it unless they found the bullet. The main thing was to make sure of the gun; he knelt to look at the lock of the case, a flimsy brass affair, and then stood his torch to shine down-ward through the glass. As he was levering the seldom-used screwdriver device out of his penknife, his throat was seized from behind. Madly he tried to use the leg-hooking tech-nique he had been taught for dealing with an assailant from the rear, but his instructor had not dealt with the case of a man who was kneeling when the assault came. Expert thumbs, cold as stone, probed direct for the jugular. He wrenched at the hands as uselessly as a baby trying to open a stiff doorknob; then even the faint light from the torch van-ished into roaring blackness. Harvey Singleton had outwaited his enemy again.

❀ ❀ ❀

Light, when it came back, was a pale rhythmic flash accompanied by the clank of heavy metal and a rumbling sound. His neck was a woeful belt of pain, but when he tried to raise a hand to touch it he could not achieve even a half inch of play for the limb—he was encased in something stiff but soft.

He filled his lungs to yell and felt the same constriction on his chest. The yell came out as a poor affair, a mild croak—the strangling had unmanned his vocal cords. It hurt even to try to twist his head, but by straining his eyes to their leftward limit he managed to glimpse the moon before a black shape eclipsed it in time to the clank, then the moon again, eclipse and clink again, moon...The rumble must be wheels; even through the padding he could sense their uneven joggle. Then the moon edged slowly into full view as the vehicle took a curve, and he could see that it had been a head and shoulders pumping up and down which had caused the interruption of its light. Then the clank made sense, too. He was lying on his back on a hand-operated rail trolley; Harvey Singleton was pumping the long arm that propelled it along the rails.

"You'll never get away, with this," Pibble croaked.

Singleton pumped on, silent, as remote from Pibble's pains and terrors as a liner must seem from dying men in a lifeboat who can just see its plume of smoke smudging the horizon. A straitjacket, a very luxurious one, encased his limbs, he realized—just the kind of handy gadget that was sure to be stored in one of the Herryngs attics: you never knew when one of your guests might not go killing-crazy halfway through a wet weekend; or perhaps it had been made to measure for some past Clavering in whom the family madness surfaced too violently for social comfort. Why hadn't Singleton simply tied him up? Answer, because the marks of the rope would show on his wrists and ankles. But the mark on his throat? Answer, it didn't bear thinking about; there was one obvious way of hiding a stigma like that.

"Did you kill Deakin?" he croaked.

Singleton stopped the trolley and opened the gates to Old England. He had to push the trolley for several yards before it had enough momentum to be driven again by the pumping handle. He stopped once more in another hundred yards and bent down to lift Pibble's rigid form across his shoulder, but in a moment of carelessness allowed their two heads to come close enough together for Pibble, despite the pang of twisting his neck, to snatch at the passing ear with his teeth, and get a good hold. With stolid patience—much the same as Pibble had earlier shown when removing the bramble from his own ear—Singleton laid him back on the trolley, their heads as close as if they had been lovers spooning under the big moon. Pibble ground his teeth, rejoicing in the taste of blood. Singleton's fingers felt for his damaged neck; they seemed to know their way about, and suddenly one of them pressed deep in under the ear to find its chosen nerve. Pibble's whole skull sang with agony. He opened his jaws.

Singleton straightened up and then bent out of sight again. There was a slow tearing noise and he rose with a strip of cloth in his hand which he used to bind around his head, with a wad over the bleeding ear. So there would be no trail of blood after all. He picked Pibble up as unemotionally as he had the time before, jerked his shoulder twice to settle his burden comfortably, and walked off along a flagged path. Pibble's head faced downward and with a shiver of unburied superstition he saw that Singleton was a monster, one whose monstrosity came by night and vanished again with sunrise: his legs ended in a pair of ballooning mushrooms, white, soft, obscene…No, he'd padded them with cloth to achieve an area of contact with the ground as broad as an elephant's foot—he'd leave no footprints at all. That's where he'd torn the strip of cloth from to bandage his ear. The path led down, breaking into steps every few yards. Each pace, each descent, shot its lance of agony through Pibble's neck, for his head was supported only by the bruised spine and mangled tissues. Singleton must have known, but cared as little for his victim's pain as he had for the chewing of his own ear, which must have hurt like hell. Pibble could still taste the blood of his enemy in his mouth, and wondered whether the pathologist would have the genius to spot it and diagnose an alien blood group. And what would Singleton do about his ear? Tooth marks are very distinctive. Cut it off? Very likely.

They stopped at another door; Singleton lifted the latch

and bore him into a wider turfed area, a courtyard among buildings. Seven steps more and he laid him on a platform and rolled him over onto his back. Directly behind Pibble's head, a big beam reached toward the stars; at its top, supported by a small timber across the angle, the L-piece stood out sideways. From this dangled, just as in the silly little toy Miss Finnick had assembled, the summoning noose of the gallows.

Pibble felt his shoes being taken off. This seemed so extraordinary that inquisitiveness overcame the apathy of his fear and he contrived to move his head slowly to a position from which he could just see Singleton low down in the corner of his right eye. The man was leaning against the pillar of a moonlit cloister, removing the pads from his feet, and cramming Pibble's shoes on—they were at least three sizes too small. Then, carrying the pads, he walked with short steps straight toward the gallows, out of Pibble's line of vision. After a few seconds he appeared again, not carrying the pads but unwinding a ball of string whose other end was attached to a part of the gallows Pibble couldn't see; he led the string around a pillar and came back to the gallows, still unwinding it; this time be came straight up the steps of the platform and tied his end of the ball to the beam above Pibble's head. He moved out of sight and there was a longish pause before Pibble felt his shoes being laced back on again—any chance that a colleague would spot that it was a non-regulation knot, supposing it was? But Singleton was a devil for that sort of detail.

Next, after another short pause, a strange sensation at his fingertips which made him shrivel with terror at the thought that he was being prepared for some agonizing torture. It wasn't until Singleton had done four fingers that he realized that he was having his fingernails cleaned with the paint of a nail file in case any telltale fragment of skin was still there after the brief fight in the Chinese Room.

So this was to be suicide. The single set of footsteps following the path of the string and then leading straight back to the scaffold would show up under normal police investigation. Presumably the string was fastened to a lever which controlled the trap, and had to be led around the pillar because the lever worked in that direction. Singleton would stand him up, put the noose around his neck, stand beside him on the scaffold, and pull the string; when the long lump of meat and bone had stopped swinging, he would untie the straitjacket and leave the body dangling, the string draped into the trap hole and the triple course of footsteps to show the world how poor Jimmy Pibble, unhinged by the shock of his dealings with the General (they might even work things to show that he had been responsible for the hero's death), had melodramatically taken his own life.

Could it come off? Not if they brought the whole apparatus of forensic science to scrutinize his death. They'd find the place where the straitjacket had rested on the scaffold, the strained seams of his shoes, the depth of footprint made by a heavier man, even the faint and mysterious indentations where Singleton's huge pads had plodded across the lawn bearing the weight of two men. All that should be detectable, given the will, but it was a lot of work and bother for an open-and-shut case.

So it all depended on whether they thought Pibble was the type to crack and kill himself. Jimmy Pibble, a bit sensitive—highly strung, you might say—never had the basic drive to make a topflight officer, clever but quirky, wouldn't put it past him...

Suddenly, with a passion which detached him from the pain and fear of the horrid machine above him, he longed to know that they would put it past him.

"I am not that sort of person," he gasped, in his ghostly whisper. Singleton hesitated in his manicuring and then moved on, silent, to another nail.

Mrs. Pibble, she'd know, surely. She thought him weak, unambitious, wasteful of his cleverness (which she absurdly overestimated), selfishly neglectful of her, but sane. She'd know he was sane. Too sane to kill himself, even as the last neglect of her. Poor Mary Pibble, she'd had a small, sour life, and she'd find it smaller and sourer tomorrow. And she wouldn't know what to do about the insurance, though he'd told her fifty times—but Tim Rackham would look after that.

But would Tim listen when she said that her husband would never have committed suicide? Four-fifths of wives say that anyway, *felo-de-se* being a distinct reflection on the inadequacy of a spouse to make the dead man's life worth living. What would Tim believe, whom he'd played chess with over beer and bangers and cheese almost every day in the last eight years on which their work had allowed them to lunch near their offices? Tim, who thought that any man's life was purposeless if he didn't find four noisy kids rioting about him the moment he got home?

And the Ass. Com.?

As Singleton levered him to his feet, taking care that his hard heels should not scrape along and mark the platform, Pibble found himself praying not to any God but to the Assistant Commissioner of Police, begging that official not to believe that Detective Superintendent James Willoughby Pibble was capable of the crime of self-slaughter.

Singleton, silent on padded feet, lifted him over to the noose; propped him up, and settled the rope around his neck.

"Stand up or you'll strangle," said Harvey Singleton, in a detached voice. They were the only words he'd spoken.

He moved off the trap and untied the string. Pibble tried to gather the nerve to throw himself sideways and, at the cost of strangling, leave better pathological evidence of what had happened to his throat before the rope got there. The wrench of the full drop must obliterate all that—there'd been that case of the sergeant in Germany—so...But he couldn't do it. The muscles of his ankles, the only muscles which the straitjacket allowed him to move, clung despite his mind's bidding to their last three seconds of life.

Singleton jerked the string.

It snagged on the pillar.

He jerked again, but still the return length hung in its low catenary curve. Without even a cluck of the tongue at the tiresomeness of inanimate things, he retied his end to the beam and padded across the lawn to remove the obstruction. This time Pibble was in control of his ankle muscles, but a faint, absurd hope bade him stand upright.

Singleton reached the moonlit edge of the cloister and pulled the string to one side; it still held. He moved it up and down under slight tension, but achieved nothing. He couldn't afford to do much waggling, Pibble thought, without producing a suspicious abrasion of the string and fragments of thread caught in the wrong places on the pillar. Singleton seemed to think so, too, for he walked around to the next opening to loosen the string from inside.

Immediately he stepped into the shadow, there was a single sharp thud and he was tossed sprawling out across the grass. A squat gorilla-like figure pounced out of the cloisters onto his body; rolled it over on its front, straddled it, and with a rapid weaving motion lashed the arms together behind the back, then tied the ankles together, then ran another length of what Pibble knew must be camera strap between these two lashings and pulled it taut so that Singleton's body was bent back into a bow. Singleton didn't stir; the blow must have been well-aimed and vigorous.

Pibble felt the noose caress the side of his neck and realized with another bout of shock that he was swaying, giddy with fatigue and pain and relief, and with no possible leverage of limbs to regain his balance. He forced his ankles to move him gingerly back to attention and tried to call to his rescuer to hurry, but no sound came. However, the squat figure straightened from its task and trotted up the steps of the platform.

"It *is* Mr. Pibble," said Mr. Chanceley. "I reckoned it was you, but I found it difficult to verify in this light. Let me have that cord off of your neck. What's this you're wearing?"

"A straitjacket," gasped Pibble. "I'm extremely grateful to you, Mr. Chanceley."

"Think nothing of it," said Mr. Chanceley. "I will be asking a favor of you in the immediate future—I'll tell you when I've untrussed you. You know, first I figured your act was a leg-pull but when I'd studied the setup awhile I guessed you wasn't play-acting, neither of you. So I knotted his piece of cord around a nail and waited for him. I reckoned I could shout or discommode him if he tried to pull that lever direct."

"He's a very dangerous man," said Pibble.

"And I was All American tackle, Idaho, afore I shifted down to Texas. You have a sore neck, Mr. Pibble."

"Yes," whispered Pibble. "He laid me out by throttling me and then he brought me down here to fake a suicide. The rope would have hidden the earlier bruises."

"I heard you say you were down here on a job," said Mr. Chanceley, with a shade of query in his flat voice.

"I'm a policeman, and I was investigating a suicide which turned out to be a murder, I think. That's Mr. Harvey Singleton."

"Yeah," said Mr. Chanceley. "I spoke with him already." The voice held a hint of social reproach; as though Pibble had committed a gaffe. He remembered the square, purple-clad figure arguing with Singleton under the fountain while the crowd milled into the coaches; remembered, too, how absurd he had seemed then.

"I hit him with my camera," said Mr. Chanceley, as if pointing out the poetic justice of the implement. "It is shock-proof, naturally. I reckon he'll live. Now, Mr. Pibble, you may consider you're a mite in my debt, but you can set the record straight before we take him to the cells. I missed the picture of my life to fetch you out of that mess, but we can set it up again, and better, too. I have this experimental film, ultra-fast, nothing like it on sale anywhere in the world, and, like the slogan says, 'It Takes Movies by Moonlight.' Now, Mr. Pibble, you and your pal were posed, ab-so-lutely posed, for *the* greatest moonlight shot in history, but I couldn't take it, first because I left my silent camera at my hotel, and second because I had to get you out of the fix you were in."

"I'll gladly put my head into the noose again for you, Mr. Chanceley," said Pibble, "but I'm afraid we'll have to do without the executioner."

"Nuts," said Mr. Chanceley. "I have a timing device for my camera. I'll strip off and be the hangman—I have more the figure for it than your Mr. Singleton, too."

He had already, while waiting in ambush, divested himself of his festooning gadgetry. Now he threw his blazer on the lawn, whisked his necktie off, and began to pull his shirt over his head, talking as he did so.

"We'll move fast. If I know photography—and I do, Mr. Pibble—that beautiful big moon will fade behind a cloud if we give her one moment's grace. Now, see here: I'll aim my camera to take in the steps and a little bit of lawn this side, as well as the scaffold. You take off your coat and necktie, Mr. Pibble, but leave your shirt open at the neck. You don't say it has a detachable collar? Holy Mother of Jesus, this is my lucky night. Take the collar off and you'll look real antique. That white shirt is fine, and your face is nigh as white as your shirt—you're sure this ain't asking too much of you, Mr. Pibble? Then I'll lead you up the steps with your hands strapped behind you; you'll turn and kneel and say a prayer; I'll jerk you up and put the noose around your neck and make like I'm going to pull the lever. Then you can step off the trap and we'll have it open. I found a crate in there"— he jerked his thumb toward the cloisters—"and we'll put it under the trap for you to stand on. Then you can go down slow, bending at the knees, while I pull the lever again slow. I can splice the pieces I need to make it seem quick when I run the film. We'll have twelve minutes and thirty seconds before the film runs out, so we should do it easy."

"Fine," said Pibble, reflecting that Mr. Chanceley and Mr. Singleton made a very near match for rapid and detailed planning. The Texan fetched a small crate from the cloisters and hid it behind the scaffold. Pibble watched him wonderingly: half naked, with the build and musculature of a real Jack Ketch, his trouser ends tucked into his socks to simulate tights, he looked like a natural force which nothing short of annihilation would deter from its ends. How easy it would have seemed to another man to wash his hands of the humane aspects of the scene, perhaps to take a still or two of Singleton pulling the lever and Pibble undergoing the drop when the lens click would be drowned by other noises. How many dedicated photographers get the chance to snap a real murder by hanging? The temptation must have been like a flood tide. Juicy blackmail afterward, too. No question of not being allowed to photograph the Abbey by moonlight, either, and then to milk the publicity for all it was worth.

Mr. Chanceley fiddled and fussed over his tripod. Pibble put his coat back on while he waited; he felt as cold as he had while brooding over Deakin's body—suddenly he remembered Mr. Waugh lying stertorous in the dank shadow under the Private Wing, rheumatism seeping every second into those alcoholic joints. As Mr. Chanceley straightened from his adjustments, Harvey Singleton groaned. Pibble bent to look at the thongs; they seemed firm enough for anything.

"Let him bide," said Mr. Chanceley. "You ready now, Mr. Pibble?"

Pibble took off his coat, let his wrists be bound behind his back, and followed Mr. Chanceley up to the scaffold. The camera whirred in the dimness. He hung his head disconsolately so that he could see where the knotty muscles bulged on the square slab of his rescuer's back. He knelt at the top of the steps and praised the Assistant Commissioner for his manifold mercies. He was hauled to his feet, stood on the trap, and again felt the harsh caress of the noose. For a crazy moment he was certain that Mr. Chanceley would be carried away by the histrionic art and would pull the lever—hard to make a motive like that stand up in court.

Then there was the juggling with the crate; slowly he did a full knee bend; when the rope was taut, he allowed his head to sag to one side while he tilted his chin upward and forward. It hurt like hell, but he owed Mr. Chanceley that much.

Harvey Singleton, when they came back to him, was threshing on the lawn like a landed salmon.

"Just let me dress," said Mr. Chanceley, "and we'll put him into that straitjacket."

Pibble went and fetched the thing, wondering whether it could be made to fit so different-shaped a man, but found that it was most ingeniously designed to suit any size of customer: there were webbing straps at the back which served the dual purpose of adjusting the scope of its embrace and tightening its grip until the victim could not even wriggle. There was a label inside the collar—it said "Army and Navy Stores."

"I'd best lay him out again," said Mr. Chanceley. "We'll have one hell of a wrestle getting him into that thing otherwise."

He swung his camera in a sharp arc, producing the same thud as Pibble had heard before. The long body jerked and lay still.

"Holy Mother of Jesus," said Mr. Chanceley as he undid the thongs. "You seen anything like that before, Mr. Pibble?" Pibble knelt and looked. The leather had cut into Singleton's wrists so that they were welling with blood and the hands were as puffy as kidneys. Pibble tore up strips of the foot-pads and bandaged the wounds. Then, while Mr. Chanceley was untying the ankles, he went through Singleton's pockets, finding a big ring of keys, a small automatic pistol, a wallet, and a roll of tape from a tape recorder. He pocketed these and helped roll the unconscious man into the straitjacket and adjust the straps as tight as they dared. He was still terrified of Singleton; the threshing had been a final desperate effort to get a hand to the pistol, and even with his arms strapped behind his back he might have managed to use it— he was that sort of man.

"Where now?" said Mr. Chanceley.

Pibble took the map Singleton had given him out of his pocket and peered at it by the light of the moon.

"I don't fancy going back to the House," he said. "I don't know how much Mrs. Singleton is involved in all this, and the place is full of guns; they might try anything. But there's a car up in the staff car park—it looks about five hundred yards—if one of us can drive it. It's an E-Type Jaguar."

"Boy, oh boy!" said Mr. Chanceley. "Is this my lucky night! If you'll carry my equipment, Mr. Pibble, I'll carry the prisoner."

"Are you sure you can manage?" said Pibble. "I don't think he'd get out if we left him here."

"I'll be happier if I know he's with us," said Mr. Chanceley. He hoicked Singleton up by the shoulders, tilting him onto his feet like a man tipping a log end over end, bent, and caught him neatly at the point of balance on his broad shoulder.

"My cameras are under the archway there," he said. "Bring what you can carry, and maybe I'll have time to come back for the rest. I'll start off—you reckon it's this track, Mr. Pibble?" He trudged into the dark with his lethal burden.

Pibble picked up the bloody straps and carried them into the cloister, where he found an untidy ziggurat of leather, glass, and chrome. It took him several minutes to thread the straps into the right buckles and to load himself up. Not a dressy man, he was still concerned lest the providential Mr. Chanceley should feel he was carrying the gear in an inappropriate manner.

He found him propping his burden up at a point where the path forked.

"You made it," said Mr. Chanceley. "Where now?"

"Left," said Pibble, glad that he'd taken an extra half minute to learn the route off. Mr. Chanceley slung Singleton up onto his shoulder without a grunt.

"Be careful how you handle him," said Pibble. "I managed to bite his ear when he was lifting me."

"He tries that on me," said Mr. Chanceley, "and I have his eye out. I was a Minuteman, back home, before they went soft, and I learned unarmed combat."

The load of photographic equipment suddenly seemed heavier as Pibble came to terms with the knowledge that his rescuer was not merely a semi-literate American figure of fun, but a supporter of the extreme right wing to boot. But an honest man, he thought. An honest man. An honest man. The load became no lighter, but at least he could carry it.

The gate was locked and none of the keys fitted. Mr. Chanceley slid his load to the ground and propped it against a tree with a casualness that suggested he would have put it down head first if it had happened to lie that way.

"I saw you took his pistol," he said. "We can maybe shoot the lock out."

"I don't think it's worth it," said Pibble. "If I take those three screws out, we can take the handle off and pull the whole lock sideways."

In the event, it was Mr. Chanceley who had to turn the screws with the gadget on Pibble's penknife. Pibble was feeling weaker every stride, and when they reached the car park he was ready to buckle under the weight of a new problem.

"We'll never fit him into a two-seater," he said.

"We'll lower the top and lay him longways," said Mr. Chanceley. "You'll have to find somewhere to squat, and you'd best look for a scarf for your sore throat, Mr. Pibble— it'll be a mite cold."

"Let's hope there's a map in the car," said Pibble. "I'm a stranger in these parts."

"Me, too," said Mr. Chanceley.

There was a map. The key was in the car. The top came down without trouble. Singleton fitted neatly in on the passenger seat with his feet in the long cavern under the dash and his head protruding over the folded top. Pibble, remembering how his own head had jogged on the journey down to the Abbey, insisted on using the two rugs in the car to wedge him into position, tying them to the straitjacket with one of Mr. Chanceley's straps. He found a Shetland scarf for his own throat; Mr. Chanceley tried on the General's deerstalker and rejected it; they settled themselves, Pibble perched on the top with his knees wedged behind the driving seat; the engine boomed its creamy note; three seconds later they were away, actually outside the purlieus of Herryngs House.

11:40 P.M.

It must, Pibble considered, be a peculiarly painful dilemma for the Night Sergeant at a provincial police station when a couple of obvious desperadoes carry in a perfect specimen of the local gentry and claim he is three times a murderer. The gentleman swears from his straitjacket that he is in the hands of madmen, in a chilly rational voice which demands obedience. One desperado—the more disreputable—produces documents which purport to show that he is a Detective Superintendent at Scotland Yard. The other desperado stands in the background uttering corroborative statements in a gangster's accent. You, naturally, incline to believe the devil you know. The British delinquent, now clearly round the bend, produces a small pistol and says he will shoot you if you don't ring up a London number which he claims to be that of the Assistant Commissioner of Police. You ask how you are to know that it is not the number of an accomplice, but offer to ring Scotland Yard and verify. Scotland Yard refuses to tell you the private number of the Assistant Commissioner of Police. The British desperado snatches the telephone from you and says, "Who's that? Hilda? Oh, Mavis, I'm sorry. Pibble here, Superintendent Pibble. For God's sake, give this chap the Ass. Com.'s number so that he can ring him up and check who I am." She does so. You ring the new number, and a dry voice answers which does not sound like that of a desperado's accomplice. It tells you that the tattered desperado is a senior officer of the force you are proud to serve in, and asks to speak to him. During the long conversation, you start trying to believe that the gentleman in the straitjacket, to whose every whim you have hitherto kowtowed, is an exceedingly dangerous criminal. The three of you lug him off to a cell, unstrap him while the American desperado points the pistol steadily at him, and lock him in. You then, on this Superintendent's advice, get poor Fred Bulling out of bed, send him round to Mr. Roberts to have a bit of paper signed permitting you to arm him, and set him to watch the criminal gentleman's cell. The desperadoes then depart in the General's red E-type, as you've often winked an eye at doing eighty-five down the by-pass.

Pibble did not consider all this, of course, until later, while the deepmouthed engine surged them back toward Herryngs. The conversation with the Ass. Com. had gone reasonably well, though Pibble's voice had given out halfway through his tale. There had been a longish pause when he finished.

"No chance of playing the whole mess down?" the sour-lemon accents had said, at last. "It sounds as if you've done very well, Jimmy, but the trouble is people won't like it at all. The Home Secretary, if I know him, will take it as a personal insult. You know the ground—is there a way of separating the Claverings' deaths from this Singleton affair? Can we make theirs accidental?"

Pibble had outlined his fairy tale in which the General died trying to rescue the Admiral from Bonzo.

"Possible. What about Singleton? Think you can nail him for killing this manservant? Pathologists ought to be able to find traces of previous semi-strangulation, but could you make it stick to Singleton?"

Pibble had pointed to his own experience, and the mild evidence of the half-painted landing craft, but had added that he wasn't even sure himself that Singleton had strangled Deakin.

"I don't feel greatly attracted to all this." The voice had sounded petulant. "The journalists are sure to get wind of something if we try to hang on until we've had a report on the manservant, and then, as you say, how do we prove it was Singleton? I am dubious about simply nailing him for trying to hang you, though I imagine we could get him for that, at least, thanks to your providential witness. Police would come badly out of it, though. Ah, well, it looks as if we'll have to go through with the whole caboosh—even then, a lot will depend on finding that bullet."

Pibble had observed that evidently the Claverings hadn't found it, or there would have been no need to fill the lion so full of lead.

"Right. Interesting point there—what would Singleton have done if Sir Ralph had picked up a Colt bullet in this pit of yours? Never mind about that now, though. I'll get on to your local Chief Constable and get him to send some reinforcements out. I'll get on to the Old Man, too, and tell him what we're up to. My inclination is to turn the whole damn shooting match into a circus, give the news hounds their money's worth and more, get the lovable British public too eager for gory details to feel the shock to our national pride. But I'll have to talk it over with our masters. You realize that this means taking you off, Jimmy? You're too involved now to be anything except a witness. I daresay you'll be glad of that."

Pibble had agreed that he would. The voice became drier than ever.

"Besides, we'll need you as a scapegoat if things go wrong. You'll see how we've decided to play it when you see who I send to take over. Meanwhile you'd best go back to Herryngs and stop anyone who's left from killing each other. Go careful, Jimmy."

So here they were, turning for the second time that

night through the magniloquent gateway. Mr. Chanceley, in boyish mood, made the car bellow down the half mile of avenue and took the curve by the fountain in a controlled skid which sent the gravel spattering across the pool. Pibble directed him around to the far side of the Private Wing.

Mr. Waugh still lay in the shadow beneath the lit study windows, but someone had been out, rolled him onto a tarpaulin and covered him with rugs. His breathing was fast and shallow. As Pibble knelt to feel his pulse, the study window was thrown up.

"Who's that?" called Mrs. Singleton.

"Me. Pibble."

"Thank heavens! I can't think where everyone has got to. Mr. Waugh ought to go to hospital—he looks awful."

"Where is the hospital?"

"In the town. I could drive him there if you could help get him into the car. I couldn't manage it alone."

"No, you stay there—I want to talk to you. But would you please ring up the hospital and tell them what to expect, and then book a room for Mr. Chanceley at a good hotel, if there is one?"

"God, they'll never take anyone at this time of night!"

"They'll do it for you, won't they?"

"I suppose so. Bring him round to the colonnade door and I'll tell your friend where to go."

The window banged shut. The art of carrying inert butlers has not been adequately studied; it is difficult to achieve a proper grip on the unresisting steppes of flesh—even the omnicompetent Mr. Chanceley let the shoulders slip twice before he changed tactics, backed the Jaguar across the blasphemed turf, and heaved the butler in in one swift movement. The big head lolled sideways, the mouth dangling open and emitting retching noises, but Pibble decided the man would have a better chance if he were shielded from the rush of midnight air, so they took time to put the top up, managing it far less neatly and surely than Singleton had earlier.

Mrs. Singleton had finished her telephoning and was ready with unflurried directions for finding the hospital. Pibble bent to the car window to thank Mr. Chanceley, inadequately, for having saved his life.

"My pleasure," said the Texan flatly, and roared off.

The fire in the study was freshly made up; the ashtrays were clean; as soon as they had sat down, Elsa stumped in with a tray of tea laid for two.

"Please tell me what has happened," said Mrs. Singleton, with about the concern shown by a parent at a P.T.A. meeting inquiring about a child's poor reports. Pibble told her. She sighed as she poured out the tea.

"Perhaps you'd prefer me to taste yours first," she said.

"Please," said Pibble.

She looked at him out of the side of her eyes, nodded, and took a good gulp.

"Damn," she said. "Burnt my throat. No arsenic, though. Now what?"

"There must be a recorder somewhere on which I can play this tape," said Pibble. She went out and came back with a green gadget which seemed to have more terminals protruding from it than was normal; it held only one spool, empty, so she threaded the new tape swiftly through and switched the machine on. Pibble rose to check that she had not set it to "Record," which would have obliterated the previous signals, and returned to his chair to listen to the faint hum. After two minutes he rose again.

"Wait," said Mrs. Singleton. "It fits onto the telephone."

More hum, and then suddenly the clatter of dialing. Then a voice saying, "Mr. Lanning's residence," and another—high-pitched, hysterical—saying, "I've got to speak to him." Brief pause, then, "Mr. Lanning is in his bath, sir." "Get him out," said the second voice, clearly on the edge of a breakdown. "Tell him it's Pibble." A click, a faint sound of feet padding away, the whiffle of feverish breathing, and then a tired voice saying, "You in trouble, Jimmy?"

The whole conversation was on the tape. It was as good as a suicide note. The Ass. Com. would have had a grisly time at the inquest if he'd tried to maintain that Pibble sounded his normal self. Unstable, remorseful, broken Pibble. And, Crippen, how much he'd told Singleton! He listened, numb at his own weakness and stupidity, until the green box settled back into its dead hum. Mrs. Singleton was looking at him with smiling concern.

"You've had a bad day, Mr. Pibble," she said. "And you haven't finished yet, I suppose—you want to know how much I knew."

"Please," said Pibble.

"I knew that Uncle Dick was dead and that the General had shot him—or, rather, that's what I thought. It didn't seem to be any concern of anyone's but us. The General was going over to Chichester after luncheon to set things up for a fake sailing accident for Uncle Dick, but you rumbled him. And then I knew Harvey was dangerous; I was going to try and warn you but I didn't realize everything would happen so fast, and I didn't know what he was up to, or why. But I did know he was up to something, the way he purred over his claret at supper—I just didn't know what."

"What would you have done if you'd realized he'd killed your uncle?"

"I don't know. Nothing, probably."

"Who took the whiskey out to Mr. Waugh?"

"I wasn't in the room, but I met Judith coming back. Harvey'd asked her to take it. I gave her a sleeping pill and sent her up to bed. It's rather sad, you know, but she wouldn't have let any of them touch her, not even Harvey. She's desperately in love in a very old-fashioned way with a rather wet young man who sells software for computers. Poor Harvey, he's so conscious of his abilities, so frustrated by Uncle Dick's refusal to let him build this place up into something really big..."

"I thought it belonged to your father," said Pibble.

"The General gave it to him when my mother agreed to marry him—it didn't belong to either of them then, of course, not until Grandfather died, but they'd had some sort of bet about who'd get her—you know their style. Anyway legally Herryngs belonged to the General, but he always behaved as though it belonged to Uncle Dick, who really hated Old England. And poor Harvey could feel the years dribbling away all the time. He should never have come here, never have married me, but the Raid trapped him, ruined him. It ruined us all."

"You, too?" said Pibble.

"Of course. If you think I'm being very callous and bloody-minded about all this, you're quite right. Everything that mattered happened so long ago, and then it was all lies. You won't have noticed it, but there isn't a picture of my mother anywhere in the place, except one Uncle Dick kept in a drawer, though he never told the General. I've never found out what happened in the end—they wouldn't talk about her. All she wanted was to live on a farm with a few horses, but first, while Grandfather was alive, she had to go bucketing round the world living in horrible quarters and taking part in Army wives' chitchat, which she was terrible at, so nobody liked her. Then she came to live here during the war. The General was away, mostly, soldiering and quarreling, but after the Raid he came back forever. I don't know what happened—I was being finished at a posh nunnery—but she died. She killed herself, I believe, but there was nothing in the papers. It may even have been something worse: I can't find out. But I know why—the General wasn't human any more, after the Raid. He had sold his soul, and my mother couldn't understand. She was the most loving person who ever walked, and the General couldn't love or be loved any more. Anyway, she tried love, and it killed her. That's why I chose callousness, and it's eaten me up. I'm the last of the Claverings, you know—there aren't any heirs, not even some ghastly Australian. I shall close Old England. I shall let the roof beams rot. I shall mumble about through leaky rooms for fifty years, living on cat food. Oh, Christ!"

She stared at her face in the mirror over the fireplace, pushing her cheeks upward with the inside of her fingers so that the little crow's-feet became the deep-etched furrows of old age.

"I'm going to bed," she said, "unless there's anything else you want to ask. I wouldn't have let him try to kill you if I'd known, Mr. Pibble. You don't belong here, so we've no right. Good night."

She swayed out, supple as a child. Pibble gloomed at the fire, trying to make his brain riffle through the day's events to see whether a card lay there which would betray her. He was sure in his own mind that she had known at dinnertime roughly what her husband was meditating, and that would mean that she knew he had killed the Admiral. But Lady Macbeth is not admissible evidence. When they'd come back from the Tiger Pit, she'd greeted them as though they'd been the General and Singleton back from some exploit, and only noticed halfway through her sentence that the little one was Pibble. But why? How could she have detached herself so from her father, her husband, her uncle, and just let them slaughter each other? With a pricking at his nape Pibble saw a possible answer: if she was the *Admiral's* daughter, then…then…it might have come out in some weeping row when the General came home for good, and so Lady Clavering died, and the old men had killed her between them—not literally, but morally, at least to a doting daughter. And so poor Harvey became just part of the machinery of revenge, his own tremendous financial schemes being nothing beside the high purpose of wiping the blood of the Claverings off the face of the earth.

Never mind. It might be true, but nothing would ever prove it. If it was, she would take vengeance again, on herself. Pibble shivered. His thought processes were becoming very dim; he went over the same point several times before he could bully his brain into moving on. She'd never called him anything except "General," not once, had she? Yes, once, when she was playing the apologetic hostess after the first attempt at murdering Pibble—and even then she'd stumbled over it. And...and...something else...yes, the General had said she'd been very "cut up" about the Admiral's death...except that she mostly called him "Uncle Dick"...cozier...and the fierce bad blood between the old heroes—it'd account for that, too...you randy old bastard...these last years Dick and I managed to steer dear of each other's obsessions...neither of them ever loved anyone else, I think (but that was Miss Finnick—let's leave her out of this)...Ah, give it up, leave it to whoever comes to take over. He dozed.

Almost at once something rattled against the window behind him. Two police cars stood out on the gravel; several torches probed the sky in a toy searchlight display; a man was bending in the drive for another handful of gravel to throw. Pibble's voice was disappearing again, but by signs and painful whispers he got the group to wait and then went around and discovered the door and flight of steps down which the General had strutted a whole afternoon ago. He led his reinforcements back into the study and addressed them. His tiredness and his damaged throat made him sound like the Ass. Com., much more impressive than if he'd been in full possession of his larynx. First a brief jeremiad about what would happen to any officer who was found to have communicated with the press; then a brief assignment of duties— two poor sods to go and guard the Tiger Pit, one to watch in the Chinese Room in case anyone tried to nobble the Colt, two down on the Gallows Ground to prevent the day staff mucking the detail up, one to go through Singleton's papers and try and warn the agency responsible for tomorrow's visitors, one on the top landing to guard the Admiral's quarters and Deakin's, a car waiting this end, another over at the staff car park. He marked maps (third drawer down on the left) for the outliers, took the house party around to their posts, and went back to his dozing on the study sofa, his ears full of a noise like the mains hum on an old radio.

When he woke, it was light; his neck was locked as stiff as *rigor mortis*. Miss Scoplow was already in the office, happy (for the moment) in a torrent of efficiency as she tried to persuade sleepy young men in Southampton that there were other things for ten coachloads of newly landed tourists to do than visit Herryngs. She bit her Biro, made accurate notes about money refunds, cooed, and cajoled. The sergeant who had made no progress in the night, having been wrongly told by Pibble to try London, gawped at her in sleepy adoration. Elsa evolved a vast breakfast and stalked furiously around the house with salvers of grilled kidneys while coppers cringed and mumbled. Mrs. Singleton stayed in bed.

Pibble mooned unhappily about, hankering for pity, dimly trying to think of an excuse to interview Miss Finnick again. Mr. Chanceley was out, the hotel said, doing the rounds of local photographic shops. The day was clear and chill, spendthrift with the last gold of summer. The hospital was cagey about Mr. Waugh's chances.

He found the control switch for the fountain in a little mahogany box just inside the main entrance, and moodily began to spell out his own name in wet, twenty-foot-high, ultra-slow Morse. He'd got as far as the second "B" when there was a hooting and a puff of dust down at the far end of the drive, where the enormous perspective of limes almost met in a point. Rapidly a cavalcade of cars, four of them, rushed toward him, swooped around the pool, and braked at the bottom of the steps. No door opened until the fourth car was still, and then all eight doors of the hinder two cars flapped forward, like the wing carapaces of beetles, and a squad of men, bearded and corduroyed and draped with the glistening gadgets of their profession, poured out and knelt or squatted or lay around the base of the steps. Only when they were ready did one door of the front car open and a man step nonchalantly out. Immediately all the cameras started to click and buzz. Head bowed, the man walked somberly up the first three steps; then, as if he'd remembered something important, he turned and barked an order to the police cars, holding his head at just the right angle for the cameras to catch the iron jaw and eagle profile.

Pibble remembered reading about an odd phenomenon of the desert; you never see more than one vulture at a time patrolling its patch of sky, an almost invisible scratch on the blueness; but when it begins to spiral down toward a dying beast, the vultures patrolling leagues away observe its change of movement and flock to see what it has found. So now.

"Hello, Jimmy," said the man when he reached the top of the steps. "Everything under control?"

"I think so," said Pibble. "You don't know how glad I am to see you, Harry."

With a noncommittal grunt (risky to be affable with a potential scapegoat) Harry Brazzil slouched into Herryngs.

If you enjoyed
The Old English Peep Show,
we hope you'll like the following
chapter from *King and Joker,*
another of Peter Dickinson's
gleefully inventive mysteries
available from Felony & Mayhem.

IT'S BREAKFAST-TIME AT BUCKINGHAM PALACE, DURING THE REIGN OF KING VICTOR II...

The first 'joke' that Princess Louise actually witnessed took place in the Breakfast Room at Buckingham Palace on the last morning of the school summer holidays.

Father gave one of his warning snorts and looked down at the typed list beside his place.

'Two hundred and five,' he said. 'Cease automatic supply of sealing-wax in guest bedrooms.'

Mother put her spoon carefully back into her dish of Fortnum and Mason's Soya Porage (by appointment).

'Most certainly not,' said Mother. 'Hue cannot expect visitors to ask for sealing-huax huenever they huish to bestow a decoration on somebody.'

'I'd have thought people who bestowed decorations carried the kit around with them,' said Nonny.

Albert, not looking up from slicing his second raw carrot into accurate rounds, said, 'Sheikh Umu certainly did. When he gave me the Order of the White Oryx he sealed it by folding a strip of silver over the corner of the skin it was written on and biting it firm with his teeth.'

'Was it oryx skin?' asked Louise.

'Of course not,' said Albert. 'Umu's an ecology nut. That's why we hit it off so well. Last bloke he caught shooting oryx he had publicly castrated.'

'I take it,' said Father, 'that there's no suggestion that we should provide strips of silver in the guest bedrooms.'

'Couldn't one of the footmen make it his business to see that there's sealing-wax in the room when that sort of bloke comes visiting?' said Albert. He then did his usual trick of looking up for a moment from his carrot, staring like a highly intelligent blue-eyed orang at the person he was talking to, popping a slice of carrot into the hole in the middle of his wild ginger beard, and instantly starting on sixty silent mastications, still staring. Strangers found table-talk with the Prince of Wales tricky, but Father was used to it. He snorted more loudly.

'How often have I got to drum it into your heads,' he asked, 'that running a Palace is a labour-intensive operation? Here we are, having to make drastic cuts in expenditure, and that means drastic cuts in labour. The more activities we embark on, even to make apparent savings in material costs, the more labour we need. Remembering to put sealing-wax in the right rooms at the right times sounds a trivial chore, but it involves labour—not just by the footman concerned but also on the part of the Protocol Secretariat who have to communicate with him about which visits are relevant. A few more jobs like that and you find you're increasing your labour force by one, not cutting it.'

'Then it huill be cheaper to keep sealing-huax in all the rooms,' said Mother. She sifted sugar into her bowl and put it on the carpet for Balfour to lick. This was her technique for seeing that Balfour ate his ration of Soya Porage, though he wasn't supposed to eat sugar at all. Father banged his pencil on the table but didn't snort, a bad sign.

'We've reached item two hundred and five,' he said, 'and so far we've accepted a total of nineteen suggestions. What's the point of hiring an O and M firm if we turn down almost every damn idea they put up?'

'Nevertheless,' said Mother, 'there will be sealing-wax in all the bedrooms.'

Only Father, half way gone into one of his rages, failed to notice the perfect English accent. Louise tensed inwardly.

'Now look here...' shouted Father.

Nonny coughed.

'Oh, all right,' said Father, making another little cross on the margin of the list.

Mother nodded, smiled and reached for her banana-shredder.

All at once, in that cough, in that yielding, in that nod and smile, Louise realised that Nonny was Father's mistress. Louise had just poured herself another cup of chocolate and had a piled spoon of sugar half way to it; she didn't spill a grain, despite the bounce of inner shock, but carried it smoothly across and stirred the chocolate to a froth. When she was satisfied she glanced across the table at Nonny. Miss Anona Fellowes was leaning back in her chair looking, as usual, both amused and bemused. She had a glistening blob of honey near the corner of her wide mouth, and like everything else that happened to her it seemed to suit her. Louise remembered a time when at a shoot at Sandringham a Land-Rover had started with a jerk and Nonny had tumbled out at the back, landing asprawl in tyre-churned mud. About five men had helped her to her feet and as she stood up, shaky but laughing, Prince Bernard of the Netherlands had whispered to Louise, 'So, now mud becomes the smart thing to wear.'

Louise's first jolt of astonishment changed quickly to a more general surprise that she hadn't realised before. Thirteen years...no, that wasn't fair—babies are so self-absorbed that you can't expect them to notice things till they're six, at least—say seven years of knowing that Nonny was completely one of the family, despite only being Mother's private secretary...perhaps that was actually what made it harder to see that she was also one of the Family.

Louise sucked the froth off her chocolate and as she did so looked round the table. She knew no one would guess that she'd suddenly found out—it was a family joke how little she showed her feelings. Sometimes that was a nuisance, when everybody assumed that you were as happy as a sand-boy when you really were perfectly miserable, but other times it could be useful. She stirred again to try and whip up another layer of froth. Did Mother know? Of course she did, because Father and Nonny could never have kept it such a secret without her help, and not even *France Dimanche* had suggested it. Did she mind? She always seemed so fond of Nonny, not only in public but also 'among ourselves'. Perhaps it even suited her. Everybody knows that short bald men like a lot of sex, and poor Father was certainly not tall and his head had been shiny right across the top ever since Louise could remember. You could be passionate about Mother—she was marvellous—but it mightn't always be easy to be passionate with her...

The second layer of froth refused to come. Louise shrugged and coldly decided not to think about it any more until she'd had a chance to talk to Durdy.

The pinger pinged its warning that they had only ten minutes more to themselves. Father gave a last snort, turned the O and M list face down, rose and crossed to the side-board. Breakfast was always the same on weekdays. Soya Porage, half a banana and low-calorie chocolate for Mother. Croissants, honey and China tea for Nonny. Orange juice, muesli and raw carrots for Albert. Weetabix, fried eggs and grilled streaky bacon and high-calorie chocolate for Louise. And for Father first a small cup of very hot black coffee, then a vast cup of milky tepid coffee, then two eggs laid yes-terday by the Palace Wyandottes, boiled for two minutes and left wrapped in a hot napkin for another five, and final-ly, when the pinger pinged, two slices of York ham carved by himself from the ham under the silver dishcover on the sideboard.

'Really, this is too bad,' said Father in a voice so curi-ously between laughter and anger that everybody looked round. He was standing back from the sideboard with the dishcover in one hand, like a distorted shield. On the dish where the ham should have been was what appeared to Louise to be a large cow-pat, palpitating with strange life.

'Hey! That's my toad!' said Albert.

Nonny gave a small scream with a giggle threaded through it. Mother rang the bell for Pilfer. Father pulled the corner of his moustache and put the cover back on the toad.

'It's got to have air,' said Albert.

'Quiet,' said Father.

Pilfer slid into the room, bespectacled, stooping, all in black.

'Your Majesty rang?' he said in his slightly nasal whine. He spoke to Mother because he knew that Father, if he'd wanted something, would have shouted and Nonny would have gone and asked.

'My ham is not what it should be, Pilfer,' said Father.

Pilfer's eyebrows rose above the rims of his lenses. He sniffed the air but seemed to detect no odour other than the usual mixture of coffee, chocolate, Soya Porage and Balfour. Then he slid to the sideboard and lifted the dishcover with a black-gloved hand. For three seconds he stared at the toad. Louise saw the toad blink back. With complete silence and decorum Pilfer fainted.

At once Father was crouched by the body, loosening the collar and straightening the limbs. Nobody said anything while he took Pilfer's pulse.

'Bert,' he said. 'Get on the house phone and tell them to send up a stretcher.'

'Is it a heart attack?' asked Nonny. Louise could detect behind the sympathy and concern a note of pleasure at the drama of it.

'No, no,' said Father. 'Just a faint. Heart quite steady. Bloody silly of me.'

'In that case,' said Mother, 'he must stay huere he is until he huakes up.'

'Are you sure he's a union member?' said Nonny.

'There'd still be no harm in having a stretcher,' said

Albert. 'There's nothing in the union agreement against that. Only against Father providing medical attention to union members without a second opinion.'

'Except in an emergency,' added Nonny quickly, but Father was already into his tirade about the idiocy of paying for a doctor for the Palace staff when he, the King, was a qualified practitioner who had worked his way up every step of the medical ladder without cutting one damned corner.

'I suppose if I'd settled for being a vet,' he shouted, 'I wouldn't even have been allowed to operate on the bloody dogs!'

At this moment Louise saw Pilfer's eyelids flicker and the colour begin to seep back into his cheeks. Father was too angry to notice.

'Stretcher's on the way up,' said Albert unnecessarily clearly. Louise guessed that he also had seen Pilfer coming to, and wanted to spare the poor man's feelings by letting his faint seem to continue until he was out of the Royal presence. But the sound of his voice drew Father's temper as a golf-club draws lightning.

'And get that frog out of here!' he bellowed.

'It's a Blomberg toad,' said Albert.

'It's terribly handsome,' said Nonny.

'What's its name?' asked Louise.

'Amin, of course,' said Albert. 'I saw the likeness at once.'

'No,' said Mother. 'You will not call it that. President Amin may well be misguided, but he is a head of state.'

'You call your dogs after Prime Ministers,' said Albert.

'That's different,' said Mother, lapsing quickly back to her Spanish accent. 'It began with Huinston. Do you remember darling Huinston, Lulu? And then there huas Baldouin, who huas rather a dull dog, but very affectionate...'

'And then,' snarled Father, 'we had to get a bloody stupid sentimental red setter and call it Attlee because some crass oaf on the Labour back benches asked a question in the House about our naming dogs after exclusively Tory Prime Ministers—just the sort of idiot interference with my private life which first stopped me going into the Navy and forced me to have a so-called socially useful training and then prevents me touching my own butler when he faints in the middle of my breakfast and anyway where's my damned ham?'

'But you like being a doctor,' said Louise.

'That's got nothing to do with it, Lulu,' said Father, suddenly mild and sensible at the sound of her voice. 'I'd probably have liked being an admiral.'

'You *are* an admiral,' said Albert.

'A proper bloody admiral,' snapped Father.

'But there will be no question of calling the toad Amin,' said Mother.

'Certainly not,' said Father. 'You can call it Fatty if you like, Bert, but you're not to tell anyone why. You hear? And now get it out of my breakfast room.'

'Please can't we keep him for a bit?' said Louise. 'I've got to do a full biology project next term, and I want to do it about Blomberg toads. What does he eat, Bert, and how do you spell Blomberg? May I have a bit off your pad, Nonny?'

Nonny tore off a couple of sheets and swung them round to her on the Lazy Susan, then rose, drifted out into the lobby and came back a few moments later carrying an ordinary china dish with the ham on it.

'It was in the dining-room,' she said. 'Lulu dear, could you make a bit of space for me on the sideboard?'

Once more the great toad blinked at the light as Louise removed its dishcover and carried the salver back to her place. She was hardly settled before the First Aid men came in, and behind them Father's Private Secretary, Sir Savile Tendence. His bluff face pinkened and blue eyes popped and the rigid little bristles of his moustache seemed to twitch when he saw Pilfer supine on the carpet and the King not yet started on his two slices of ham.

'Sorry we're a bit late this morning, Sam,' said Father, carving carefully away while the stretchermen fussed behind him with the body. 'We've had a bit of a brouhaha. Pilfer saw a toad, fainted. Come and sit down. Give the poor man some tea, Nonny. What have we got on today, Sam?'

He always asked the same question and it was always unnecessary. All four members of the Family had in front of their places a typed form, one column for each member, showing all engagements for the week. Louise's entry for yesterday read, for instance, '11.00 a.m. HRH shopping. Clothes for new term. Jean Machine. Laura Ashley. 2.30 p.m. HRH open Sports Centre, Romford, Lady Caroline Tonge in attendance.' Today was blank, at Louise's insistence. Tomorrow disgustingly said '08.50 a.m. HRH starts new term at Holland Park Comprehensive. Photographers.' After that it was plain 'School, School, School,' and back to living a bit more like real people.

'This luncheon for Prince Albert at the London School of Economics Canteen,' Sir Savile was saying. 'We've made strong representations that nothing special should be laid on by way of food. They normally include a vegetarian menu. I understand, though, that a demo is expected.'

'That's all right,' said Albert. 'I'm hairier than your hairiest Trotskyite, and a good deal further to the left, if the truth were known.'

'It's a demo by the British Meat Traders Association, I'm afraid, Sir.'

'Well, I'll demo right back at them.'

'Now, Bertie, huill you please be careful?' said Mother. 'Poor Mr Peart huas telling me only on Monday about how huorrying the EEC beef mountain is.'

'Who would be heir to the throne of a nation of beef-eaters?' said Albert. 'At least it's better than...'

'All right, all right,' snapped Father, just in time to stop him teasing Mother about bull-fighting. 'We've got to get on. This is a new one here, Sam. What the hell's a semi-informal walk-about? I don't know how to walk semi-informally. I wasn't taught.'

Louise decided that her first experiment was a failure. Blomberg toads didn't eat bacon-rind. She was turning the Lazy Susan to get at Mother's Soya Porage packet when the light rumble of wood seemed to break the toad's nerve. It lurched forward off the salver at a fast, ungainly waddle, scattering cups and cutlery over the mahogany. Nonny threw her napkin over it but it barged on, a spectral blob moving with the gait of nightmare. With his usual gawky deftness Albert nipped to the sideboard, picked up the dishcover, whisked the napkin away and brought the cover down on his pet like a candlesnuffer. Still it drove on, a silver tank, to the edge of the table, where Albert had the dish ready. Gripping the handle of the dishcover he coaxed the toad onto the dish, then lashed the cover neatly down with Nonny's napkin.

'Good God,' said Sir Savile. 'When you said Pilfer saw a toad I didn't think...'

'You're not the only one who didn't think,' said Father. 'Damn silly of me to spring the brute on Pilfer like that. I suppose it was OK Bert having me on, but what I did was distinctly over the line.'

(There were three important but vague concepts that had ruled Louise's life ever since she first understood words—'Among ourselves', 'Over the line', and 'Putting on a show'. Nonny was clearly 'among ourselves'. So, in his quiet way, was Pilfer. But Sir Savile was not and nor was Mrs Mercury, the housekeeper. McGivan, mysteriously, was, in a way which the other security people—Theale and Sanderson and Janet Fletcher, for instance—were not. 'Among ourselves' you could say and do what you liked—things which if you'd done them elsewhere would have been 'over the line'. When you weren't 'among ourselves' you were always to a greater or lesser extent 'putting on a show', wearing your public face, behaving as though it were the most natural thing in the world that forty photographers should turn up to take pictures of a teenage girl going to school. If Sir Savile hadn't been in the room it would have been possible to hold quite an interesting discussion about whether playing a practical joke on Pilfer was in fact 'over the line' because although Pilfer was a servant he was also 'among ourselves' and had been ever since, as an underfootman, he had shown Father how to build his first radio set and speak along the crackling ether to other radio nuts in places like Brazil and Oregon. You could discuss and disagree about 'over the line', but 'among ourselves' was a set of relationships which you simply knew, without thought, in much the same way that baby chimps know from the grunts and grimaces of their elders the hierarchy of the group they live in, without even knowing that they know.)

Father's last remark had caught Albert at about his fortieth chew at a carrot-slice, so he had to wait another twenty before he could protest.

'Me!' he said at last. 'It wasn't me! Damned silly thing to do! Somebody might have put that dish down on a hot plate! And anyway I've more respect for toads than to play practical jokes with them.'

'Then who was it?' said Mother, accentless and angry.

Everybody made not-me shrugs and grunts.

'What's this?' said Louise, picking a torn scrap of paper off the table. 'I think it must have been under the toad. I think I saw it fall off the dish when Bert picked it up.'

'Yes, that's right,' said Albert.

The paper was blank. Louise turned it over. On the other side was a single scarlet cross, scrawled with a thick felt pen.

'Oh, Lord,' said Sir Savile. 'It's another one.'

'What do you mean?' said Albert.

'We've had a couple of other practical jokes, while you and the Princess were still in Scotland, Sir. The joker left a red cross like that both times.'

'What were the jokes?' asked Louise. 'Were they funny?'

'We won't go into that now,' said Father with a sudden snap of temper. 'D'you think this really matters, Sam? I mean, it's a nuisance, but we're used to this sort of thing. Only this joker has a bit more sense of humour than most.'

'That's what's bothering me,' said Sir Savile. 'OK, there's always going to be the odd frustrated little tick who gets his own back with a silly practical joke. We've seen 'em, time and again. But I can remember old Toby, before I took over, warning me about the other sort. I can see him, clear as if it was today, sitting in the arm-chair in my office and puffing that horrible black pipe of his and saying "What you've got to watch out for, me boy, is a *real* joker. They're the type that don't let up." And he told me a long story about the trouble they had with a run of practical jokes right back in your great-grandfather's time, before the First World War. Never caught the blighter. Turned out to be a junior equerry. Died in the trenches, and his lawyers sent old Toby a sealed envelope confessing everything. Point about his jokes was that they could be funny, in a rather vicious sort of way. For instance, Trooping the Colour once, he managed to scatter getting on for a thousand stink-bombs all over Horseguards Parade. He knew the drill, you see, and didn't put 'em where anyone was going to walk till you got several companies of guardsmen tramping about. Never knew when they weren't going to step on another one, you see. Ghastly stink, ladies fainting in the stands, guardsmen going bright green, horses shying like a circus—wish I'd seen it, though I expect if I had I'd have been too angry to laugh. Another time, visit of the French President, 1909, he managed to get itching powder on the harness for the Glass Coach. Horses bolted halfway down the Mall with King Edward, Queen Alexandra, President and his missus all aboard. Half the stable staff got the sack, but our joker didn't care. He'd seen the Glass Coach bucketing down the Mall at a hand-gallop, with the King and Queen sitting there stiff as pokers, looking as though that was the way they always received State Visitors.

And another thing about that joker—he left his signature too. So if old Toby didn't like it then, I don't like it now.'

For Louise there were several ghosts in the Palace—not the sort of hauntings that get into books, but memories so strong that the person remembered seemed almost solid enough to come stalking along one of those stretching corridors. For instance, Queen Mary, after whom the liner had been named, had died nine years before Louise was born, but there were still people in the Palace who could imitate her icy accent and super-regal stance with such accuracy that Louise seemed to know and fear her more than some living people. Sir Toby Smythe was another such ghost, having come to the Palace to work for the Master of the Household in the reign of Edward VII, and in 1922 becoming Private Secretary to Louise's great-grandfather, Victor I, and only retiring on Father's twenty-first birthday at the age of seventy-six. Louise knew all about Sir Toby; and his pipe; and his annual hiking holiday in German *lederhosen* which had got him thrown into Norwich jail as a spy in 1917; and his gallant but vain swim for help from the yacht in which Louise's grandfather, the Prince of Wales, had drowned in 1937; and the ins and outs of his campaign against the other great ghosts (including Queen Mary) to see that Father, when he became King a year later at the age of ten, knew something about the actual lives of his subjects; and the fire-watching on the Palace roof during the Luftwaffe raids; and all that. Louise didn't much care for Sir Savile, mostly because he'd been on what she thought was the wrong side in the fight over whether she ought to go to a state school or to a dismally snob fee-paying establishment, but she knew that if he called up old Toby's ghost to witness that something mattered, then it did. This was no time to bait Father, so she crossed out the word 'Todes' she'd put at the top of her notes and wrote 'Toads', then listened carefully to everything that was said. Immediately after breakfast she planned to go up to the Nurseries and ask Durdy about Nonny and Father, and whether it was all right, but it would be useful to have something else interesting to talk about in case Durdy clammed up. The joker would be ideal for that.

In fact not a great deal more was said about him, because the fuss with the toad had already taken up half Sir Savile's twenty minutes. Nobody needed to look at a watch—Louise herself never wore one—because Mother had a clock in her head and at exactly the same instant each day she would fold her napkin into its ring and say 'Huell, Nonny...' It was a signal for Father to rise. When the King stands, all stand. The formal day—the day not lived 'among ourselves'—had begun.

'I'm afraid we're a bit behind schedule, Sir,' said Sir Savile. 'I'm supposed to brief you about the Mali Ambassador—the FO are a bit jumpy there. I've made a tape of their briefing.'

'Toshack's a damned fusser,' said Father. 'I wish the FO would move him to another desk. I read the dispatches last night, but I suppose I'll have to listen to the bloody tape on my bog. Thanks.'

Father marched away. Sir Savile held the door for Mother and Nonny, saw that Louise and Albert weren't ready to leave, gave that curious heavy nod of his which was the vestigial remains of a court bow, and went. Albert yawned with relief.

'That makes you look like a sea anemone,' said Louise. 'All tendrils sticky red.'

He snarled at her like an ogre and picked up Father's list of suggestions from the O and M firm.

'He oughtn't to leave this about,' he said. 'We don't want a lot of rumours floating around about who's getting the push. Where'd we got to?'

'Two oh five. Sealing-wax.'

He flipped through sheets.

'That's the last of that section,' he said. 'Ah, now we're really getting down to brass tacks. "Section Four. Domestic

Arrangements for Royal Family. Two oh six. Princess Louise
to advertise her services as a baby-sitter."

'Come off it. They wouldn't put that first.'

'Careful, Lulu. You mustn't get a reputation for being
brainy. The GBP doesn't go for brains.'

(This abbreviation for the Great British Public was
clearly 'over the line' but just as clearly ineradicable. Even
Mother sometimes slipped into using it.)

'Shut up,' said Louise. 'I'm going to go and tell Durdy
about the toad. Bert, can I do next term's project on it?'

'Course you can. I'll give you a hand,' said Albert, still
running his eyes down the list of royal comforts the O and
M men wanted to chop.

'I suppose I couldn't take him to school tomorrow. I'd
love to see some of those photographers faint.'

'Princess Louise and friend. Is this her first romance?
Better not, Lulu...Hey! Look at this!'

Startled by the tone of genuine shock Louise craned to
read the line he was pointing at. '312. The transfer of Miss
Durdon to a suitable nursing-home would represent a saving
of £1,620 p.a. in medical and other expenses.'

'Durdy!' whispered Louise.

'They must be mad!' said Albert.